Copyri

Celia Micklefield hereby asserts the moral right to be
identified as the author of this work of fiction

All rights reserved

No part of this publication may be reproduced, stored in a
retrieval system, or transmitted in any form or by any
means, electronic, mechanical, photocopying,
recording or otherwise, without the prior permission of
the author.

*All characters in this publication are fictitious and any
resemblance to real persons, living or dead, is entirely
coincidental.*

ACKNOWLEDGEMENTS

A Measured Man is set mostly in Norfolk. It's my adopted county and I love it and its people very much. We have characters here. I've never met anybody quite like the main character in this book but I suppose you might say he's NFN. I say this in the knowledge that only the good folk of Norfolk could take what was originally a derogatory description and turn it into a term of endearment.

Nowadays, *Normal for Norfolk* means that you are accepted. Regardless of all your quirks, foibles and unusual habits, as long as you have a good heart and cause others no harm you are a good sort.

For the sake of 'yew furriners' reading A Measured Man I've included very little dialect.

A Measured Man

A man's character is his fate
Heraclitus (*c. 535 – c. 475 BC*) *Greek philosopher*

The First Year

Chapter One

June

His mother was the one who'd first called him a *back-room-boy*. He'd queried her intention at the time. When he'd tried to ascertain her exact meaning he couldn't correlate the lyrics of Nazareth's nineteen eighty three version of *Back-Room Boy* with his position at Piper Precision Engineering, nor the lyrics to Marlene Dietrich's version of *See what the boys in the back-room will have* in the nineteen thirty nine film *Destry Rides Again*. Furthermore, even though he professed himself something of a film buff, he could see nothing in the nineteen forty two British comedy *The Back-Room Boy* which demonstrated clearly his mother's meaning and he told her so.

"It means people who do important things but only in the background," he remembered she'd told him. "Unsung heroes and people who don't get noticed."

Aubrey Tennant didn't consider himself a hero in any sense of the word, nor was he the type who enjoyed being noticed but his work was so essential to the company it could be called critical and he occupied an office in the rear of the building, therefore he was able to accept his mother's definition of a back-room boy and take it as a compliment of sorts. In any case compliments meant very little. He didn't need them.

He'd always taken pride in the knowledge he'd saved the company thousands of pounds. Tens of thousands. Maybe even hundreds of thousands. He'd probably also saved lives about which nobody could put a monetary value. Even the smallest aircraft parts were vitally important to people's lives.

Aubrey Tennant's office squeezed itself into the far right rear corner on the ground floor of Piper Precision Engineering. Located between the gents' toilet and rear staircase to the smarter office suites above, the windows in his workspace nevertheless afforded him a pleasant outlook over green space at the edge of the industrial park. He didn't feel pressed or encumbered in any way by this backroom position. Indeed, he couldn't be handier for the facilities when he needed them and, if his presence was required at a meeting upstairs, he could attend promptly without all the fuss of walking through the building to front reception and the grander set of stairs there. Headquarters of PPE in Cambridge was an unassuming building compared with the futuristic edifices on the nearby science park. It might have been a private clinic or a Department of Work and Pensions office block. Its pale walls and unfashionable dark-stained doors and window frames belied government and civil contracts worth billions negotiated within.

Aubrey appreciated the contradiction. He didn't see it as a clash of interests, rather he thought it appropriate that Piper Precision Engineering headquarters possessed none of the swagger evident on the rest of the industrial site. On the contrary, he thought, the building was much like himself. Even though he had to dip slightly to get under the doorframe to his office, his compact workspace tucked into that ground floor corner had provided him with everything appropriate to his needs throughout his thirty years' service. He had no desire to be nearer the offices of his work colleagues nor had he the slightest interest in having instant access to the communal kitchen area upstairs and the wordplay badinage that took place there. He had his own kettle, easily refilled at one of the sinks next door in the gents' toilet and, in the bottom drawer of one of his filing cabinets, he kept his own stock of tea, coffee, a canister of dried milk granules and sachets of his favourite hot chocolate mix.

Piper Precision Engineering, designers and manufacturers of non-magnetic mounting nuts, high temperature two-lug anchor nuts, nut plates and the like had sufficient reason to be eternally grateful for Aubrey's sharp eye and meticulous attention to detail. Precise measurements were paramount when one aircraft part must fit inside another. Aubrey Tennant could spot an error before a design left the draftsman's printout.

On the third Friday in June the monthly meeting had finished early and Aubrey was tidying his desk and gathering his things together for his upcoming week's holiday when a sharp rap at his door was followed by the appearance of Reynolds, PPE's former health and safety officer. Aubrey hadn't been surprised by Reynolds' re-appointment to building maintenance and supervision of the premises' cleaning team even though it would seem an ignominious shuffle sideways if not a peg or two downwards. One must epitomise the qualities required from one's job description and poor Reynolds' first attempt at a company presentation had rendered him the butt of every health and safety joke imaginable ever since. Reynolds had rendered PPE no choice but to replace him as Health and Safety officer when he'd set up the executive meeting room for a Powerpoint demonstration of the finer points of risk assessments, waited until the whole company was assembled facing the screen and then promptly tripped over the laptop wire from the power socket which he'd left trailing across the floor. Still, Aubrey thought, Reynolds had adapted to his new position with grace if not gratitude and it seemed unfair he should be judged for evermore on that one mistake. Aubrey dismissed the thought and grabbed a rolled-up pair of socks from the small pile on his desk.

"Oh," Reynolds said. "I was going to ask you if you needed a lift to the train station as usual, Tennant, but I can see you perhaps have other plans."

"I do. Indeed I do," Aubrey said and continued stuffing the pair of socks into his tan leather summer brogues. "But if you're going in the direction of the supermarket I'd be grateful if you could drop me off at the Travelodge on Newmarket Street."

"Going away somewhere?" Reynolds said, eyeing the holdall on Aubrey's desk.

Aubrey laid the shoes on their sides inside the bag and said, "It's my week off. I'm going down to the south coast."

"Torquay again?"

"I like it there. The hotel is without question, in a word, superb."

He adjusted the clothes already rolled into sausages and lined down one side of the bag and slid the brogues right to the end of the other side leaving space for his bathroom bag next to the shoes. He always rolled clothes when he was packing. His mother had shown him years ago how the method avoided too much creasing. It was how the airforce did it, she said.

Reynolds said, "So, when are you off?"

"Tomorrow morning. There was no point in going home tonight. The coach picks up here in Cambridge."

"I'll be ready to leave in about half an hour," Reynolds said. "I'll meet you in the car park."

"Thank you. I'll be there," Aubrey said and zipped up the holdall.

It had been a sensible decision to remain overnight in Cambridge. If he'd gone home to Thetford he'd only have to get up extra early to catch the train to be at the coach station in Norwich where the journey began or else come all the way back again to the pick-up point in Cambridge. For some reason the tour operator didn't include a stop in his home town along the way although Thetford was en route. He congratulated himself that he'd avoided having to rush. A leisurely start to his week off work would set the right tone and help him relax.

Reynolds was as good as his word. The two men arrived at Reynolds' car at the same time.

"Just the one bag?" Reynolds said as he opened the boot.

"Yes. Casual but smart is the order for the week," Aubrey replied. "I've got everything I need."

He said nothing about what he was hoping to find while he was away.

Aubrey glanced around his room at the Travelodge and wondered whether he should unpack everything from his bag for his one night's stay. He removed the summer brogues and placed them on the floor at the side of the bed intending to wear them during the journey to the south coast. He also removed one pair of summer trousers and the rest of his travelling outfit, shaking out each piece before he arranged them on hangers. He took his bathroom bag to the compact en-suite and put his toothbrush in the glass holder. His mobile phone rang. He looked at the readout and accepted the call.

"Reynolds?" he said. "Is anything the matter?"

"Aubrey, we're away from the office. I may call you by your name, may I? It's like this. I did the extra bit of weekend shopping. You know, fresh cream, extra milk as usual and took it straight home. But Daphne isn't here. She's left me a note. Apparently I have forgotten she is visiting her sister this weekend in Dumfries."

Aubrey said, "I see." He didn't *see* at all so he waited for Reynolds to continue.

"I was wondering if you'd care for some company at dinner tonight."

Aubrey sank onto the bed. He wanted to say, *why?* Instead, he said, "Where?"

"Over there where you are. I could invite you over here as I now have surplus supplies but, as I'm not much good at cooking . . .?"

Aubrey had planned a quiet evening with an *Amazing Value Meal Deal* and an early night. The family restaurant wasn't his usual choice of eatery but he was nevertheless looking forward to a simple meal near his accommodation without having to go to the trouble of organising taxis into town. Sharing the first night of his week away from work constituted an unwelcome disruption to his schedule but he didn't want to offend. He'd always had a rather soothing affinity with the ex-health and safety officer, being of a similar age and with apparently similar backgrounds judging by their style of speech and general mannerly behaviour around the workplace. Timothy Reynolds was the closest thing to a friend Aubrey possessed.

The restaurant was busy and noisy. Friday night, it would seem, was a relaxed family night. They waited at the entrance to be seated as the notice there requested. Aubrey wondered what he and Timothy would find to talk about in this unfamiliar setting. Nearby, a family got up to leave and someone came to clear. Shortly afterwards someone else invited them to take the vacant table. They sat together in the booth near the door.

"I was at a bit of a loose end, as they say," Timothy said, as they took their places, "and as I knew you were here by yourself for the evening I thought we might get together, so to speak."

"What will you do for the rest of the time," Aubrey said, "if you can't cook?"

"I'll have to manage. Normally, when Daphne goes away on one of her trips, she leaves the freezer full of meals she's prepared for me. Not this time."

"Why not this time?"

Timothy puffed out a sharp breath. "I think it's because I forgot she was going away."

Aubrey considered this. "I don't understand why your forgetting would make her change her routine," he said.

The waiter came to take their order. When he went away Timothy let out a groan.

"It's my own fault," he said. "Daphne complains I don't listen to what she's saying. The thing is, when you've been together as long as we have you simply keep on expecting everything to be the same as it always was."

"I can give you some simple recipes," Aubrey offered. "Since Mother died I've had to cook for myself. I do occasionally eat out but on the whole I make my own meals." He began recounting some of his staple recipes and Reynolds made notes and lists of ingredients on his iPad. When Aubrey had dictated enough ideas to cover a few days he gazed up at the ceiling as if he were daydreaming and said, " I think it would be a source of contentment to have someone cook for you everyday."

Timothy Reynolds suddenly looked aghast. His mouth dropped open and his eyes seemed surprised.

"Aubrey," he said. "Of course, you're quite right. You have hit the proverbial nail on the head there, my friend."

Aubrey flushed with warmth at the mention of the word *friend* and a slight kind of discomfort nibbled at his innards but he had no idea to which nail Timothy was referring. He coughed a little and smiled to cover his embarrassment. Quietly he said,

"I do think of you as a friend, erm, Timothy."

The food arrived and conversation ceased for a while. A family group came through the entrance doors, chatting loudly to each other, the children obviously excited and not watching where they were going. A young boy stumbled and knocked Timothy's elbow as he was reaching across the table for the salt.

"Say sorry to the man, Ethan," the mother said.

"What for?"

"Because you bumped into him."

"It's quite alright," Timothy said.

The boy spluttered a *sorry* and ran off.

"He's only six," the mother said.

Timothy said, "No harm done."

"I think most of the salt went on the floor not on your food," Aubrey said.

"I should pay more attention to my wife," Timothy said as if he hadn't heard Aubrey's comment. "And I must thank you for pointing that out to me."

Aubrey wasn't aware he *had* pointed anything out to his companion. In the few moments' silence that followed he replayed the conversation in his mind. When he remembered his wishful thinking about having someone to cook every day he realised he'd almost revealed his secret, the purpose of his trip to Torquay.

Chapter Two

Lisa Miller had chosen her holiday in June at the Clarendon Grand Hotel in Torquay quite by chance. She'd been in the middle of sorting through all her belongings after her recent house move when her daughter, Amy turned up out of the blue, ushered her out of the kitchen and thrust a magazine in her mother's direction. Lisa blew an annoying strand of overgrown fringe out of her eyes and took the glossy brochure her daughter offered. With her other hand she lifted an empty cardboard box out of her armchair, dropped it on top of another box on the floor and sat with a thump against the cushions. She let out a sigh as she flipped through full colour pages of smart hotels with manicured gardens under a blue sky.

"Well, I don't know," she said.

"Mum, it would be good for you to get away. Do something different. When was the last time you had a holiday?" Lisa screwed up her eyes. "I'll tell you when it was,"Amy went on. "It was when you took Danny and me to Majorca shortly after Dad died."

Lisa let another sigh escape. "It was already booked and paid for," she said. "At the time I thought it was the right thing to do. For you and Danny. Take your mind off things. Give you both a bit of fun after all that hospital visiting and what came afterwards." She leaned back in the armchair, reached up and patted her daughter's comforting hand stroking her shoulder.

"Mum, that was fourteen years ago. I was fifteen. Danny was only twelve." Amy lifted a pile of books to clear a space on the sofa and sat facing her mother.

Lisa took a deep breath and exhaled slowly. "Yes, you're right, Amy," she said. "Time flies. I've still got all the pictures Danny took with his first camera." She glanced around the cluttered sitting room as if she was searching and meant to get them. "They're in here somewhere. I haven't unpacked everything yet. I've run out of places to put things." Another sigh.

"You did do the right thing, Mum. Danny and I have good memories of that holiday but it must have been hard for you."

Lisa blinked at the memory and said, "It was. I remember feeling horribly lonely sitting on the beach watching other people. I couldn't stop looking at other women with their husbands, other children with their fathers. Happy families. I missed your dad all the time."

Amy nodded. "So, it's time you did something for yourself now," she said.

"Maybe you're right."

"I know I'm right, especially after this last couple of years."

Lisa pushed back the same piece of fringe and shook her head to put a stop to wistful daydreaming.

"I'll be all right, Amy," she said. "You don't have to worry about me. I've still got my job and I'm not without friends. Anyway, you don't hanker after things so much at my age."

Amy jumped up from the sofa. She paced and waved her arms about.

"At your age? What do you mean at your age? I hate it when you talk like that. I don't want you to grow old before your time, sitting about like an ancient with only your memories for company."

Lisa popped her eyebrows and said, "Well, thank you, Amy. Neither do I."

"Well, I just won't have it," Amy said. "You're only fifty two. You've still got a lot of life to live. Don't you dare give up hankering after things. But please, Mum, don't go falling for any more losers like *that thing* you married last time."

"You shouldn't call him that, Amy," Lisa said, browsing the brochure.

"I can call him whatever I want. He was a complete waste of time."

Lisa was thinking the hotels in the southwest looked pretty when she said, "You ought not to speak ill of the dead."

"Mum, if it wasn't for him you wouldn't be where you are now. Just look at this place."

Lisa's newly refurbished apartment above the veterinary surgery in Great Yarmouth looked out over a supermarket car park. With her living room window open she could hear the constant noise of it: shoppers loading and unloading trolleys and bags; car doors and boots slamming closed; engines, gears, brakes. Weekends were the worst when there'd be hundreds of high-pitched children's voices soaring above the general clamour, shouting for sweets or wailing because they were bored.

At night the empty car park morphed into a different creature. Security lamps illuminated a silent expanse of naked black asphalt. Cone-shaped shafts of yellow light pierced the darkness of the night sky and transformed the lifeless ground into a scene from a mystery movie especially when river mists rose from the Bure to curl around the car wash and skeleton lines of empty trolleys.

The entrance to her first floor apartment was at the rear of the building accessed through an archway into a courtyard where people came with their sick pets to see Mr Hague, the vet. The noise from the courtyard below was often blood-curdling. Lisa didn't like to think about it too much.

The only greenery she could see was a spider plant in her windowsill at the front. There were trees beyond the supermarket car park, scrubby, stunted things along the banks of the Bure, bent double by winds from the North Sea but they were too far away to see any green and much of the time they were lost in those damp mists.

Packed in cardboard boxes and stacked in neat piles against the walls, Lisa's belongings left little room to move between her furniture. Small windows in the converted coach house over what had been a livery yard admitted little daylight. Even on the brightest days she had to switch on the light in the tiny galley kitchen.

Looking around at her new home Lisa said, "Well, Amy, it was all I could afford."

"And whose fault was that? You should never have married him. I tell you what, if I'd known the kind of debt he was landing you with I'd have killed him myself."

Lisa closed the holiday brochure with a snap and said, "Well, that's all over and done with now. There's no point in keeping raking it all up."

Amy went to make coffee.

"Look at the brochure, Mum," she said. "It looks like just the thing to me. You'll meet new people. Make new friends."

Lisa flipped the pages again. When she looked more closely she recognised the company name.

"Amy!" she shouted. "These are holidays for *old* folks. I thought you said you didn't want me to grow old before my time?"

Amy laughed and shouted from the kitchen. "You didn't think it was Club Med, did you? What did you fancy, a week in Shag-a-luf?"

"Amy! For goodness sake. You know I'm not interested in having any more men in my life. No, but, this? Coach tours for desperate grannies?"

Amy came in and set down two mugs.

"Give it a chance, Mum. You're always saying there are places in England you've never seen. What about that programme last week on television? You said Devon and Cornwall looked lovely."

Lisa agreed the pictures in the brochure were inviting. She sipped her coffee and scanned the pages again.

"This looks nice, Amy," she said.

A woman who has already buried two husbands needs to be careful what she wears, Lisa mused as she prepared for the first evening's welcoming party and celebration dinner in the Chippendale restaurant at the very grand Clarendon Grand Hotel in Torquay. Twice widowed women wouldn't want to give the wrong impression. She settled on her mushroom crepe. It was nearly as old as Danny but the boat neckline and three-quarter sleeves whispered *classically smart*. Tan leather heeled sandals that she'd bought with her staff discount from Marshall and Simpson and pearl stud earrings were the perfect complement. Amy was right after all about getting away. As Lisa brushed her hair and plucked out a stray grey she was already beginning to feel more herself.

The other members of the party were a mixed bunch. Lisa hadn't spoken to many of them yet. The woman who got on the coach with a group at Cambridge and took the seat next to her was a widow too but her conversation had been all about how she was going to miss her cats. The woman had begun controlling the conversation at the Membury service area in the queue for the ladies'. She'd had to shout over the noise coming from gaming machines in the nearby arcade.

"Oh, I'm going to miss my boys," she'd shouted. "Lovely boys they are. I said, lovely boys. Would you like to see a picture? That's Smokey with Ginger and this is one of Tabby on his own."

The woman's shrill voice was thin and reedy. Lisa thought it epitomised the sound of an *old* woman.

Thoughts of growing old before your time pricked at Lisa's conscience but she listened politely. She continued listening when the woman followed her out of the toilets and joined her at a table in the coffee shop.

"Course, I've had 'em all done. It makes 'em so much nicer, you know. Well, you wouldn't want them spraying everywhere and getting too excited. Do you have cats?"

"No." Lisa put her head on one side. Her tight smile accompanied apologetic eyes but she wasn't sorry she didn't have a cat. On her days off work she could hear them yowling downstairs at the vet's. Dreadful noise.

"You should get two if you're going to get one. They like company, do you see?"

"I see."

"We all sit down together at night. They watch the telly, you know. Oh, yes. They like to watch the telly."

"Lovely," Lisa said and hoped it sounded like she meant it. She checked her watch although she knew there was still plenty of time before the end of the lunch break.

Back on the coach Lisa still managed to nod her understanding when this woman, Joyce, went into all the details of the rota she'd set up for which neighbour was going to do the feeding in her absence. The Monday, Wednesday and Friday person had cats of her own and the Tuesday, Thursday and Saturday neighbour was a good soul who simply enjoyed helping out. Joyce was going to buy both neighbours a nice little souvenir as a thank you. Sunday feeding seemed to have been forgotten, Lisa thought, but didn't want to ask for fear of another lengthy explanation and when she glanced out of the window she realised they'd left the M4 and were cruising slowly along city streets to the coach station in Bristol.

Fifty-eight miles of Tabby and Ginger and Smokey in that ear-piercing voice.

Lisa's conscience stabbed her again. She knew Joyce meant no harm and was only being friendly in her own way but it rankled that a conversation in which Lisa had no interest was being forced on her.

But I mustn't be selfish, she thought. *It's Joyce's holiday too. Surely she won't talk about cats forever.*

Ten more women and two gentlemen were waiting to get on. Joyce passed comment on the new arrivals. Lisa wasn't listening. She said she felt like taking a nap and closed her eyes. Fortunately, she had the window seat and could rest her head against the glass so Joyce couldn't see whether her eyes were open. Lisa heard the passengers alight and shuffle along the aisle to find their seats. There were a few murmured good afternoons. The luggage hold closed with a bang and with a great sigh from the air brakes the coach pulled away.

With her forehead pressed against the window Lisa opened her eyes and watched the countryside flash past. It was looking green and fresh. June was a good month to travel, she told herself. A small flutter of excitement tickled her insides. *This* was the feeling she wanted. She welcomed the stirring of her inner child looking forward to adventure and she didn't want anything to spoil it. She decided to steer clear of Joyce in future when it came to seating arrangements. She could do it without hurting the woman's feelings.

I can say I'd like to meet the rest of the group, she thought. *It wouldn't be a lie.*

The party was made up of more women than men. It was to be expected, Lisa supposed. Two ladies travelling together looked like they might be sisters. They'd been in the early morning queue with Lisa at the start in Norwich along with a group of six women who were probably members of some group or other, several single ladies like herself and five solitary gentlemen. Added to that there was the group from Cambridge and the people who got on at Bristol making forty-eight passengers to complete the onward journey to Devon.

It wasn't quite a full coach. There'd be plenty of opportunity to move seats if she found herself in the position of needing to. The driver was nice, probably in his early sixties. Very friendly with a smart uniform and a neat haircut. Beautifully polished shoes. His name was Jim.

Another flutter of excitement welled up when the coach swung into its allotted parking space at the hotel and its passengers gathered up their things to get off and wait in line for Jim to bring out their luggage from the hold.

My goodness, Lisa thought. *The word grand doesn't do it justice.*

She couldn't take her eyes away from the view across the bay. The sea gleamed like a glassy reflection of the sky: blue with shiny streaks of turquoise and flashes of silver sparkling in late afternoon sunlight. Palm trees and other exotic plants gave the place a continental feel. A foreign smell of suntan lotion and cigars drifted on the air. No wonder they called it the English Riviera.

"Stunning, isn't it?" a male voice sounded as she dragged her wheelie case behind her. She stopped and turned to face him.

"Yes. It's wonderful. I'd no idea."

"People tend to forget what a beautiful country we live in."

He had a lovely voice, deep and rich, the sort of voice that ought to advertise chocolate. Or sell insurance. You'd have to believe anything a voice like that told you. He was very smart, too. Lovely summer slacks and a lemon-coloured sweater over a pale blue shirt. They suited his auburn colouring.

"This way, Mrs Miller," the coach driver, Jim said to her. "Let's get everybody checked in."

She said, "Right you are."

"You'll be in your usual room, Aubrey, I expect," Jim said to the man.

Aubrey? I've never met an Aubrey before. Auburn Aubrey.

After freshening up, putting on her mushroom crepe and wearing her pearl studs Lisa waited in reception with Jim and a few others for the rest of their group to assemble. Dinner was booked for eight and, before that, they were going to have a brief tour of the premises. She looked out over the swimming pool area to the terrace where people were taking drinks.

Jim said, "Everything in order, Mrs Miller? Are you satisfied with your room?"

"Oh, yes. Thank you. It's beautiful."

The reception area was beautiful too, Lisa thought, with its lush terracotta and cream carpet and sofas and lampshades placed just-so in the height of style. There'd be no children running around and laughing in a place like this. Her years of family holidays were over. Maybe they'd come back if ever she was lucky enough to be a grandmother. That was something about growing older you could look forward to. She smiled at the memory of watching children splashing about in the swimming pool. She looked again at the people outside enjoying their aperitifs. Only one family was accompanied by a child and he was sitting quietly and politely with his bottle of coke.

School holidays haven't started yet.

The rest of the group arrived in dribbles. Jim led them outside. Lisa noticed the man called Aubrey wasn't with them.

"Are you sure we're all here?" she asked Jim.

"All except one," he said. "Mr Tennant knows where everything is."

Aubrey Tennant. A distinguished sort of name. She couldn't stop her imagination running away with her thoughts. *Why would an Aubrey Tennant be on a coach holiday for the over fifties?*

The tour took in a circle around the outdoor pool and terrace, the indoor pool and fitness room and the beauty centre. Lisa already knew about the facilities. She'd painstakingly looked through the brochure and Amy had brought up the website on her laptop to show her mother how grand The Clarendon Grand actually was.

"You should treat yourself to a makeover while you're there, Mum," Amy had suggested.

"Well, I don't know . . ."

"Tell you what. My treat. Let's book you in before you go," and Amy had made the appointment and paid online right there and then.

Standing outside the premises, looking through the windows at the swish interior, Lisa felt another small thrill. She'd never heard of some of the brand names featured on the advertising boards. She would turn herself over to the experts, lie back and enjoy like Amy said she should.

The group re-assembled at reception and Jim handed out name badges.

"You don't *have* to put them on," he said. "We're not at a business conference after all but I always think it helps to break the ice."

Everybody pinned on their badges. The women giggled a bit. The men coughed and jangled coins in their trouser pockets. In the restaurant their tables awaited. Lisa felt the springiness of the carpet beneath the soles of her sandals. It must be an excellent underlay, she thought, wondering how much it cost and comparing it with the kind she had in the flat.

Jim made another announcement. He indicated name cards already in place on the tables.

"This is just for tonight," he said. "Just to get you all started. I always think it's a good idea to swap places each night at dinner to get to know each other better. But it's up to you."

Lisa wondered how many times Jim had accompanied these trips and said *I always think it's a good idea to* do something or other. She took her place and put her handbag on the floor by her feet. She saw she was sitting between a woman called Nancy who was wearing lovely chunky jewellery, the sort Lisa admired but didn't have the nerve to wear, and a man called Malcolm. Lisa was the first to speak.

"Hello, Nancy," she said. "I noticed you got on at Bristol. I'm from Great Yarmouth."

"That's Norfolk, isn't it," Nancy said and her earrings bobbled about, clusters of bright beads catching the light with flashes of purple and amber.

"That's right."

The man labelled Malcolm fiddled with his cutlery and did a little cough.

Lisa said, "And how about you, Malcolm? Where are you from?"

"Swaffham."

"You must have got on in Norwich like me," Lisa said.

Nancy said, "Oh, so you're both from Norfolk. How nice." She tucked one side of her hair behind an ear and the earring twisted and sparkled. The huge ring she wore shimmered with the same contrasting colours. Maybe women her age in Bristol all wore chunky jewellery like that. As much as Lisa admired the woman's choice of accessories, the way she'd said *how nice* sounded sour, as if coming from Norfolk was beneath her. Lisa had only ever passed Swaffham on the way to somewhere else but out of some sudden allegiance to her home county didn't want to admit it.

"They have a wonderful market in Swaffham every Saturday," she said instead.

The two sister ladies were sitting opposite. The one whose name badge said Barbara piped up.

"We used to have a holiday home near Sheringham," she said. "Didn't we Suzy? Mother wouldn't leave Norfolk, would she, Suzy? All her life she never left the county, did she, Suzy?"

Suzy pursed her lips and nodded. She pursed and nodded, nodded and pursed all the way through Barbara's sermon about Mother and how Father adored his wife and would do absolutely anything for her so that *he* never got out of the county either.

"Different times," Malcolm offered. "People didn't expect so much back then." He put his hand on Lisa's shoulder and craned his neck to read her badge. He let the back of his hand slowly stroke her left breast as he took it away. She jolted and he apologised but the words didn't match the smirk he was wearing. His chin jutted out of a shirt collar two sizes too big for him and his wrinkled neck made him look like a tortoise peeping out of its shell.

"Have you done much travelling, erm, Lisa?" he said as if he'd done nothing wrong.

She didn't want to cause a scene.

"Not for a long time, she said. "This is my first visit to this area."

"Ours too," Barbara said and Suzy pursed and nodded.

Lisa's stomach sank. This wasn't how she'd envisaged her first night's holiday. She added Tortoise Man and Two Dotty Sisters to her mental list of people where she'd need to keep the conversation short. She wouldn't want to make it obvious she was deliberately avoiding them exactly, but a furtive monitoring of contact with them would give her more time to meet the people who were more *her tribe* as Amy had often told her she should find.

Lisa turned to her right. She would have liked to ask Nancy about the striking silver collar she was wearing with a stunning pendent but Nancy was involved in conversation with a man on her other side. Lisa sneaked a look at her watch. It was only ten past eight.

Chapter Three

The next day was Sunday. Jim's itinerary included an afternoon trip into the Devonshire countryside. Lisa rose early and took breakfast alone. She'd made up her mind to make the best of things and not let the disappointments of her first night's holiday stop her from finding things to enjoy. She spent a pleasant morning walking into town, browsing gift shops and choosing postcards to send to Amy and Danny even though she'd probably be home before the postcards arrived.

The sun felt warm on the back of her *ivory-to-go-with-everything* jacket. When she returned to the hotel lunch was set out on the terrace and most of the coach tour people were already seated. Clattering cutlery punctuated the hum of conversation. The aroma of fresh bread and coffee made Lisa's nose twitch. She checked her watch. There wouldn't be time to go to her room to freshen up. She should join them.

"Hello, I'm Lisa," she said to a group at a table with a vacant seat. "Do you mind if I join you?"

"That seat's taken," one of the women said and looked away.

A hand touched her shoulder and the chocolate insurance voice of Aubrey Tennant said,

"I'd be honoured if you would join me for luncheon."

Luncheon. How grand.

She collected a plate from the buffet and made her selection from the tempting display. At the table she brought out hand wipes from her handbag: un-perfumed, antibacterial tissues for those little emergencies. She rubbed her hands with one and dropped the soiled tissue into a drawstring plastic pouch.

"May I?" Aubrey said and used one himself. "I see that you like to be prepared. Well organised."

"I always carry wet-wipes," Lisa said. "They're so useful. I mean, if the cutlery is not too clean. You know. Not that I'm saying that would happen in a place like this, of course."

"I think you're very wise," he said and Lisa could tell he was impressed.

"Yes," she said, "when it comes to organising I like to think I'm usually well prepared."

She hadn't been prepared for losing both her parents within two years of one another and mother having to sell the house to pay for her own care. She hadn't made provision for her first husband dying and leaving her with two children to raise alone, and she hadn't expected the way the second husband went and left her in the lurch with large debts she knew nothing about. But she had regrouped, recharged and got on with things. There was no point in regrets and longing for *what might-have-beens.* Life happened to you and you made the best of whatever hand you were dealt.

Aubrey Tennant and Lisa Miller ate prawns and salad on the grand terrace of the Clarendon Grand Hotel under a June sky peppered with puffball clouds.

"I didn't see you at breakfast," Aubrey said.

"No. I was up early. I went for a walk."

"Ah, an early riser." He looked impressed again. "And where did you walk to?"

"Just into town to buy postcards to send to my children."

"How many?"

"Postcards?"

"Children."

"Two. My son, Danny is twenty six and my daughter, Amy is twenty nine."

"At home still?"

"No. They have their own homes."

"And what field are they in?"

Field? Oh, he means what do they do for a living.

"Amy is a psychiatric nurse. She works in a residential care home. Danny is a photographer."

"Grandchildren?"

"Not yet. You?"

"No. I've never been married."

Alarm bells.

⚖️ ⚖️ ⚖️

Lisa looked for Nancy as she boarded the coach for the afternoon excursion but the seat beside her was taken by one of the other women who'd joined at Bristol. Before Lisa realised what was happening Joyce was standing up a few rows back beckoning her. Joyce removed a shopping bag from the seat next to her and beckoned again. Lisa managed a smile and sat down.

"Haven't you brought a shopping bag?" Joyce squeaked in her old lady voice.

"No. I thought this was a trip into the country."

"It is but we always stop for shopping on the way back. That's where I buy my souvenirs."

"You've done this holiday before?"

"I come every year. I wouldn't miss it for anything. You meet such lovely people. And the hotel? Well, what can you say? Everything about it is top-notch. I like to do the round tour with Jim every time to see what's changed. What did you think of the meal last night?"

"Very good."

"They're all like that. They couldn't do better on *Masterchef*. It's a real treat coming here."

Jim pulled the coach out into traffic and Joyce stopped talking. The absence of soprano squawking was a relief. Lisa leaned over to take another look at the sea.

"You live near the coast, don't you?" Joyce said, her intonation at the end of the question enough to crack glass.

"Yes, but the North Sea never looks as blue as that."

"I saw a programme on television once about how the coast in your part of the world is falling into the water."

"Not where I live, Joyce. Not where I live."

Totnes was a quick walk up the hill and back down again to the coach park. Buckfastleigh allowed just enough time to whizz through the abbey and buy some honey at the gift shop. Ashburton wasn't a stop at all and finally they arrived at Joyce's favourite destination.

The coach pulled in at an outlet centre, *Trago Mills*, a huge complex surrounded by walls with imitation battlements and turrets. Within the walls alleys of craft and gift shops, food outlets and souvenir stalls encircled an enormous store at the centre, big as three football fields housing clothes and shoes, garden equipment and DIY supplies, kitchen and bathroom accessories. Joyce made a beeline for the discount shelves.

"You'll find the best bargains in here, Lisa," she said. "Don't go spending silly money in Torquay's posh shops."

Lisa said she'd browse. "I'm not looking for anything in particular," she said. "You go ahead. If I lose you it won't matter. I've got my watch on and I know where the coach is."

She left Joyce rummaging through displays of cat ornaments: metal cats with wire whiskers; wooden cats with skinny, elongated necks and oversized heads with enormous painted eyes; fat ceramic cats glazed in a daisy design. Lisa went outside.

She strolled the streets. A smell of fried onions and doughnut grease wafted from nearby refectory tables where people were having a late lunch. She followed the path up the incline and found a small leisure park with children's rides and a miniature railway.

She bought an ice cream and sat on a bench watching pre-schoolers and their parents running from ride to ride. She wondered where all her time had gone. Danny had liked miniature railways when he was their age. He would have loved to ride the Trago park miniature train, sitting in one of those carriages with tiny windows and cute little door, rattling along the narrow track and through the tunnel. He'd been obsessed with Thomas the Tank Engine. He had a Thomas duvet cover and collected all the models. He used to line them up on the living room floor and went mad if anybody moved them.

"I'll never get them back in the right place," he'd say and they would have to stride over his layout being careful not to nudge anything until the day her husband had tripped on Gordon and spilled his coffee all over the sofa.

Danny grew out of Thomas eventually and then it was Star Wars. He ate, slept and breathed Skywalker. When Lisa took the children to Majorca Danny wouldn't go without his light sabre.

Now, stop that, she thought. *Don't get maudlin.*

"Lisa. Lisa! There you are." Joyce was running up the hill but not exactly running. Her movements were more of a swift shuffle. Joyce's feet hardly left the ground. Her shopping bag was bulging.

"Let me show you what I bought," she was saying. Her voice came in gasps, breathy bursts in high, sharp soprano. Not pleasant. A bit like cats. Joyce flopped down on the bench beside her. The shopping bag came up on Joyce's knee and she delved inside. "Look what I found," she said and brought out two lustre cats in mottled, almost psychedelic colours. They had startling green eyes. "Aren't they beautiful? My neighbours will love these. What do you think?"

I don't want you to grow old before your time, Amy had said. *Is this what that looks like? Dear Lord, it's what it sounds like. Poor Joyce. She must be lonely.*

A pang of guilt stabbed at Lisa's gut. Her face felt suddenly hot. She smiled at Joyce and, although she couldn't imagine where anybody would want to put the monstrous felines, her voice was warm as she said,

"Yes. They're lovely. I'm sure your neighbours will be delighted to have them."

Joyce re-wrapped her purchases carefully, rolling them in tissue and sliding them back into their gift boxes. She looked pleased. She leaned back on the bench and settled.

"I saw you with that Aubrey Tennant earlier," she said. "You want to be careful there."

Lisa said, "Sorry? What did you say?"

"You've got to be careful of that one."

"Aubrey?"

"Yes. Him."

"Why? What's the matter with him? He seemed very nice to me."

"That's what I mean," Joyce said. "He *seems* very nice and polite and charming and all that. But, you just wait."

"I'm sure I don't know what you mean."

Joyce puffed out her chest. Her chin went down and her mouth curled up. "He's odd."

"Odd?" Lisa said and an echo of the early warning system alarm bells she'd experienced at the lunch table reverberated under her ribs. Joyce puffed out her chest further. She looked around as if she wanted to check nobody was listening. She leaned in close and softened her voice.

"He's looking for a woman, Lisa. He's definitely looking for a woman."

"What's so odd about that?"

"It's the way he does it. You'll see," Joyce said and nodded sagely. "You'll have to watch out."

If Joyce hadn't said what she had about the strange way Aubrey Tennant was looking for a woman Lisa might have paid more attention to her own gut feelings. Even though she'd had no intention of taking up with a man ever again she couldn't shake off her curiosity about him. It *was* odd that a man his age had never been married.

She lay on her bed in her underwear waiting until it was time to go down for dinner and thought about it. Her spirit of inquisitiveness fired her imagination and she gave way to its enticement. Like instructing a teenager not to do something and then they go out and do it straight away, Joyce's warning made Lisa look for reasons to explain away Aubrey's unusual circumstances. Her thoughts battled with each other.

Maybe he's been looking after an aged parent.

That would make him a caring sort of man, the kind who put duty before self.

LOOK OUT. HE COULD BE A MAMA'S BOY.

Maybe he was engaged once and had his heart broken when she called off the marriage.

That would make hime the sort who fell deeply in love and he's been guarding his heart ever since.

LOOK OUT. HE COULD BE RIGID.

Maybe he's very particular and has simply never met The One.

That *would* make him the kind of man who was definitely still looking for a woman.

LOOK OUT. HE MIGHT BE IMPOSSIBLE TO PLEASE.

But what did he do about his URGES when he was young?

There was no answer to the last one. At least, Lisa couldn't think of one. Didn't want to think of one. Her stomach felt uncomfortable. Alarm bells were ringing again but she said aloud,

"I'm just hungry."

She decided there was no point in aggravating herself further when there was no obvious answer to her questions. Time would tell. In any case, she wasn't looking for romance. She got up from the bed and went to the bathroom. She brushed her teeth. She put on her new summer best outfit for the second evening's dinner. She left off the ivory jacket, chose garnet earrings that had been a present from Amy and when she looked in the mirror decided she was presentable. She smoothed her skirt, picked up the ivory bag and went downstairs.

Jim had put out name cards again and they were in different places. Lisa scanned the room to see where Aubrey was sitting. He was at a table behind her. She had a plan to keep an eye on him, just out of curiosity, but it wasn't going to be easy if she had to keep twisting around to see what he was doing.

"Did you buy anything this afternoon?" the woman beside her said. Her badge said Alison. Lisa hadn't put her badge on.

"No," she said. "Did you?"

"I chose some jars of herbs and spices. Big ones. Cracked black pepper, Italian seasoning for when I make lasagne, oregano which is in the Italian seasoning anyway but I always like to add a little more. Oh, and cinnamon. I use a lot of cinnamon. They were all very good value."

"Oh."

"Do you like cooking, erm, I'm sorry I don't know your name?"

"Lisa. Cooking? Do I like cooking? Well, I suppose the answer to that is *sometimes.* We have to eat after all. But sometimes I'm happy just to have a fried egg sandwich."

"I love trying out new recipes. The food here is excellent, don't you think? I'm attempting to deconstruct the dishes so I can try them out myself at home."

"Lovely," Lisa said and swivelled around to look at the table behind.

Aubrey Tennant was in conversation with a lady sitting at his left. Lisa couldn't get a good look at her face because of the back of the man's head sitting opposite them.

"I was saying, Lisa, how much my Charlie will miss my cooking."

Lisa swivelled back. "Charlie? Didn't your husband come with you?"

"Charlie is my dog. He's my *fur baby*." The woman put her hand to her chest and gave a shivery sigh the way children do when they've just stopped crying.

Not another one.

"I wonder where Jim will take us next," Lisa said in a rush. "I was hoping we'd get the chance to see the moors. We don't have moors in Norfolk. It's all quite flat, you see. Except for the north coastline where there are a few ups and downs but mostly Norfolk is flat. Well, we wouldn't have the Broads otherwise, would we? Now *there's* a place worth visiting. The Broads. Have you ever been to the Broads, Alison? Oh, you should try to see them if you haven't already. The Broads are quite outstanding. But flat, you see. That's why I would very much like to see the moors. I once read Wuthering Heights. Have you ever read Wuthering Heights, Alison? It all takes place on the moors in Yorkshire. There's something very special about moors, I always think. Wild and romantic and, well, moorish. I do hope Jim is going to take us to see Dartmoor. I once read The Hound of the Baskervilles. Have you ever read The Hound of the Baskervilles, Alison? It's all set on the moors. Dartmoor, in fact, if I remember correctly. Oh, yes, I do hope Jim is going to take us to see the moors."

Lisa had never read either book. She'd seen only films or television adaptations but, judging by the expression on Alison's face, it was game, set and match to Lisa. Alison did an awkward smile and turned to her other side.

Mission accomplished.

Lisa swivelled again. Aubrey Tennant was talking to the woman on his right and Lisa had a clear view of Nancy, bobbling her earrings and patting her hair with that big be-jewelled fist of hers.

Chapter Four

Aubrey Tennant was sitting between two women. In fact, apart from the man sitting opposite him across the table, Aubrey was surrounded by females. He knew it was Jim's way of sharing out the menfolk in the evening dinner seating plan.

The Nancy person to his right was an attractive sort in a nurse *Gladys Emmanuel* way. She was buxom and jovial without being too loud. She had reasonable conversation and didn't want to talk about herself all the time, although he *had* managed to glean from her that she was divorced and all of her offspring were well out of the way. She took care of her appearance, too, and her hair had those streaks running through it that made it appear full of sunshine and shadows. On the whole she was quite *presentable.* Apart from the jewellery. Aubrey didn't much care for the large earrings and other accoutrements the woman favoured. *They* were way too loud. In any case, he reflected as he summed up, the woman lived in Hampshire which was much too far to travel on a regular basis.

He'd already dismissed the woman on his left. As soon as she'd mentioned she had a son still living at home he cut the interview short. He had no intention of taking on other people's baggage. You never knew what was lurking at the bottom of the bag.

"Aubrey," the man opposite was speaking to him. "Good evening. How do you do? Pleased to make your acquaintance." The man held out his hand across the table. "I'm Barney. Ex C.I.D."

Aubrey shook his hand and said," Piper Precision Engineering. Design and Technology."

"Not retired yet, Aubrey?"

"No."

Aubrey scrutinised the intruder. The man was well put together, quite a physical type. He looked like he might have played rugby at some point. He had a full head of hair and good skin.

Early retirement.

He was wearing a well-cut jacket over a Ralph Lauren polo shirt. His teeth were capped. Aubrey couldn't see all of the man's wristwatch but it looked like the real thing.

On a good pension.

He oozed confidence.

Bugger.

The man seeped his oily confidence all the way through the meal, chatting to the ladies, flashing his too-white veneers, nodding and smiling. He had excellent table manners, Aubrey noticed, and he passed on dessert, patting his waistline and saying he had to watch his shape now that he didn't have criminals to run after. The females laughed at that but they all had a twinkle in their eyes.

When the meal was finished Aubrey watched Barney get up from the table and leave the dining room. The man was limping. Aubrey slid back his chair and followed on behind to get a better look. He was right. The man definitely had a pronounced limp.

An old rugby injury?

He had to find out. One of his *friendly approach* phrases should do it. He came alongside.

"Fancy a digestif, Barney?"

"A biscuit?"

"An after dinner drink. I like to take a measure of cognac from time to time. Would you care to join me?"

"That's very kind."

They sat on the terrace overlooking the bay. Daylight was fading and lights from the town reflected in the water like wobbly coloured balls. Aubrey decided on another friendly opener and said,

"So what brings you on a coach tour to Torquay?"

"Ah," Barney said. "Several reasons really."

Aubrey didn't know where to go next so he waited. Barney tapped his left leg. "I'm not driving at the moment," he said. "I got involved in a RTA. Would you believe it? All those years in the force and the week after I retire some lunatic sideswipes me and I finish up rolling over in a ditch."

Aubrey said, "Oh, dear."

"I'm waiting for a proper prosthesis." He balled his fist and knocked on his lower left leg.

Aubrey said, "Oh, dear."

"Well, a week in Torquay is not my usual choice of holiday but I needed a break, one where somebody else was driving. And, it gave me the chance to look up an old buddy of mine who retired to Brixham."

Aubrey said, "Ah."

"I can't wait to get behind the wheel again," Barney said. "What do you drive, Aubrey?"

"I don't drive."

"You *don't drive*?"

"No. I never felt the need to learn."

"You need a good set of wheels to attract the ladies, Aubrey. When your hair's going grey and," he patted his waistline again, "when the muscle tone's going south for the winter, you've got to have something good for them to look at."

"How will a false leg affect their impression of you? Won't it make them squeamish?"

Barney laughed. Aubrey didn't see what was funny. He waited.

"On the contrary," Barney said. "The ladies love it. It brings out their mothering side. They can't do enough for you. They treat me like I'm some kind of hero."

Bugger. Competition.

Aubrey was tired of forcing his face into a smile by the time Barney said he had an early start next morning and took his leave. He waited until the competition had limped off and made for his own room. He had plans to make, possibly he would need to adjust them due to the unexpected intrusion of this Barney fellow and his Hollywood smile. He let himself in and immediately set about his business. He opened his bedside drawer and took out a notebook and pen. He sat on the edge of the bed.

Day Three:

Find out more about the Lisa female, he wrote. *Where does she work? Homeowner? Widowed or divorced?*

He realised he'd been so impressed by the antibacterial hand wipes the woman carried with her and the handy pouch she kept to put in used ones, he'd forgotten to ask all his usual first questions. An unfortunate oversight. As a rule, Aubrey Tennant did not forget things. He considered for a moment and decided it was a good sign he'd forgotten his usual routine. It must mean there were real possibilities.

He got up and went to the tray holding a miniature electric kettle and sachets of tea and coffee. He thumbed through the dispenser till he found a sachet containing powdered chocolate and he opened the miniature packet of malted biscuits. He slipped off his shoes and placed them neatly side by side in the bottom of the wardrobe. Then he held the back of his hand against the heels of his shoes to make sure they were in perfect alignment. He slid the wardrobe door back into place.

He switched on the television for the ten o' clock news but he was paying little attention. He sat at the small table by the window with his notebook and pen, eating biscuits and drinking hot chocolate.

He pondered what his next movements should be and checked through his stock phrases for a suitable one to enquire about the Lisa female's financial situation. It mustn't sound too obvious. He didn't want her to realise what he was doing but it was an important matter and he must find the right words. Before he'd come into his inheritance he'd had no real concern over the female's finances. It was different now. It wouldn't do to have the female too comfortably off. She wouldn't be grateful enough. On the other hand, he'd have to watch out for gold-diggers.

Some biscuit crumbs had fallen onto the polished table. Aubrey went to the bathroom and pulled out two tissues from the wall dispenser. He scooped the crumbs into one tissue, brought the corners together and knotted them tightly. With the other tissue he wiped the table and buffed it back to its original shine. He wrapped the first tissue in the second and tied up the corners of that. Then, he put them in the waste container under the luggage shelf. When he went back to sit at the table by the window he shook the heavy drapes and smoothed the folds in case he'd disturbed them.

He picked up his notebook and began to write again under his Day Three heading.

Cleaning. What are her household standards?

If the antibacterial hand wipes were anything to go by her housekeeping skills ought to be optimum. He leaned back in his chair, sipping the last of his hot chocolate and pictured her.

Tidy. Presentable. Perhaps a touch plain. Slim, though. Yes. Not overweight at all which meant she must be still quite active. But plain.

With his tongue he teased out a crumb lodged in his molar and picked up his pen again.

Cooking, he wrote. There must be nothing with garlic. She must be adept at producing good old-fashioned English home cooking.

And then there was the question of Barney. What was he going to do about *him*? The man had a lot to offer with his good pension and trim waistline and hair like the actor Richard Gere. Women liked that sort of thing. Even a plain sort like the Lisa female could have her head turned. He must up his game. He might have to lower his own standards of requirements and settle for seventy-five per cent of his boxes ticked.

It soon became apparent to Aubrey that he would have to spend some money. He'd have to work faster. He decided to book himself on the Monday excursion and treat the Lisa woman to lunch.

Chapter Five

The Lisa wasn't in the queue waiting for the Dartmoor trip next morning. The air was cool and a breeze blew in from the east like an Arabian dream, carrying with it the aroma of a thousand and one full English, wafting from hotels and boarding houses across the bay. Even after eating his fill at the breakfast buffet, Aubrey's nose twitched and his taste buds danced on his tongue making his mouth water.

He hadn't had bacon for breakfast. Aubrey preferred his bacon *grilled.* The bacon in the bain-marie on the breakfast buffet at the Grand looked suspect and it wasn't full back bacon either. It certainly wouldn't have been his favourite sweet-cured. Not maple-cured as that was *too* sweet. Nothing could compare with Wiltshire sweet-cured, full back bacon and it would be as unthinkable as refusing to sing the national anthem to sit down to a plate of anything less. Aubrey had had muesli and a pot of strawberry yoghurt, wholemeal toast and apricot jam. He stuffed a banana in his pocket for later. Afterwards he went outside to find Jim to see if he could look at the passenger list for the day. Jim was already on board making his checks. Aubrey could see him looking underneath seats for litter. Jim's clipboard was on the dash but the coach door was closed. Aubrey contented himself with being at the head of the queue so he could be first on.

He chose a seat near the rear and regarded the females as they arrived. Lisa wasn't among them and he felt a pang of disappointment but there were still other possibilities on his list. The Nancy and the one with a son still at home could be disregarded, also the two sisters who never left one another's side. He wouldn't want to be encumbered with two of them. The Joyce had been crossed off his list long since. Her voice drilled into his head and made him shiver. He couldn't imagine having to listen to her screeching around him all day long. It would drive him mad. It was bad enough that the woman kept showing up in Torquay every year. One of the six females from Bungay looked worth a try and there was another who'd joined at Cambridge as he had.

On reflection, Cambridge wasn't a bad option, headquarters of Piper Precision Engineering being based there. He knew Cambridge well. It was easy on the train. Peterborough wouldn't be out of the question either, or Diss or Ely which was an attractive place. Yes, Ely would be a distinct advantage but the villages were not worth considering. They were too difficult to get to without a car. But his thoughts kept drifting back to the Lisa woman. She had started at Norwich which was even better, living as he did in Thetford. One stop on the East Coast Network.

He looked out of the coach window to see if she was a late arrival to the Dartmoor party but Jim was walking down the central aisle counting his passengers and ticking off on his clipboard. Lisa wasn't coming. In order not to waste his morning Aubrey selected his next prospect.

He made his approach during the coffee stop. He had his *friendly opener* ready.

"Are you enjoying your stay?" He couldn't use the woman's name because he didn't know it and he didn't think to say his own and introduce himself properly. The woman looked behind her to see who was talking and when she realised the question was intended for her, she smiled at him.

That's a very nice smile, he thought, *but she must be little slow on the uptake.*

"I am. Thank you for asking," the woman said. "I don't believe we've had the chance to speak before, have we? My name's Alison."

Aubrey shook the woman's hand.

"Aubrey Tennant," he said. "I'm very pleased to meet you. Would you allow me to join you for coffee?"

They went to find seats at The Café on the Green at Widecombe-in-the-Moor. The wind had got up and was blowing dust into their eyes. It was an indoors coffee day but all the tables were taken. Jim was with a group at a table near the door and explained how to find The Rugglestone Arms a short walk away. Aubrey led the way, two paces ahead of the woman.

He ordered coffee for himself and the Alison person asked for a glass of white wine. Aubrey watched to see how fast she drank it. They were seated near a window.

"Isn't that wisteria outside beautiful?" the woman said.

"I think it must be past its best now. Wisteria flowers in early May, possibly earlier in this part of the country."

The woman looked surprised by his response. Perhaps she was in awe of his superior knowledge.

"It must be very old judging by the size of it," she countered.

"It can take wisteria twenty years to flower if it's not in the right position."

She took a sip of her drink and looked as though she was deciding what to say next. She put down her glass and looked straight at him.

"Perhaps I should say that I am president of the Cambridge branch of the Ladies' Gardening Association, Aubrey. Although I have a fondness for beautiful flowering shrubs like the one outside I am more interested in growing for the table."

Excellent.

He knew how to move things forward from here.

"Tell me about your table, Alison. What kind of things do you like to cook?"

She seemed pleased that he'd asked her something about herself and she launched into an explanation of how she loved picking vegetables fresh from the garden and cooking them straight away. Aubrey listened with delight at the way she knew how to tend garden peas, beans, cabbage and cauliflower, and tomatoes and cucumbers in the greenhouse.

Aubrey said, "I like cake. Do you bake cake, Alison?"

She did. Angel cake with coloured layers , proper sponges without fat, the mixture whipped over steaming hot water to the right consistency, and something called Chocolate Devil's Food Cake which set his mouth to watering.

Excellent. Excellent.

The Alison female was ticking a lot of boxes. He offered to buy her another drink.

"That's very kind," she said, "but, no thank you. One is enough during the day."

Tick.

When they returned to the coach Aubrey went to his seat toward the rear and the Alison female took hers nearer the front. Jim was saying something over the loudspeaker system but Aubrey was concentrating on what he should do next.

So far, so good with the Alison from Cambridge. He could catch up with her again at the lunch stop and delve further, or he could use the afternoon to interview the Bungay woman. Kill two birds, as it were. That way he'd be in a better position to map out his evening plan.

He watched out of the window as the coach climbed up past the tree line and the landscape opened out like the dual rotating anamorphic lenses of Panavision in a scene from *Warhorse*. When he looked up again the Alison was twisted round in her seat looking at the back of the coach. Looking at *him*. His decision was made for him. When Jim stopped for photographs at a panoramic viewing site the Alison approached.

"I was thinking, Aubrey," she said, one hand holding her hair out of her eyes in the strong wind and the other hand keeping down her skirt, "as you were such a gentleman this morning, perhaps it might be an idea to have our lunch together. And *I* will buy the drinks this time.

Tick.

Aubrey inclined his head in a gesture he'd seen once in a film. He didn't have the colouring of a Captain von Trapp, or the Austrian national costume but he'd used the gesture before and he knew it helped to impress. It was elegant and masculine at the same time. He'd seen it copied on Downton Abbey.

Back in his seat near the rear of the coach Aubrey watched the moors slide past the windows. In his mind he was rehearsing his next conversation so that when Jim pulled into a pub car park in Yelverton Aubrey was prepared.

They would have to share a table with four others. Aubrey hadn't considered this eventuality and wondered whether it would be feasible to go ahead with his interviewing procedures in front of them. He had an idea. He needed to move her away from the others.

"Alison," he said. "Might I persuade you, just this once, to break your rule and have another glass of wine before we sit down to eat?"

She smiled and agreed.

He said, "Shall we take our drinks outside and look at the garden?"

She made no objection.

There wasn't much garden to look at and after they'd named the shrubs and trees and flowering perennials they sat on a bench with their backs against the wall, sheltered from the wind.

"Have you met many of our party?" Alison said.

"A few. I was talking to a man called Barney at dinner last night. He's gone to visit a friend in Brixham today. I had an exchange with a woman called Nancy, too."

"I was talking to a very strange lady. She has a passion for the moors. I'm surprised she isn't here."

Aubrey said, "Strange?"

"Oh, yes. Very odd. She went on and on about the moors and all the books she'd read with moors as the background setting. I thought she'd never stop. Some people have some very unusual interests."

"What was her name?"

"Lisa."

Aubrey did his Captain von Trapp and added raised eyebrows. He didn't know what to say next. He didn't think it the least strange that people might have odd interests, but more than that, he acknowledged that the Lisa female's unusual passion had aroused in him a certain, secret admiration for her. He knew deep in his heart how it felt to be different and he could imagine Lisa tramping the moors with her antibacterial wet wipes safely stashed somewhere about her person.

He dismissed the thought and concentrated on the job in hand. He was just about to voice his finances question when Alison put her handbag on her knee and began rummaging inside it.

"It's my only vice," she said, and brought out a packet of cigarettes. "You don't mind, do you?" She stuck one in her mouth and lit the filthy thing.

Aubrey said, "Actually, yes. I do mind. I mind very much." He stood up and looked down at the Alison female. "I'm very disappointed," he said and walked off.

Under the proviso that it's better to keep your enemies close, Aubrey was sitting on the terrace before evening dinner listening to Barney recount the events of his day in Brixham when someone stepped out from the residents' lounge to take the air.

Her fair hair shone in the glow of evening. She had on a pretty outfit with a skirt that came just to her knees and showed off a finely turned calf. Her face was beautiful. From where he sat he could see finely arched eyebrows over sparkling eyes that were *familiar.* Barney's words dissolved into the ether and floated out of Aubrey's hearing. They wafted from Barney's mouth, fluttering empty and meaningless, drifting over the table like silent mouthings, wisps of nothing at all.

The Lisa female had undergone some kind of transformation. Aubrey hadn't realised what fine bone structure she possessed and what an elegant neck now that he could see it. In the lobes of her ears golden shells glinted, pert and pretty. His eyes dropped to her legs again: slim ankles and, yes, big feet. It was definitely the Lisa female. Many Norfolk women had inherited large feet and, even though he knew the reason was something to do with their forebears spreading their weight as they walked marshy fens, he comforted himself with the knowledge that it tended to be those females who could trace their ancestry all the way back to Boudicca.

She turned on her heels and saw him. She smiled and her rosy lips parted to show even teeth. He pushed back his seat, stood to attention and Captain von Trapped.

"Bloody hell, Aubrey," Barney said. He had his back to the vision of wonderment and whipped his head around but missed what Aubrey had seen. "What on earth are you doing?"

"Acknowledging a friend, Barney."

"Royalty was it? Sit down man, and have another drink."

Jim knew better than to seat the Joyce anywhere near him and, since Aubrey had also managed to have a word about the Nancy and the Alison and the one with a lazy lout still living at home playing on his X-Box all day long, at the dinner table he found himself right in the middle of the Bungay Women's League. Bosoms and ballast as far as the eye could see. Lots of laughter and talk of things he knew nothing about. One of their group was on his list but the vision of loveliness he'd just encountered outside had over-ridden his intentions for the evening.

He scanned the restaurant. Lisa was at the same table as Barney on the far side of the dining room, not close enough for Aubrey to keep a close eye on them.

Dammit.

Barney would surely notice the change in Lisa's appearance.

Dammit.

And all Aubrey would be able to do would be to sit there and watch from afar.

Dammit. Dammit. Dammit.

It couldn't be helped. He would have to bring into action Plan B of the afternoon and get to know the other female on his list. There was no point in wasting the evening as well as the afternoon. His eyes roved across the faces of his dining companions and he waited for a lull in their conversation to make his *friendly approach*.

He fell at the first hurdle. All six women from Bungay still had husbands. They were on what they called their girlie week while the menfolk did their own thing. Three of the husbands were birdwatching up at Sea Palling, looking for Little Terns and the other three were on a walking week with their dogs.

The women included him in their conversation but, whenever he could, he looked down the room to where Lisa sat. She was looking very comfortable and confident, surrounded by a new group of friends.

"And what is it you do, Aubrey?" one of the Bungay women was saying.

"Piper Precision Engineering," he said. "Engine parts. For aircraft."

"That sounds very specialised."

"It is. Next question?"

The woman said, "Well, pardon me for asking," and turned away from him.

Aubrey scratched at his neck. The feeling he'd said the wrong thing prickled in his hairline. No matter. He had no further interest in Bungay.

He endured the meal. He left the starter after his first tasting of scallops in a creamy, white *garlic* sauce but he managed most of the pork *filet-mignon-en-croute* with accompanying garnish of vegetables. The chocolate dessert was more to his taste and, for a moment, he was able to forget that Lisa was sitting across the room not more than a few yards away from him where she was enjoying her time with her companions. Every now and then he heard her laughter, delicate and tinkly, feminine and nice.

He made a decision. He wouldn't let Barney muscle in on his prize. He would go over there and get between them. Just as soon as he saw them make a move from the dining room he'd excuse himself from present company and . . . . . .

. . . . Barney was taking Lisa by the arm and they were moving toward the cocktail bar. Aubrey sat rigid, staring. They disappeared from view and then came back. They both carried fancy glasses with sticks and cherries and paper parasols and they were going out onto the terrace. Barney had his hand against Lisa's back, guiding her to a table near a palm tree with a blue uplighter. He pulled out a chair for her and Aubrey watched as Lisa smiled at Barney in a way she hadn't smiled at himself. His intestines shrank and he needed the toilet.

Chapter Six

Aubrey kept himself to himself for the next three days. His list of prospects was exhausted and he didn't have the heart to reassess the females he hadn't already considered. On Tuesday he picked up a leaflet from reception and wondered whether he should book himself in for the Agatha Christie style November Murder Mystery weekend or even the advertised Christmas Special for Singles. He took the leaflet with him outside and walked toward the sea. The wind had strengthened again and the sky was grey, reflecting his mood. The beach was as empty as his Day Four plan. The situation was becoming more urgent. He couldn't realise his future plans until he found the right woman.

His stomach twisted as he thought about returning to work once more without an *intended*. The contentments of his backroom boy position at Piper Precision Engineering were no longer satisfying. It wasn't the work itself. He enjoyed the exactitude required and, overall, the company appreciated his scrupulous skills. It was the *people*. Apart from Reynolds he'd never got on with them, even when he was younger and they'd make jokes about him batting for the other side or even swinging both ways just because he didn't have a wife, or a fiancée or even a steady girlfriend. He couldn't join in with their talk of nights at the pub with the lads or how the team was doing in the league. Aubrey didn't drink much alcohol and had no interest in football or any other sport. During his days at work he filled his kettle and made his solitary brew at break times and ate his companionless packed lunch looking out of the windows as the seasons changed.

Since mother's passing he spent his weekends alone cleaning his house and restocking the larder. On Saturday evenings he went to the cinema and became an aficionado, watching how male/female relationships developed on screen and learning his stock phrases. As the years passed he paid into his pension fund and looked forward to the day he could leave Piper Precision Engineering and its people behind him forever.

But old age was approaching. Aubrey didn't want to spend it alone. He wanted a companion, a female to look after him and be a true friend. Now that the inconvenient desires of his youth had dissipated, surely there would be a woman who would enjoy the same kind of companionship. The recent and unexpected inheritance from his late father's brother had made early retirement a possibility. The amount of tax due on his inheritance had dented his savings considerably but still left him in a very comfortable position. It galled him that now he had the means to fulfil his dream the opportunity to put it in place was as far away as ever.

He dropped the leaflet in a waste bin and watched as the wind sucked it out again and up into the air, buffeting it, spinning and twisting it ahead of him as if it were a tease. He didn't look out for Lisa at dinner that night. He didn't even bother to see where she was sitting and with whom. He ate with some people from Bristol, excluding the Nancy, and retired early to bed.

On Wednesday he went to the cinema to see *Aftermath.* He admired Ridley Scott. He bought chocolate raisins from the Pick-and-Mix counter and the heavy feeling in his stomach lifted as the lights dimmed and the curtains drew back. At the dinner table that night he talked about his enjoyment of the film and recounted the plot in detail to his fellow diners until they retired early to bed.

He spent Thursday on a full day excursion organised by a Torquay travel company rather than one of Jim's trips. It included a boat ride and packed lunch and he was able to spend the whole day not talking to strangers at all. During the boat trip, as Aubrey sat watching the Devonshire coastline drift by, he was surprised to feel his phone buzz in his pocket. It couldn't be anything to do with work. PPE had never interrupted his time away before.

"Just thought I'd give you a quick call, Aubrey. See how the holiday's going."

Reynolds. Strange he should call.

"It's going well, erm, Timothy," Aubrey said. "But I'm at sea at present."

"In a muddle, old boy? Why? What's happened? Not like you to be all at sea."

"I'm on a boat. An excursion."

"Ah. I see."

Aubrey searched for something suitable to say. "How are things with you? Have you heard from Daphne?"

"Funny you should say that, Aubrey. I have heard from her, yes. She isn't coming back just yet."

"Oh."

"The thing is, dear fellow, I've run out of ideas of what to cook for my evening meal. I wondered if you could text me a few more of your bachelor specialities."

"Certainly. How many will you need?"

"You'd better send another week's worth."

Aubrey went to McDonalds for dinner. He'd seen the hotel menu and knew there'd be garlic in it. He sat alone, eating fries and texting Timothy Reynolds his chicken and pasta bake, a simple barbecue-style pork menu and a few ideas of what to do with left-overs.

On Friday, the last night at the Claredon Grand Hotel, Aubrey was surprised to see Lisa sitting with Joyce in the lounge area having a nightcap after dinner. He scanned the table next to the sofa where they were sitting.

Two glasses.

So there were just the two of them. He bought himself a soft drink and sat at the bar where he could watch.

⚖️⚖️⚖️

On the last night, Friday, Lisa agreed to have a drink with Joyce and prepared herself to listen to how much Joyce was looking forward to being with her boys again. They exchanged addresses for future Christmas cards although there was little chance of them ever meeting again. Joyce wrote in a diary and slid it back into her handbag.

"I thought you'd be spending your last night here with your new friend," she said with the fussy old lady expression that had become familiar to Lisa. "Whatsisname. Barney."

Lisa screwed up her nose.

"Not my type, Joyce."

"Oh?"

"Far too full of himself. Presumptuous. I mean, it wasn't that I was put off by the fact he has a false leg. No, that didn't bother me in the slightest but why would he assume I was thinking about his legs at all? How soon did he think I'd be getting anywhere near them in the flesh?"

"Oh, I see. Yes, I see what you mean. Still, it's a shame, though. Wouldn't you say?"

"No. I wouldn't. I prefer a more . . . *measured* man."

"What do you mean . . . measured?"

"Someone who has a strong sense of self-control."

"Well, don't look now, Lisa," Joyce whispered, "but there's that Aubrey Tennant sitting at the bar."

"There's nothing wrong with that, Joyce."

Joyce puffed herself up. Her mouth went tight and she whispered again through a thin line of stretched lip.

"He's looking straight at you."

"Is he?"

"Yes. No, don't look now. He'll know we're talking about him."

"Joyce, he isn't doing anything wrong."

Joyce pursed, a lot like the Suzy sister.

"Well, he's odd. That's all I have to say."

Lisa sneaked a quick look and said, "He looks a bit lonely. Why don't we invite him over?"

"You've got to be wary of that one. Don't say I didn't warn you. There's something not quite right about him. He turns up here every year just like a bad penny."

"Perhaps he likes his routines, Joyce. We all have them, don't we? Things that make us feel comfortable. I rather like that. You know where you are with routines, Joyce. You can depend on routines. I like dependability in a man. I know what it's like to have the other kind."

Lisa smiled at Aubrey Tennant. She made a gesture to invite him to sit with them.

⚖️⚖️⚖️

Aubrey wondered whether he should Captain von Trapp. He slid from the bar stool and padded across the thick carpet to where the two women were sitting.

He said, "Good evening, ladies."

Lisa said, "Good evening, Aubrey."

Joyce said nothing.

Lisa said, "Would you like to join us?"

Aubrey said, "I would. Thank you."

Joyce said nothing.

Aubrey said, "Can I get you a drink?"

Joyce said, "I'll have a gin and tonic."

"And for you, Lisa?"

"Thank you, Aubrey. I'd like a dry sherry."

Aubrey beckoned a waiter and ordered. He sat in an armchair at right angles to the women's sofa. He could see the back of Lisa's head reflected in the dark window behind her. From all angles she was a picture, a welcoming, comforting picture, like coming home after a hard day's work or a cup of hot chocolate held in cold hands. He knew he was smiling.

They talked about going home and he agreed with Joyce that while it was good to get away it was always lovely to be back home with your own things. Lisa pulled a face and said she always used to feel like that but, due to personal circumstances, she'd had to downsize recently and she didn't really like the place where she was living at present.

Tick.

Joyce emptied her glass quickly and began yawning. She picked up her handbag and excused herself.

"Early start in the morning," she said. "I'll see you at breakfast."

Before she shuffled away she leaned in close and said something in Lisa's ear. After Joyce had gone Lisa said,

"She wants to sit with me on the way home tomorrow."

This is your last chance, said a voice in Aubrey's head.

"Do you have a mobile phone?" he said.

While Aubrey was tapping in Lisa's number she leapt suddenly from the sofa and marched over to the far wall. Aubrey leaned sideways in his seat to get a better view of what she was doing. She stood in front of one of the paintings hanging on the wall and nudged it slightly to the left. She stood back, inspected it and gave it another small nudge.

"Sorry about that," she said when she returned. "I can't stand to see things not straight. Especially paintings. It's so annoying if they're at a wonky angle."

Tick.

"It's my training, Aubrey. I've got the Marshall and Simpson all-seeing eye. They teach us to notice these things. Now, I just can't help putting things straight."

Tick.

"Even when I'm putting out food on plates. I want it to look nice and neat."

Tick.

"Not that it's anything very fancy, you understand. I never learned how to do foreign food."

Double tick.

Aubrey Tennant listened to Lisa's nervous rambling with a faraway look on his face. He was watching her mouth move. That nice pink colour on her lips went well with her lovely shiny hair. Her dainty jewellery sparkled in the light from the table lamp. She smelled of something clean and fresh like apple blossom. His cup was overflowing and his checklist was almost complete.

Tick. Tick. Tick.

Almost complete.

He leaned forward and ahemed. "You don't smoke, do you?" he said. "And do you know how to make Chocolate Devil's Food Cake?"

Chapter Seven

On her return home Lisa threw open all the windows in her apartment. She screwed up her nose at the unpleasant smell drifting up from the courtyard outside the vet's below. She scurried through the rooms spraying air freshener and hoped somebody would wash away the unwelcome deposits outside her entrance door or she'd have to go down there and do it herself.

"Poor things," she said. "I bet they're scared. But really, that's nasty. I'll have to have a word with the manager."

She picked up her phone to call her daughter. There was no answer. She looked at her watch and decided Amy and her flatmate, Jessie must be both working the nightshift. She texted to let them know she was back home safely. There was no point in calling Danny. He'd probably forgotten she'd been away and anyway, it was Saturday evening. Danny would be out with his friends.

She made a hot drink and took it to bed, exhausted from travel and listening to the sound of Joyce's voice. The noise from the supermarket car park below her bedroom window was nothing more than a rhythmical bass hum compared with Joyce's off-key soprano all the way from Torquay, through Bristol and then at the service stations on the way to Cambridge where, at last, they said goodbye to one another and promised to keep in touch. Lisa had breathed a sigh of relief.

As she lay waiting for sleep Lisa thought about the journey home. Aubrey hadn't left the coach at

Cambridge. Lisa had got up from her seat when she saw Aubrey was asleep and mentioned it to Jim as he was getting ready to retrieve luggage from the hold.

"He got on at Cambridge, that's right Mrs Miller. I'll be dropping him off at Thetford. It's no trouble. Just one extra quick stop. It's on the way."

"He didn't tell me he lives in Thetford," Lisa said and felt a small smile at her mouth.

It would have been rather pleasant to sit beside him for the remainder of the journey home. She wanted to ask him about where he lived and all the other things they hadn't had time for but he was hard and fast asleep. As it turned out, they waved and smiled at one another when Jim pulled up in a lay-by and let him out.

Lisa slept till nine-thirty next morning and would have slept even longer if it hadn't been for somebody's car alarm going off outside in the supermarket car park. She woke with a start and realised she'd have to get a move on. She was having Sunday lunch with her friends Madge and Wallace Sparrow at their house.

Madge Sparrow had been Lisa's friend since they'd given birth to their daughters on the same day and occupied neighbouring beds in the Maternity Ward at the James Paget hospital in Gorleston. It seemed they were destined to keep bumping into one another: at the market, at play school and then through their children's primary and secondary years. They'd lost touch for a while and then one day in the 1990s when Lisa was manning the sales desk at Marshall and Simpson Madge came to pay for a pair of school trousers and two school shirts.

"And how would you like to pay?" Lisa had asked after they'd caught up with family news.

"I'd like to pay by debit card."

"I'm sorry we don't take them."

"I know you don't take them but you asked me how would I *like* to pay."

That conversation repeated for years. Every time Madge came in she'd ask to pay by debit card. Sometimes Madge would ask to see the manager and she'd go through it again with him.

"I would like to pay by debit card."

"I'm sorry we don't accept them."

"Why not? Everywhere else does. Are you going to be the last store on the High Street to move with the times? I thought you valued your regular customers."

"We do, Madam."

"Don't you *Madam* me. I would like to pay by debit card and I can't be the only one."

Madge loved to move with the times. She'd been pestering Lisa for years to get a smart phone or an iPad. Maybe now would be a good time to ask Madge's opinion and Lisa could learn how to send email photos as well as phone texts to her new gentleman friend.

Lisa threw on her coat and dashed downstairs. She hurried across the car park to the supermarket. She had her own shopping to do before work on Monday and she wanted to buy a nice bottle of wine to take with her for Sunday lunch. Strong wind was whipping up white tops on the Bure channel as it raced past on its way to the North Sea and nearly sucked her handbag from her arm.

Wallace was on duty at the front entrance. He had on his Addison's staff uniform and a *Customer Greeter* badge pinned to his chest showing his name.

"Good morning. I'm your Greeter today. Welcome to our store," he said to everybody as they came through the doors. Lisa collected a trolley and wheeled on through.

"Good morning. I'm your Greeter today. Welcome to our store," he said.

Lisa said, "Good morning, Wallace. Not on trolleys today?"

"Fuck's sake, Lisa," Wally said and clapped his hand over his mouth. "Pardon my French. I didn't recognise you."

"It's still me."

"Look at you," he said. "You've had it all cut off. It suits you."

"Thank you, Wally. What's all this greeting people at the door?"

Wallace looked around and dropped his voice.

"New initiative from management," he said. "Got to make customers feel they're part of our *family.*"

"I see."

"Well, I bloody don't. Bloody stupid, if you ask me. I said to the manager, I said, *Leave it with me Mr Waterhouse. They all know me. Trolley Wally'll see 'em right.* Do you know what he said? He said, *No, that's not quite what I had in mind. You must say Good morning. I'm your Greeter today.* I told him nobody would understand a word but he wouldn't have it. Are you still coming to eat with us? Madge is getting it all ready."

"I'm looking forward to it. What time?"

"Come back when you've finished your shopping. I knock off at twelve. I'm parked in my usual place."

Lisa knew where everything was at Addison's. She grabbed some fresh vegetables from the front of the store, dashed down the bread aisle to the back where they kept beer and wine and chose a bottle of rosé, back up the chilled food cabinets and picked up a 'three for a tenner' ready meals, skirted around the tea and coffee to eggs and cheese, turned around and headed back down by the furniture polish to the cash desks and had everything put away in her fridge and cupboards within the hour. Perfect. She plugged in the new automatic pump action room freshening dispenser and turned it up to full. Downstairs cats were yowling and dogs were yapping at the Sunday morning emergency appointments. She switched on her radio and turned that up too.

She took a shower and stood in her underwear pressing her M and S supervisor's navy blue ready for morning. Then she got out her makeup and had a go at applying it the way they'd shown her at the Clarendon Grand.

Wally was waiting in the staff car park at Addison's. He greeted Lisa with a peck, opened the passenger door and Lisa got in.

"Thank you," she said. "And thanks for looking after my car for me."

Wally pulled out into the middle lane by the traffic lights ready to make a right turn.

"No trouble at all," he said.

"It would probably have been all right to leave it in the car park here like I usually do. I don't know why I made a fuss this time. I mean, I can't keep my eye on it every night when I'm at home asleep, can I?"

"No. But I know what you mean. Anyway, far better to have your mind at rest. She's been sitting nice and safe in my garage while you were away. How was your holiday?"

"It was very nice. The hotel was absolutely beautiful."

"Don't tell me any more. Madge wants to hear all about it."

Wally made the turn for Bradwell and cursed. A long queue of cars was coming out of a car boot sale, snagging up the flow. When they arrived at the house Madge was on the doorstep looking out for them.

"Here you are. Here you are," she shouted and came running down the drive to meet them. "Lisa Miller! Look at you and your fancy new haircut. Get you indoors right this minute. I've got Yorkshire puddings ready to jump out the oven."

"A *gentleman* friend?" Madge said as they sat with a second glass of rosé before dessert. She folded her arms beneath her ample bosom. Her mouth went into a tight round shape and she made a humming noise.

"Well, don't leave it at that, Lisa," Wally said. "Madge won't settle till she knows it all."

"His name is Aubrey Tennant."

Wally put down his glass and gestured in the air with his finger.

"I used to know a Tennant," he said. "Years ago, it was. I was just a kid and I'd just started working for the gardening business. Funny old bloke. Lived near the Broad in one of those big houses up Peachtree Rise."

Lisa said, "Oh, I've heard it's lovely up there."

"It wasn't before we set to work on it. The whole garden was overgrown like it had never been touched for donkey's years. Took us weeks just to clear it. Then the old feller went away. Went to live abroad somewhere, so they say."

Madge waved an impatient hand.

"Go on, Lisa. How did you meet him?"

"At the hotel. He has a lovely voice. That's what I first noticed about him."

"A widower, is he? Or divorced?"

Lisa cleared her throat and said, "He's never been married."

"What? How old is he?"

"I don't really know."

"Well have a guess. You haven't gone and got yourself a toyboy, have you?"

"In his fifties."

"In his fifties and never been married? What's wrong with him?"

Wally said, "That's a bit harsh, love."

Madge shook her head and said, "Lisa knows what I mean."

"I'll get the apple pie," Wally said and left the two women alone.

Lisa emptied her glass. "I don't think there's anything wrong with him," she said. "I didn't get the chance to find out why he never married. I'm sure there's an explanation."

Madge leaned back in her seat and unfolded her arms. Then she leaned forward again with her palms flat on the tablecloth.

"Lisa, love," she said. "I've only got your own interests at heart. You know that. I wouldn't want to see you making any more mistakes like you did last time."

"I know you mean well."

The microwave in the kitchen pinged and there was the sound of Wally getting out plates for the apple pie. Madge was tapping her fingers against her bottom lip as though she was wondering whether she should let her next words out.

"Have you told him?" she said.

"Have I told him what?"

"Have you told him yet how your second husband went?"

Chapter Eight

Lisa enjoyed the half hour or so before the store opened. Everything looked neat and tidy and in its proper place. The whole shop floor smelled fresh and clean. Clothes hung unruffled on the racks; shoes and slippers lined up like little soldiers on parade and the food department was as glorious as the flowerbeds in St George's park, all nicely laid out and colourful with lettuces and tomatoes, carrots and French beans gleaming in their cellophane shrink wraps under the store lights.

It reminded her of how a school must be during the long summer holidays when there were no pupils leaving their clutter all over the place. Lisa thought her place of work looked better with no customers in it: no scuffing on the polished and buffed floors; no tramlines over the carpets where mothers had dragged pushchairs; above all, there was no noise.

Tills waited in silence at the cash desks and there were no bells summoning a supervisor to assist with a customer problem. There were no loud voices. The shop floor gleamed like a show house. Pristine walls looked out from their pegboard pink.

"Mrs Miller!" the voice of the staff manageress broke Lisa's contemplation.

"Yes, Miss Vaughan."

"I hope you had a nice break."

"I did. Thank you."

"Good. Have you read through all your mail this morning?"

"Not yet, Miss Vaughan."

"We're expecting Mr King."

Oh, bother.

A visit from the Divisional Superintendent, Mr King, was like a visit from the Queen. Nervous tension percolated downwards from the manager's office, through the staff manageress and general office staff, worked its way through the warehouse and on to the supervisors on the shop floor. Lisa picked up her mail and walked to her department.

Justine Belton, Lisa's new junior was unpacking pretty, retro shortie nighties to replenish the rack before opening time. She was wearing white cotton gloves to prevent static as she slid out the garments from their poly wrappers to arrange them on metal hangers.

"Can you remember the display ratio?" Lisa said.

"The what?"

"Have you forgotten already? You can't just put them out willy-nilly, Justine. Look, what would happen if a customer came in wanting a size fourteen and you'd filled the rack with size tens?"

Justine bit the inside of her cheek and said, "Would I have to go and get one?"

"Yes, you would."

Justine said, "Okay."

"No. It's not okay. Where would you have to go to get one?"

"I'd have to go to the stockroom."

"That's right. You'd first have to ask permission to leave the shop floor. You remember that bit, don't you?" The girl nodded. "Right, and you'd have to mark down the stock bins like I showed you. Remember?"

"I think so, but I could always ask Mrs Bush to remind me. Have I got the name right? Mrs Bush the stockroom manager. Her that always looks cross."

"Yes, you've got the name right. And all of that would take you ten minutes, maybe more. That's why we try not to go to the stockroom for odd items. We fill up the racks according to what the best selling sizes are. So when the customers come in, chances are we've already got the size they're looking for. Display ratios Justine. There's always a reason for everything we do at Marshall and Simpson."

"What if eight size ten customers came in one after the other?"

"It's very unlikely, Justine."

"No, but, what if they really did?"

"You'd have to go to . . ."

"The stockroom!"

"Yes."

"So, it's okay to go to the stockroom for size tens but not for size fourteen. That's not fair, Mrs Miller. And anyway, I'll never get my head round all these rules."

Lisa looked at her watch. Down on the ground floor Stewart from the warehouse would be unlocking the doors to let in the public and she hadn't yet dealt with the I.D.Ls and the R.T.Ms. She shuffled the morning's mail. No Returns To Manufacturer. Good. There was a decrease on the Increase or Decrease list though, over in beachwear, the department she was covering for staff holidays. She rushed through the store and pulled out the price card on the rack of polka dot beach playsuits. She sent an assistant to collect a card with the adjusted price and did a quick count of stock on display.

"Mrs Waveney," she called to another assistant. "Take this stock count up to the office for me, will you, please? And Mrs Elmhurst would you red star stamp the labels on all this stock? Thank you."

Lisa emptied the rack and carried the playsuits to the space next to the pay desk. Mrs Elmhurst followed.

"Did you have a nice holiday, Mrs Miller?" the woman asked.

"I did. Thank you. It was lovely."

"I like what you've done with your hair. I might have a go at that myself."

Lisa thanked her again for the compliment and hurried back to her own department to check on her trainee. When Mr King was coming Lisa had to make sure everything was as it should be. Back in Night and Underwear, Justine was still folding up empty cardboard cartons.

"Miss Belton, " Lisa said, "we need to get these boxes out of the way right now. The store's open." Between them they loaded cartons and poly bags on a stock trolley and wheeled it over to the lift. "Miss Belton, go back to your post now, please. I'll call Stewart and tell him we're sending up this trolley."

I feel like taking another holiday, Lisa thought as the pressures mounted. She dealt with the phone call to the warehouse then got out her figures. One last session with her department's sales percentages should see her ready to answer anything Mr King might throw at her. She hoped he didn't do the old *knickers* joke. If she'd heard it once she'd heard it a thousand times when sales were down on the corresponding period the year before.

Knickers are down. Ha, ha, ha! Mr King, whatever shall we do with you?

Lisa had a good idea exactly what Mr King would like to have done to him. You only had to see the way he looked at the juniors.

Lisa was dealing with a customer when the divisional superintendent made his appearance on the shop floor with the manager and staff manageress in tow. A woman had brought in a nightgown given to her as a birthday gift from her mother-in-law and she wished to exchange it for something she liked. Layers of flocked nylon with embroidered cabbage roses were not her thing, she said. When Lisa checked the manufacturer's item number on the back of the label she had to make an uncomfortable decision. And Mr King was watching.

"It's really old, isn't it?" the customer said.

Lisa said, "It isn't a current design."

"Go on, you can tell me. Just how old is it?"

Lisa knew it was so old it pre-dated decimal currency, but she said, "It's difficult to be precise but we can exchange it to the value of, let me see," and she made a rapid calculation from the original forty-nine shillings and eleven pence, "two pounds fifty."

The woman punched the air and said, "I knew it. I knew it. The old crow. She's done it again. Two pounds fifty? How long is it since nightdresses were two pounds fifty?"

"I really couldn't say. Would you prefer a full refund?"

Lisa escorted the woman to the refund desk and explained to an assistant. Management waited.

"Well done, Mrs Miller," Mr King said after the woman was out of earshot. "I wouldn't like to be that customer's husband tonight."

He strode through Lisa's department, flicking at the displays and nudging the rack feet with the toe of his shoe to see if the floor underneath was clean. Then he ran a handkerchief over the rails and inspected it for dust.

"Good. Good," he said. "Eight weeks forward estimate on men's pyjamas, Mrs Miller?"

Miss Vaughan said, "Mrs Miller has only just this morning returned from holiday."

Lisa said, "Six point five per cent down on last year over all styles, Mr King." She picked up a pack and used it as a visual aid. "I expect this style to continue its decline, bearing in mind that young men prefer the more sporty styles." She showed the divisional superintendent a pack of shorts and matching tee. "Twenty eight per cent up on these, Mr King."

"On all sizes?"

"Could be if we could get them in all sizes. We're waiting for a delivery on extra large. I'll make a call to the manufacturer today to see what's happening."

Mr King treated her to one of his satisfied smiles.

"Thank you, Mrs Miller," he said. "Always dependable. Well done."

She took an early tea break and had a ten minute think with a toasted teacake in the staff canteen. She was the only member of sales staff there. She sat by a window and watched hurrying shoppers on the street below. A sharp shower rapped at the glass and then she couldn't see the people outside any more beneath their umbrellas. They looked like one enormous, scaly-backed animal swaying down the street like a dragon at Chinese New Year. The shower strengthened. Drops of water on the window joined together to run down the glass and the Chinese dragon became a colourful water snake all the way from River Island to the Market Gates shopping mall.

In the canteen, behind the stainless steel counter top, kitchen staff were preparing vegetables for staff lunch. They all had their capped heads down, hair neatly tucked away, and there was the sound of scraping and chopping, rinsing and wiping clean the surfaces afterwards with their tins of *Lemon Cream Cleaner* and their scratchy paper towels.

Kitchen hygiene, Marshall and Simpson style. No cloths allowed. Only paper towels. A sensible rule. Umbrellas for the rain outside; paper towels for the work surfaces indoors. Horses for courses. If life was like work, you'd know what you were supposed to be doing.

She took another bite of her teacake.

You'd always know what to use, what to say, what to do and how to do it. There'd always be a procedure so you'd never get caught out.

But life wasn't so predictable. In fact, Lisa thought as she sat munching her hot buttered toast, life was a series of attempts to catch you out. A bit like Mr King. Life: the everlasting divisional superintendent.

Aha, life might say to you. Think you've got it all worked out do you? Then have some of this. And your husband drops dead. Now let's see if you can sort yourself out.

She ate the last mouthful.

And just when you think you're back on track — wham!

The second husband had been a bad mistake. Everybody said so but there'd been no handy rule book to rely on. No amount of percentage increase, decrease or eight weeks' forward estimating could have prevented her from wandering so far off her tried and trusted ways. It had been a disaster from start to finish. And she hadn't *meant* to kill him.

Chapter Nine

July

Aubrey waited for a week before he invited Lisa out for luncheon. He thought long and hard about the correct way to approach her and what would be an appropriate venue for their first meeting since Torquay. He felt nervous as he called her number but was eased by the sound of pleasure in her voice. They made arrangements to meet in Norwich the following Friday, her day off work. He took the train from Thetford and waited at the station for her train to arrive from Great Yarmouth.

His stomach was churning. He had a proper assignation at last and a lot depended on the outcome of it. Nervous apprehension interfered with his system of self control. A sinking feeling that it was all going to go wrong made him tap his fingers against the seam of his trousers. He hadn't tapped once in Torquay. He was on familiar ground there. He knew his *friendly openers* and *friendly interest questions* so well he didn't have to think about them.

To stop himself from picking at the stitching down the outer seam of his trousers he browsed the bookstore while he waited but bought only a small bottle of water for his dry mouth. He found a seat on the station forecourt and went through his friendly openers again.

There wasn't one to fit. All his openers and approaches were designed for first meetings, for people he hadn't got to know yet. He couldn't use - *so what brings you to Norwich?* That would sound ridiculous as both of them knew what was bringing her to Norwich: the train. And he couldn't say -*so what brings you on the train to Norwich?* They both already knew the answer to that too: lunch. Maybe he could put something together connected with lunch but not - *I'd be honoured if you'd join me for lunch* because she'd already agreed to it. He tried out some new ideas.

Are you hungry?

That was no good because whichever way she answered he wouldn't know where to take it next. If she said no what would they do until she *was* hungry? If she said yes should they then march to the nearest place? He tried another.

What time do you normally eat lunch?

He looked at his watch. It was twelve thirty. Suppose she normally had lunch at twelve. How would that question help? It wouldn't. The fact was, this was not a normal situation for him. The last time he'd had lunch in Norwich with a woman was when his mother was still alive.

They'd eaten at the restaurant in Bonds department store, now under the banner of the John Lewis Partnership. Mother had ordered beef and ale pie and he'd had cod fried in crisp batter with chips and peas. Afterwards they'd both had a Knickerbocker Glory in a tall glass with a long spoon. You could see all the different coloured layers through the side of the glass. Aubrey wondered if you could still have a Knickerbocker Glory. It was a very long time ago. When he thought about it he realised he hadn't seen a Knickerbocker Glory for twenty years. They'd probably have cheesecake now, or Tiramisu or whatever was currently fashionable in desserts. What had they been served in Torquay? Fancy little cakes and pastries with dots of coloured fruity sauces around the edge of the plate or sometimes one wide smooth stripe. But they wouldn't make those in the restaurant he used to go to with Mother. Fancy little things would be too time consuming for the cooks. They had to make big dishes of trifle and similar to dish out in shoppers' restaurant sized portions.

Mother loved department store shopping. Aubrey remembered the time when he was home from boarding school and they'd gone into Norwich for curtain fabric. He'd always enjoyed helping her choose furnishing or curtaining textiles for the house in Thetford where he still lived. He used to imagine furnishing a home of his own and choosing its decor but life had other plans; apart from his years at school he never left the house where he was born. Whenever he pulled on the sitting room drapes he remembered Mother, sitting at her sewing machine with the fabric spreading across the dining room table and onto the floor as there was always so much of it to accommodate huge bay windows. A family house with large rooms, the Thetford house would make for a tidy extra income in the rental market when he was able to move out to Oriole Broad and take advantage of Uncle Van's generous bequest.

Laburnum House. Uncle Vanguard's English residence would make a comfortable home for Aubrey and his lady. The detached house on Peachtree Rise with its high gables and genuine leaded windows must surely captivate any woman who made it her home. The garden would need landscaping again and they'd probably need to modernise the kitchen and bathroom but it was the perfect retirement hideaway.

But first things first. Where to go for lunch? Perhaps Lisa had a favourite place. He could ask about that. Something like, *Is there anywhere in particular you would like to go?* That one sounded considerate of her wishes. Females liked that. They wanted to be consulted and then they wanted the man to take charge. He played the question one more time in his thoughts. Someone sat beside him. He could smell perfume and feel her warm body beside him.

"Hello, Aubrey," she said. "It's lovely to see you again."

He looked round and, forgetting to greet her properly, said, "Is there somewhere in particular you would like to go?"

"Oh," she said. "I hadn't really thought. Let me see. No. I haven't got any particular place in mind."

They strolled from the station up the rise of Prince of Wales Road into the city. Bearing right, on to Upper King Street they talked of Lisa's work and Aubrey's work and what they'd been doing since the week in Torquay. Soon they approached Tombland.

"It's such an attractive area, this, isn't it?" Lisa said as they crossed over Queen Street. "All these pretty old buildings and lovely shops. But its name gives me the shivers.

"Ah," Aubrey said. "I can help you there. The name has nothing to do with tombs. Some say the original wording came from a Scandinavian language. There is historical evidence of the Vikings settling here. Others describe it as Old English. Either way, the word *tom* meant an open space."

"Really?"

"Yes. It was where the people of the time, the Anglo Saxons would hold their market. That was before 1066, of course. When the Normans came they made a lot of changes, including building the castle."

"Yes. I knew about the castle being Norman. You can tell by the shape of it, can't you?"

"That's right. It is classic Norman architecture."

Aubrey would have liked to continue a deeper conversation into the architecture of the ancient city of Norwich but the street ahead of them became so busy with lunchtime shoppers they had to walk in single file.

"Shall we find somewhere to eat?" Lisa suggested. "Let's go up here."

Aubrey followed as she turned left into a narrow street. Elm Hill with its quaint, bow-windowed shops each side of the cobbled street led them to a side alley where an appetising smell drifted from an open doorway.

"Oh, Aubrey. I'm feeling hungry now. Doesn't that smell wonderful? I wonder what it is."

Aubrey knew how to take his cue.

"Shall we go in and see?" he said.

They climbed wooden stairs to a compact room decorated with posters of far-flung places. The tables were dressed with different coloured cloths and none of the chairs matched. Neither did the crockery. Aubrey could see green cups on purple saucers. But the smell was making his mouth water. A young man showed them to a table and handed them vegetarian menus. Aubrey didn't know where to begin. He had no idea what couscous was, had never tasted butternut squash and thought lentils were what you put only in winter soups. *Honesty is the best policy*, his mother used to say whenever you were faced with a dilemma and so, when the young man came back to take their orders, he said, "This is my first visit to a vegetarian establishment. I'd like something without garlic. I quite like the flavour of nuts."

"I like it in here," Lisa said, looking around. "It's different." Aubrey said nothing. He was wondering what he would do if he couldn't eat what the waiter had recommended. "Joyce told me you go to Torquay every year in June, Aubrey. Is that something you've always done?"

"Yes, that's right," he said. "I was just a boy when I first went with my uncle Vanguard."

"Vanguard? That's an unusual name. I haven't heard it before."

Aubrey did a mini Captain von Trapp just enough to show he'd appreciated Lisa's comment. He settled back a little in his chair.

"He was a most unusual man, Lisa, and very intelligent. I loved the times I spent with him."

"And he was the one who first took you to Torquay."

"That's right. I was seven years old. Father wasn't well and mother suggested we took uncle Vanguard's offer to take my younger sister and me away for a while."

"You have a sister?"

"I don't know."

"What do you mean, you don't know?"

"I don't know if I *still* have a sister. We lost touch a long time ago."

Lisa made a sympathetic sound and said, "Oh, that's so sad when families lose touch with each other. What happened?"

"She went travelling when we were in our late twenties and she never came back. We received postcards for a time and then they stopped."

"Didn't you try to find her?"

"No."

"No? Aubrey, something terrible might have happened to her."

"I don't think so. Sigourney was a strong woman. She could look after herself. She was very popular and always had a lot of friends. If something terrible had happened to her we would have heard." The waiter brought their dishes and Aubrey leaned over to smell his. He picked up his fork and sampled. "Actually," he said. "That's very good."

"So, Sigourney, like the actress?" Lisa said. "Your family liked unusual names, didn't they? It makes me feel quite plain."

Aubrey missed the opportunity to tell Lisa he thought her far from plain ever since the evening in Torquay when he'd first seen the results of her makeover. Instead, he said, "Sigourney was the most captivating female any man ever set eyes on. At least, that's what they all said."

"All?"

"She had admirers queuing up for her hand."

"Oh."

Aubrey leaned toward Lisa and said, "Your dish looks interesting."

"Yes. It's very nice. So which admirer did she choose?"

"She didn't choose any of them. She went off travelling. I think it must have been uncle Vanguard who had given her the wanderlust."

"Since Torquay?"

"Yes."

"So, where did she go?"

"To see the world."

"Where was the last postcard from?"

"Argentina."

"Oh."

Aubrey had almost emptied his plate. He was pleasantly surprised by his first foray into vegetarian food. He finished the last mouthful and dabbed with his napkin.

"You must have stayed at the Clarendon Grand Hotel many times," Lisa said.

"Yes."

"Was your uncle a wealthy man? I think you must have needed a lot of money to stay there in those days. I bet they didn't have special offers then."

"You're right. It was more exclusive back then. Father used to say that uncle Vanguard was a man of mystery. He had business abroad for much of the year and spent a lot of time in Thailand. I once heard my parents discussing a rumour that uncle Van had a secret wife and family over there but nobody knew for sure. My sister used to invent stories about what he really did, *who* he really was."

The waiter returned and asked if they would like dessert.

"Something with chocolate," Aubrey said with confidence and Lisa asked for the same. A frothy concoction of dark and milk chocolate arrived in seconds.

"I must remember where this place is," she said. "I'd like to come again. Was she like you, your sister? Did she have your colouring?"

Aubrey laid down his spoon and said, "I remember her hair was darker than mine. Very shiny. It didn't look red until the sun shone on it. Then it blazed with hidden fires. Her eyes were grey-green. They sparkled like her favourite champagne."

Lisa patted her own hair and Aubrey wondered why she suddenly looked uncomfortable. He finished off his chocolate dessert and was just about to ask Lisa what time train she was taking home when she sat up straight, shook her head and said, "There's a film on today I'd like to see. We could catch the early evening showing. You're not in a hurry to go home, are you?"

"You like film?"

"I love films. I love going to the cinema."

The prickling sensation at the back of Aubrey's neck moved round to his ears but he knew he hadn't said the wrong thing.

"Which film is it?"

"It's Ridley Scott's new one. I forget what it's called."

"Aftermath."

"That's the one."

"You like Ridley Scott? He doesn't direct this one."

"I know. But I've always admired his work. I've seen them all. Some of them more than once or twice."

Aubrey grinned. Things were going very well indeed. If it all continued to fall into place he would have someone who could discuss one of his favourite subjects with him. He made a mental note to sit down with his notebook over the coming weekend and make serious plans about their future.

Chapter Ten

August

Lisa didn't want to tell Amy or Danny about Aubrey Tennant. Not yet. It was too soon. Life being as it is, she thought, anything could happen and the whole thing could be finished before it had even got going. She'd met Aubrey a few times for lunch or the cinema but there was no point in making a big thing of it. She had a new friend who just happened to be of the male variety. That's all there was to it. Nothing more.

Yet. If ever.

On her next weekday off she met Madge Sparrow in the Addisons' car park. The Bure channel was less grey than usual, gnarled trees on the banks looked less wind-battered and white hire cruisers rolled drunkenly as they manoeuvred between marker buoys on their way upstream to the Berney Arms and Polkey's Mill beyond.

Schools had finished for summer. The car park was full of visitors' cars and camper vans. Tied to the trolley park railings a line of holidaymakers' dogs waited with glum expressions. Their owners smelled of sunburnt skin and wore brand new, very white Reeboks, vest-tees revealing beer bellies. Madge made a cutting remark about women in muffin-top cut-off denims.

Wally was there to greet them at the door.

"Good morning, ladies," he said. "I'm your greeter today. Welcome to our store."

"Thank you, Trolley Wally," Madge said. "And what do you have on special offer today, my good man?"

"Chickens. Three for the price of two."

"What a pity we don't have space in the freezer."

Lisa said, "I suppose they've moved everything round."

"You've got it," Wally said. "Six packs and fizzy drinks in prime position."

Lisa grimaced.

"I wish they wouldn't do that," Madge said. "Who do they think their best customers are? People who are here for only two weeks or their year round faithfuls?"

"I've got a break in half an hour," Wally said. "Do you think you'll be finished by then? I'll meet you in the coffee shop."

Lisa and Madge wheeled their trolleys up the aisles together.

"Look at this," Madge said. "It's like a flaming carnival in here." At the head of each aisle plastic toys hung from hooks next to water pistols big as machine guns and pool 'noodles', brightly coloured cylinders of foam stacked upright in enormous cartons. "How is it going with your new friend?"

"Very nice." They wheeled into canned goods.

"So have you asked him yet why he's never been married?"

Lisa put two cans of baked beans into her trolley and said, "No. It feels too soon. It's not something you can just come out with. Is it?"

Madge picked up a tin of tuna and studied the label. "I don't want it in oil," she said. "I want it in brine." She put the tin back on the shelf and chose a different one. The store speakers crackled and a male voice announced *rolling back* prices on pickles and sauces.

"They're in the next aisle," Lisa said and they wheeled on, stopping briefly to look at specials on the end gondola. Lisa picked up a sachet of ready-made sauce for fish.

"So, what happens next?" Madge said.

"We're thinking of going away together for a few days. I still have holiday to take. But it won't be until after the main season's over. All the August dates are fully booked at work. Maybe some time in September." She picked up the buy-one-get-one-free offer on Branston even though she'd have to keep the extra jar under the sink.

Wally joined them for his morning break. A popular meeting place at any time, the Addisons' café was even more packed than usual with pensioners having the senior citizens' early specials and pushchairs full of toddlers greedily cramming in chips, their parents sporting burnt red shoulders and peeling noses.

All the trolley parking bays next to the café were full. Madge and Wally Sparrow and Lisa squeezed around a table for two and left their shopping bags against the wall where they could see them.

Madge said, "She's going away with him for a long weekend."

"Do you think that's wise, love?" Wally said. "I mean, you hardly know him."

"Well, I'll know him better after we've been away won't I?"

"Have you introduced him to the family yet?" he said.

"I was thinking I might do that after we've had our trip. You know, if it doesn't go that well, there'd be no point, would there?"

Madge said, "So where are you thinking of going?"

"Aubrey suggested Yorkshire or maybe Derbyshire."

"Why Yorkshire or Derbyshire?"

"He wants to show me the moors."

"Why?"

"I don't know."

Wally took a gulp of his coffee and said, "Will you go on the train?"

Lisa took a moment to think. She put down her cup in a determined fashion and cleared her throat.

"You know what?" she said. "I think I'll drive. We were going to take the coach but it takes forever, stopping here, there and everywhere. My car could do with a good, long run. Yes, I think I'll drive."

"Drive?" Wally said, his eyebrows raised. "Oh, Lisa it's a long way for you to drive, love. Especially after . . ."

Madge interrupted. "You haven't told him yet, have you?"

⚖️ ⚖️ ⚖️

"You can drive?" Aubrey said when Lisa called him on the phone that night.

"Yes. I want you to think about it. That's why I called. I wanted to stop you from booking coach tickets. You haven't booked already, have you?"

"No. Why do you come to Norwich on the train if you have a car?"

"It's easier on the train. Parking's a nightmare at the moment in Norwich. There's a park and ride and I sometimes use that but I'm so close to the station where I live. It's right next to Addisons."

"You didn't tell me you had a car."

"You didn't ask."

Aubrey realised she was correct. He hadn't asked. He had assumed. *First rule of business: never assume anything.*

Lisa was still speaking. "Well, I know you're not keen on travelling in cars, Aubrey, but . . ."

"How do you know I'm not keen on travelling in cars? Who told you?"

"Nobody told me. I put two and two together and worked it out myself. And I want you to know that, whatever anybody says, I am a safe driver."

"What do you mean, *whatever anybody says?*"

"Well," Lisa said, "some people have a thing about women drivers."

Aubrey had a thing about *all* car drivers. They were not to be trusted. They caused accidents. They killed other people as well as themselves. Coach drivers were different. They took their responsibilities more seriously. And anyway, if the worst were to happen you'd stand more chance of survival in a coach crash than in a little tin box that could easily slip underneath the wheels of a giant truck or slam into the back of a double decker bus.

"So, if it's because you get travel sick," Lisa was saying, "we could make regular stops. And you'd be sitting up front, of course. People who get travel sick are often better in the front."

"I don't get travel sick."

"Well, that's good, then, isn't it? We'll take a spin up the road and have ourselves an adventure."

Aubrey felt the back of his neck prickling. The room was closing in on the tight corner where he found himself and the fingers of his free hand were tapping against his trouser leg.

"Aubrey? Are you still there?"

"Yes."

"So, have you thought about it?"

"Well, I . . ."

"My little car needs a good run out."

"*Little*?"

"Well, I know you must be at least six feet tall, Aubrey, but you can slide back the passenger seat all the way. My son's used it and he's a big boy. He's never had any trouble getting in and out of it."

Little cars were worst of all. *Little* cars had no headroom and gave you a stiff neck after half an hour. *Little* cars made you sit with your knees under your chin. In little cars you felt as if you were too close to the road surface. Moreover, little cars squashed like concertinas at the slightest bump and crushed your legs. Little cars were nothing short of death traps.

Aubrey's free hand wandered up his trouser leg, drummed across his chest to the phone receiver and his fingers began tapping on the speaker.

"Aubrey? Aubrey? What's that noise?"

"What noise?"

"I can't hear you, Aubrey. There's a funny noise."

"I can't hear it."

"I can't hear you, Aubrey. You'll have to say that again."

"Say what again?"

"I can't hear you, Aubrey. There's some interference on the line."

"I can hear you perfectly well."

"Sorry?"

"I can hear you perfectly well."

"I can't hear you, Aubrey. There's a funny noise. I'll call you tomorrow after you've had more time to think about it."

Chapter Eleven

September

Lisa drew up her car in the street outside Aubrey's house in Thetford. She pulled on the handbrake, switched off the engine and leaned back with a sigh. It had been a long day. On reflection, it probably hadn't been a good idea to squeeze so many different activities into the last twenty four hours of their little holiday. She cast a quick glance at Aubrey in the front passenger seat. He was looking diminished. Even in the dark she could tell he wasn't feeling himself. His head was lolling forward to his chest. He seemed suddenly much older than his years. He'd said very little on the journey back from Yorkshire and even less since she'd detoured on the way home to attend the last couple of hours of the 1940s day in Sheringham. But she'd wanted to make the most of her time off work and it wasn't her fault that the Sheringham 1940s weekend happened to coincide with her and Aubrey's trip to see the northern moors.

"Are you feeling unwell?" she said, flicking on the car's interior light.

"I'm fine, thank you."

"Only, you look a little jaded."

"Just tired, Lisa. Just tired. Why have you stopped here?"

"Because it's where you live."

"I mean here. In the road. You passed the drive to the house."

"That's right, Aubrey. I did. I don't reverse into dark driveways."

Aubrey didn't question her further about her reasons for not wanting to reverse into his drive. When she looked at him more closely she could see he seemed too tired to talk. She dismissed all thoughts of dark driveways and said, "So, shall we go in then? I expect you'd like a nice cup of tea."

Aubrey's kitchen felt cool after the warmth of the September evening. Lisa switched on the lights and pulled down the roller blind. Aubrey had disappeared upstairs. Probably gone to the bathroom. She filled the kettle and found tea cups in their usual place. Aubrey's kitchen was well organised. It was one of the things she admired about him.

Since meeting Aubrey in June at the Clarendon Grand Hotel in Torquay their relationship had developed slowly but comfortably, Lisa thought. They were understanding more about one another. It seemed to Lisa that Aubrey had been something of a mama's boy when he was younger. She'd gathered this from the things he said. Whatever the conversation might be about he always managed to include something about what his mother would have done in the same situation.

Mother would have cooked her roasts **this** *way,* he might say. Or, *Mother would have my shirts washed, dried, ironed and back in my wardrobe as soon as I took them off.*

When Aubrey and Lisa visited somewhere new to them such as the glass museum at Langham and watched a demonstration of glass-blowing or the

Museum of the Broads at Stalham, Aubrey would say, *Mother would love it here* as if he planned to go home and tell her all about it.

Lisa thought a younger, less experienced woman would be disheartened by such remarks, finding herself being measured against a superior female who held the biggest part of her son's heart and would never let it go. In her own younger days she would have retorted with a response something like,

Well, I'm not your mother, Aubrey Tennant. I don't want to be like your mother. If it's another mother you're looking for you'd better look elsewhere.

But, Lisa was nothing if not stoical in her own measurement of the man who was courting her. It didn't matter how many times Aubrey mentioned how his mother would have cooked her roasts or ironed his clothes or planned their days out. Mother was dead. If the day ever dawned when Aubrey and she became a permanent couple Lisa would set her own standards of housekeeping and cooking roasts. If Aubrey didn't like it he knew what he could do.

Madge Sparrow had offered a different explanation of why Aubrey Tennant had never married. Lisa had invited them to her flat to share a meal one August afternoon when Lisa had a day off work and Wally's shift at Addison's finished early. They'd met in the store car park and strolled along the banks of the Bure working up an appetite and breathing in the salt air coming in on the tide from the east. Under a cobalt sky cruise boats tackled the channel below them, doing their best to avoid hitting the marker buoys, the wind urging them on their journey inland. They dipped and weaved against the pull of the tide, bright white holiday boats, beach towels flapping from the decks, pilots wearing *Captain*'s hats and young girls stretched out on the sun decks aft of the cabins. Sometimes the boats' occupants would wave at the three of them and they waved back, catching the holiday atmosphere that engulfed the town at this time of year especially when the sky was the colour of cornflowers and boats sliced the water into thousands of marquise-cut, watery diamonds blinking under the summer sun.

Windswept and hungry, Madge and Wally Sparrow returned to Lisa's home where the table was already laid with salads and cold cuts, pies and pastries, relishes and sauces, all set out in bowls or on platters and all covered in hygienic plastic film.

"Tuck in," Lisa said. "Don't wait for me." She left them helping themselves while she went to the kitchen for a bottle of wine.

"Caramelised onion relish," she heard Wally say. "My favourite." He was still spooning it onto his plate when she came back with the opened bottle.

Lisa had baked a cake for afterwards, her third attempt at the chocolate devil's food cake Aubrey had mentioned more than once during the course of their meetings since June. This third attempt was good enough to put out for guests and Lisa was looking forward to Madge and Wally's feedback on it.

"I think I've got it right this time," Lisa said. "You've got to give the milk enough time to sour in the lemon juice."

"Well, it's a funny sort of recipe, if you ask me, Lisa, but I've got to say I like the flavour. It's not too sweet, is it? Not too chocolatey."Madge said. "What do you think, Wally?"

"Bloody lovely."

"And how is your Mr Tennant with a voice like chocolate?" Madge went on. "What does he think of your chocolate devil cake?"

"I haven't given him any yet. I want to get it right first."

"You mean it's got to be better than what his mother used to bake?"

"Sort of."

Madge Sparrow shook her head and her mouth pursed. "I've been thinking about what you told me the other day," she said. "You know, about how you thought Aubrey might have been a bit too tied up with caring about his mother."

Wally looked up from his wedge of chocolate devil's food cake and said, "What do you mean, Madge? You don't mean . . ."

"No I don't mean anything seedy, Wally. Nothing like that. No. Lisa wondered whether the reason he never got married was because his mother got in the way."

"You mean, like, she disapproved of his girlfriends or she didn't want to be left alone if he went off and got married?"

"Yes, love. Like that. Well, it's common enough, that sort of thing. So, what I was thinking is, maybe, just maybe, he wasn't too close to his mother at all. In fact, he resented her influence in his own life so much he actually detested her."

Lisa screwed up her eyes in thought. "Oh, I don't think so, Madge. He always talks with such reverence about all the wonderful things she could do."

"Yes, but, listen a minute. That could be a cover-up for how he really felt. I mean, you're supposed to love your mother, aren't you? And boys do admire their mothers more than daughters do. Don't you think? Anyway, what I'm suggesting is, it might not be what you think it looks like. When he's saying *mother used to do this and mother used to do that*, he might really be glad that she's not around any more controlling his life for him."

Lisa took another slice of cake and said, "So that could be a good thing, then?"

"Not necessarily, Lisa, love. From what I've read in my monthly *My True Heartbreak Stories*, men who constantly refer to the mother they secretly hated spend the rest of their lives hating the woman they're with!"

The upstairs toilet flushed and Lisa heard Aubrey padding down the stairs, shifting her out of her reverie and back into the job at hand.

"Are you staying tonight?" Aubrey said as he came into the kitchen. "The spare room is made up."

"Not tonight, Aubrey, thank you. It's Monday tomorrow. I've work in the morning. I have to get back home."

"It's late."

"Yes, I know. I'll just have this cup of tea with you and then I'll have to be off."

He didn't look disappointed.

Aubrey waved his lady off and watched the tail lights of her car disappear into the night. When he went back inside he looked at the clock. He couldn't remember the last time he'd stayed up until this far past eleven thirty. His back ached. His legs throbbed. His brain hammered against his skull as if it were trying to get out through his ears. He made another hot drink and took it into his living room to sit and think. He slumped into his favourite chair.

Discomforting feelings gnawed at his innards and he couldn't make sense of them. He didn't know why he felt troubled. He sipped at his hot chocolate and mulled over the time he and Lisa had spent in Yorkshire. Briefly, it occurred to him it might be better if he brought out his notepad and listed all the things on his mind so he could put them into some sort of order but he was too tired to think straight. He would have to postpone his pros and cons list. He let the thoughts wash over him in whatever order they presented themselves and decided to make his list in the morning when he felt refreshed.

Overall he'd enjoyed the trip to Yorkshire to see the moors. Lisa had found a very presentable lodging for them in Haworth close to The Black Bull where, apparently, Branwell Brontë used to partake of his nightly libations. Aubrey took another sip of his hot chocolate and contemplated the Brontë brother. He could not find it within himself to feel sympathy for anyone who drank himself into alcoholism and use of opiates but, as Aubrey felt the comforting warmth of his favourite armchair cushioning his body and supporting his aching limbs, he acknowledged a certain understanding with a complex character who questioned himself so much he painted himself out of his own family portrait.

Branwell Brontë must have been a man who was dissatisfied with himself. A disappointed man. A man who felt he didn't belong. Aubrey had always known that feeling. Trying to be ordinary took a lot of effort. Fitting in with everything that happened to ordinary people in their ordinary lives required of Aubrey Tennant a level of undertaking the majority would never be able to understand. Sometimes he thought the illusion of ordinariness he created in his daily activities was his finest performance.

Yet Lisa seemed to understand him. At least, she didn't pass comment on anything about him she might find odd. As he sat cupping his mug of hot chocolate in his hands Aubrey tried to remember if during the week there had been any occasion when he himself had felt there'd been any of the interpersonal discomforts that usually accompanied his having said something or acted out of the ordinary. He couldn't recall one.

From the beginning of their trip to the north of England Aubrey had been surprised by Lisa's accomplishments. In truth, he'd been impressed. She'd planned the route meticulously and worked out an estimated time of arrival taking into account time for two stops along the way. She'd picked him up promptly at the train station in Norwich and as they travelled along the A47 towards Kings Lynn he realised he was quite comfortable in her little car. She'd been correct about the amount of leg room once he'd pushed the passenger seat all the way back. There was headroom enough, too. She was a competent driver. He'd felt himself relax a little. When he'd suggested an alternative route she was remarkably forthright in expressing her preparedness.

"Wouldn't it be better to pick up the A1 at Peterborough rather than using the A17 out of Norfolk?" he'd said.

"I considered that, Aubrey," she said. "I know the A17 well. It's a drag, I admit. In fact, it's particularly boring in places but when did you last drive it, Aubrey?"

"I don't drive."

"Exactly," she said and put her foot down.

She was quite right, of course, and he didn't object to the way she'd defended her decision. Indeed, Aubrey thought, her succinct summing up of the situation filled him with confidence in her and he relaxed even more.

She'd booked separate rooms at the hotel and it comforted him that there were to be no expectations from her on that particular front. On the few occasions she'd stayed at his house in Thetford he'd made up the spare room for her and she'd never questioned it. They'd had no more than a tentative hug at bedtime and, once, he'd pecked her on the cheek. The arrangements for their week away together had been a huge concern. Separate rooms had saved him much anxiety.

He slept soundly on their first night away and woke with a hearty appetite for his favourite breakfast. It wasn't *Wiltshire Sweetcure* but he'd waived his usual requirements with regard to the quality of his breakfast bacon. The Yorkshire variety proved tasty enough and they set out to explore the village of Haworth to discover its attractions.

The Brontë Parsonage museum had interested them both. Lisa bought postcards and a copy of Jane Eyre at the gift shop. After lunch she'd discovered the delights of the various retail establishments with their traditional shop fronts and large bow windows. They'd walked the length of the cobbled main street, all the way down looking at shops on their right and all the way back up again looking at shops on the other side. She'd bought a soap bar that looked like a large slice of cake for her son and in the shop specialising in Thai silk she bought a lipstick holder for her daughter. By the time they returned to their lodgings Aubrey realised his legs were aching.

"I didn't realise it was so hilly," he said over dinner at The Black Bull.

"It's the Pennines, Aubrey," Lisa said. "We're not used to walking up and down hills in Norfolk, are we? It'll do us good."

"I was wondering whether we might postpone our walk tomorrow up into the moors," Aubrey said. "I understand it's quite a trek to High Withens."

They'd driven out to Skipton instead, the gateway to The Dales and afterwards taken a circuitous route along country roads before their evening meal in a wayside hostelry with stone floors and replica antique light fittings.

Lisa had insisted on making the moorland trek the following day. The forecast had promised fine weather and she was keen to see the ruins of the isolated farmhouse that had inspired Emily Brontë's Wuthering Heights. Aubrey remembered they'd set out in high spirits and he was looking forward to witnessing Lisa's delight at being surrounded by genuine moorland. They began the gentle climb beyond the tree line.

The Yorkshire air tasted fresh and sweet; clouds scudded in a gentle breeze. Sheep grazed below them in fields surrounded by dry-stone walls and sheltered by trees just beginning their autumn change of colour. Aubrey welcomed a feeling of contentment as he padded along, the mossy path beneath his feet soft and yielding. Heather was still in bloom and as they made their way through the heath the path changed to gravel bordered by bright pink heather bells.

At the thought of the moorland path Aubrey's stomach lurched. As soon as he imagined crunching along that path through heather that spread as far as he could see, the strange, discomforting feeling gnawed at him again. He put down his drink.

"I should have fetched my notebook," he said aloud.

He got up and went into the kitchen then spun around to retrieve his hot chocolate mug. His mind was muddled. He couldn't make it focus on why he had suddenly felt nervous. Without thinking he switched on the kettle and made a third hot drink. He took it upstairs and put it on his nightstand. His getting-ready-for-bed ritual passed in auto-pilot. Eventually he found himself sitting up in bed with his drink cogitating on the day they went to see the moors.

"Beautiful, isn't it?" Lisa had said, stopping to breathe in deeply. Aubrey had lowered himself on to a boulder and stretched out his aching legs.

"It's further than I thought," he said. "Do you think it's much further yet?"

"I should think we're half way there, Aubrey." She bent down to sit beside him and ruffled her hands through the heather. "I think I'll cut a bit of this on the way back to put on the front of my car. You know, like a whats-it-called."

"Insignia?"

"Yes. I think that's what I mean. Like a badge." She leaned forward clasping her knees and sniffed at the air. "Isn't there an earthy smell up here?"

"We're sitting on ancient peat underneath this rock, Lisa," Aubrey said, "and the rocks beneath the peat on most moorlands are one hundred and fifty million years old."

"No."

"Yes. From the middle Jurassic period. They were deposited by great rivers. The surrounding land was rich in plant life and supported many animals, including dinosaurs."

"Well, I never."

"But the rocks of the Penistone area, here in Haworth are from the Upper Carboniferous period."

"You don't say."

"I do say. That makes them three hundred and twenty million years old."

"Get away with you."

"The continent was then close to the equator."

"Who would have thought it?"

"Yes. It would have been warm and wet."

"Instead of mostly cold and wet."

"It would have been covered in tropical rain forest."

"And now it's covered in heather. I think I prefer the heather, Aubrey. I shouldn't think we'll come across any animal bigger than a grouse today."

Sitting up in bed Aubrey didn't understand why Lisa had shown so little interest in the geography surrounding them and its history. Why, when she had professed to an acquaintance in Torquay her passion for such landscapes, did she seem interested only in trekking through the heather at an alarming rate only to turn around and trek all the way back again?

He fell asleep lost in the mystery of it.

Chapter Twelve

Even though Lisa was used to Aubrey's pattern of waiting a few days before contacting her again she wasn't surprised when he phoned her the very next evening after their return from the north. She'd sensed there was something on his mind straight after their walk on the Brontë moors and there was no doubt he'd seemed unusually tired when they arrived home in Norfolk. It pleased her that he was thinking about her enough to break his habit but her stomach was rumbling.

"Aubrey," she said, "it's lovely to hear from you but can I call you back in about an hour? I've only just got in from work and I'm ravenous."

She kicked off her shoes and padded into the kitchen, pulled out an Addison's ready meal from the fridge and thrust it in the microwave. By the time she came back from the bathroom her evening meal was pinging ready. Normally she would have flicked on her television and watched the evening news with her plate on her knee but she had things to think about. She wanted to concentrate. Noise from the television would have been a distraction.

Why had Aubrey broken his pattern and telephoned tonight? What was bothering him? Maybe, after complaining about his legs aching so much, he'd come to realise the truth about the level of his fitness. Or, lack of it.

Well, what do you expect? she thought. *Sitting down at your work all day and watching films all night?*

She was exaggerating, she knew, but truth be told, Aubrey hardly ever had any exercise at all. It was a wonder he managed to keep his slim physique especially with his love of all things chocolate. It must be in the genes, she decided. Some families are like that. Just like some families are all fat, others are all slim whatever they eat.

As she ate her evening meal, Lisa tried to conjure up an image of Aubrey's family. She hadn't seen photographs of any of them at his place in Thetford. She wondered if he actually possessed any old photograph albums. Most families have them, she thought. In the days before computers and digital photography everybody had a camera to record special occasions and albums to keep the memories in.

She tried to imagine his mother's face. In her mind's eye Lisa could see a small face with a tight mouth. Would her voice be pleasing like Aubrey's or an unpleasant squawk like Joyce's? His mother's eyes would be small, too, and probably a bit too close to the prominent nose. Her body would be small and wiry, like a terrier always on the go, always doing something. She'd always be busy what with all that washing and ironing and making sure Aubrey's clothes were back in his wardrobe before he'd taken them off. She wondered if Aubrey's mother had devoted the same care to her husband's clothes.

Lisa couldn't picture Aubrey's father at all. Perhaps he'd been much like Aubrey himself. Maybe he had a voice like chocolate insurance as well. She supposed the alluring Sigourney was still as voluptuous as ever with her sparkling eyes and burnished hair. How old must she be now? What did Aubrey say about his younger sister? How many years younger? She'd be into her fifties now. Lisa pondered what Aubrey's sister might look like after thirty years of champagne and travelling the world. Probably fabulous. Who wouldn't look and feel fabulous after a lifestyle like that?

Ah, well, she thought. *I don't much care for champagne anyway.*

She laughed at herself for her juvenile reasoning. "You're too old for this tomfoolery," she said aloud. "Why don't you just ask him?"

She cleared away her plate and picked up her phone to call him.

"Aubrey," she said. "Sorry about that. I feel better now I've eaten. What did you have on your mind?"

There was a pause before he answered.

"I've been thinking," he said.

"That's funny. So have I."

"What were you thinking about?" he said.

She couldn't very well tell him all the details of her imaginings so she said, "I was wondering what had happened to your sister and where she might be now. What were you thinking about?"

"It's time we had a serious talk, Lisa."

"Is it?"

"Yes. But first there's something I want to show you."

"Really?"

"Next weekend. Are you free?"

"Yes, but what is it?" Lisa said, her imagination sparked. She wasn't sure what to think. She knew from experience that not all surprises were pleasurable.

"I want you to see it first," Aubrey said.

As soon as they made arrangements and finished their conversation Lisa couldn't wait to ring Madge.

"Hang on a minute, Lisa,' Madge said. "Let me turn the telly down. He wants to do what?"

"He said he wants to show me something."

"*Something*?"

"Yes."

"Like what, for instance."

"I don't know."

"Like the moors? Maybe he wants to take you to see the moors in Derbyshire next time. Or Dartmoor. He likes Devon."

"No, I don't think so. He said it wasn't far to go. What do you think it could be?"

Lisa heard Madge suck in a breath with a whistling sound. Lisa could imagine her expression, her mouth as round as her eyes."It could be anything," Madge said. "Don't you go driving down lonely country lanes, Lisa, love. It might turn out to be no further than his groin if he's into doing it in public."

"Madge Sparrow!"

"Well, you never know. He might have got a new lease of life after your week away. How did it go? We haven't spoken about it since you came back."

"Sorry Madge. I was going to call you straight after work today but I was starving when I got in. And then Aubrey called."

"So it went all right, then?"

"Yes. I enjoyed it."

"And did you . . . you know."

"No."

"No?"

"I booked separate rooms, Madge."

"Lisa, I've never known separate rooms stop anybody before."

Lisa paused a moment before she said, "I don't think he's all that interested."

"There you go. I told you there was something wrong with him. Maybe he wants to show you his operation scars."

"Madge Sparrow, you're in a funny mood."

"Well if you're thinking about taking this relationship further, Lisa, you need to know all there is about him. If he can't get it up you'll need to decide if that's what you can be happy with."

"I'm not looking to light any bonfires, Madge."

"So, what *do* you want out of it?"

"I don't know."

"You'd better make your mind up before it's too late."

"I'll come over tomorrow after work."

"Good idea. Fish and chips okay?"

"Perfect."

Tuesday proved to be a quiet day as usual at Marshall and Simpson. It was a consolidation kind of day before Wednesday which was always the busiest day midweek when the town's open market was in full swing and shoppers came into Gt. Yarmouth in their numbers. Lisa was glad of the Tuesday lull. She had enough to contend with as Miss Belton had once more confused procedures for displaying goods according to best-selling ratios.

"Here," Lisa said, handing the junior a diagram. "I've written this out for you and asked the office to plasticise it so you can keep it clean. Keep this under the cash desk where customers can't see it and when you forget what the best-selling sizes are you can refer to it."

"Refer to it?"

"Look at it."

"Oh, I see."

"If you look at it enough times maybe you'll start to remember it."

"You mean like learning the words to your favourite song? You know, when you have to go over it again and again and again and . . ."

"A bit like that, yes."

"I hope it works, Mrs Miller. I really, really, really hope it works."

Lisa smiled. She couldn't think of a suitable response.

At the end of her working day Lisa hurried home to change out of her uniform and pick up her car from the Addison's staff car park. Wally's car was still in its usual place but she didn't go inside the store to look for him.

He might be on a later shift and anyway it would be good to have a few private words without him especially with Madge being so outspoken about subjects Lisa tended to shy away from.

Madge was making tea as Lisa arrived.

"Come you in, girl. Come you in. Kettle's on," Madge said and pulled out a chair for her at the kitchen table. "Wally should be back in about an hour. He's picking up the fish and chips on his way home."

"Can I do anything to help?" Lisa said.

"No, no. Sit you there, girl and we'll have a mardle." Madge poured tea and sat down. "So. Now then. Better get it said. There seems to be a little downstairs problem with your friend Aubrey."

"I can't say for sure, Madge. How would I know? I've never seen his downstairs."

Madge clapped her hands. "That's what I mean, love. After four months I think it's fair to say if you haven't had as much as a fumble between you then there's something missing. Probably his hormones."

"Four months isn't a long time," Lisa said. "At least, not in my book."

"Yes, but we're talking about a new relationship here, love. Not once you've been together for twenty five years. You know what I'm saying. The novelty of a new relationship when you can't keep your hands off each other."

"You've been reading too many *My True Heartbreak Stories*, Madge. I can't remember ever being like that."

They both picked up their mugs of tea and took a drink at the same time.

"Anyway," Madge said, "I thought you weren't looking for another serious relationship. You know. After the last one. You said you'd had enough. So what's changed?"

Lisa pondered the thought. "You know what? I'm not sure anything has changed. It just feels nice to have the companionship of a man-friend, a man who has similar interests."

"And has he?"

"We both like the cinema."

"Lots of people like going to the cinema. There's nothing special about that. What about this thing he has about the moors?"

"Hmm. Yes. To be honest that did get a bit boring. I enjoyed the walking but I didn't need to know about Jurassic Park and peat that's millions of years old. I just wanted to enjoy the scenery."

Madge's smile looked a bit strained and her eyes were questioning when she said, "Is he lively enough for you?"

"I'm not sure I need him to be lively, Madge."

"Well, does he make you laugh, Lisa? Is he fun?"

Lisa said, "Not really."

Chapter Thirteen

October

Lisa waited in the driving seat as Aubrey unfolded himself from her car and went to push open an enormous pair of iron gates at the front of the property. He motioned her through and she pulled up on the drive waiting for him to close the gates behind them. They met with a dull clang. The ornate wrought iron work she'd first noticed from the road repeated on the interior side of the gates: a central boss with a tree design and radiating branches decorated with flower and leaf motifs. They'd already passed an identical pair of gates lower down the hill.

"What is this place?" she said as Aubrey climbed back into the passenger seat.

"Wait. You'll see."

The drive curved away to their right and on each side high rhododendrons and other shrubs and trees concealed the view ahead. Slowly Lisa pulled away and followed the curve till the house came into sight. The gravel drive swept up to the house and then branched off again further to their right sloping all the way back to that first pair of gates, Lisa assumed. She parked in the wide space in front of a huge double garage to the side.

She stared at the magnificent house. Central steps gave onto a balustraded terrace topped by weathered urns crusted in lichens. On either side of the entrance doors two sets of leaded windows spanned the brick and flint facade. They got out of the car and Lisa noticed Aubrey had a set of keys in his hand. He took her by the arm and led her to the steps.

"Laburnum House," he said indicating the impressive residence. "This is the rear of the property. Uncle Vanguard had it built to take advantage of the view on the other side."

"Your uncle's house?"

"It's mine now. This is what I wanted to show you." He mounted the steps to unlock the door then stepped inside and disarmed an alarm near the entrance. "This way, Lisa."

She followed. If this was the rear of the house, she thought, how much more grand must the front of it be? The door opened onto a wide parquet-floored hall with rooms either side and a corridor leading to the far side of the building. Just in front of them a baronial staircase climbed to the upper floor. With the entrance door closed behind them the house was calm and cool and quiet. Lisa could tell the place hadn't been a home for many years but she found its tranquility peaceful rather than foreboding, inviting rather than unfriendly. Like the shop floor at Marshall and Simpson before the doors opened to the public, Laburnum House carried an air of unspoiled serenity far removed from the noise and cramped rooms of her apartment over the vet's surgery in Great Yarmouth.

"We must ignore the state of it," Aubrey was saying. "I had most things covered in dust sheets to protect the furniture. Some of the pieces are genuine antiques. Uncle Vanguard always had an eye for beautiful things."

Silently she followed on behind Aubrey marvelling at everything she saw. Even Aubrey himself had somehow acquired a different bodily stature. He seemed more upright and he walked slowly with his hands clasped behind his back as if he'd taken into himself a kind of nobility not required in Thetford or on the Yorkshire moors. They passed the staircase and entered a room where Lisa watched as Aubrey pulled on a cord by the window to draw back heavy drapes in a pattern Lisa recognised.

"Oh, look," she said. "Aren't those curtains just like yours?"

"That's right. I think this particular chintz must have been very popular when they were made." The drapes swung back revealing Lisa's first view of the garden.

"Oh, my goodness," she said. "That's stunning."

"It needs work. When you draw closer down at the bottom by the water you can see the quay heading needs some attention. Uncle Van didn't always steer in so well after one of his summer picnics on the Broad. Would you care to take a gentle stroll?"

He opened the French doors and they stepped outside onto another raised terrace with steps leading down into the garden, partly crazy-paved and part laid to beds of roses. Lisa couldn't take it all in at once. There was too much to look at: a tunnel covered in wisteria, well past its flowering season but with its unmistakable leaves and curling stems winding around the supports, mature shrubs of varying hues and trees too many to count. Beyond the paving and the flower beds the land sloped away and ran gently down toward the water where wooden decking led to a boathouse alongside a small lagoon.

"It's absolutely superb, Aubrey. You are so very lucky to own all this."

"We won't go all the way down to the water, Lisa. The decking is not safe, I'm afraid. It's been left untreated for too long."

"But the garden has been cared for," Lisa said.

"Yes. I employed a gardener to take care of it. I didn't want it to become too overgrown. Let's go back inside." He led the way to the kitchen and flicked on the lights. "It's past its best. I've been looking at ideas for refurbishment. I should think uncle Van didn't replace anything in here since the nineteen fifties."

"It's the height of fashion again now, Aubrey. They call it retro," Lisa said.

"So you would leave it as it is?"

"Not exactly."

"I value your opinion. I would very much like to hear what you would do with the kitchen, Lisa. And the bathroom. Let's go and inspect."

⚖️⚖️⚖️

A mid-October Indian summer brought settled conditions. A sunken sun winked through quiet branches of trees that had begun their autumn colouring gilding them with the warm radiance of backlit foliage. The Bure sparkled under pale light as Lisa drove over the Breydon bridge on her way to Madge and Wally's. She looked down at the water below as she passed over it. Summer blue had faded. The river ran silvery, soft as a dove. She turned into the Gorleston by-pass and then around the roundabout where a pleasant display of pink nerines gave a last burst of cheerful colour. She arrived at the Sparrows in time for Sunday lunch and found them in the rear garden where their patio table was already set for three. The late warmth had prompted Wally to fire up the barbecue one last time before the wind changed round to the east again and brought with it the first hints of colder weather.

"Got to make the most of it, Lisa," Wally said. "It'll be a long time before we can sit outside again without a coat on."

"I know. We turn the clocks back next weekend."

"Oh, don't remind me," Madge said. "Early dark nights and even darker mornings. I could shiver just at the memory of it."

"I was thinking about the weather on the way over here. Coming over the bridge, I thought it won't be long before everything looks grey and wintery."

"A bit like us, eh?"

"Not just yet, I hope. You know, Madge, I used to enjoy winter," Lisa said. "I always preferred winter clothes to summer ones. I like thick fleecy jumpers and winter woollies."

"I don't. I always feel like the Michelin man all wrapped in layers," Madge said.

"Huh," Wally joined in. "It doesn't matter how many layers you wear. You always want the heating turned up. Bloody expensive is winter."

"Well, you could always take me on a long winter holiday instead, Wally. I'd be able to handle the tropics a bit better than the east coast."

"Okay," Wally joked. "Here, love, watch the barbecue for me a minute while I run inside and book us a world cruise."

Madge wafted a playful arm at him and he ducked to one side.

"So, come on then. Fill us in. Tell us your news," Madge said. "You said on the phone he took you to look at his uncle's house last weekend."

"It's called Laburnum House. It's nearly at the top of Peachtree Rise. It's a beautiful spot. The garden goes all the way down to the Broad. There's a boathouse and a kind of landing stage. I didn't go all the way down there. We spent most of the time looking round the house. The rooms are big with high ceilings."

"Laburnum House? Yes, that's the one I remember," Wally said. "I never saw all the inside of the place. Most of the time there was nobody home. But every now and then the lady of the house would invite me in the kitchen for a cup of tea. Sometimes she'd offer a piece of cake."

"The lady of the house?" Lisa said. "Aubrey told me his uncle lived alone."

"Well, that's definitely the same place where I used to work in the garden when I was a lad. The old feller had a fancy cruiser in that boat shed. All shiny wooden decks and brass fittings everywhere. It reminded me of something you might see in an old Hollywood movie. Very upper class. It'd be considered old-fashioned today.

Boats are all shiny white plastic stuff now aren't they?" He flipped sausages on his barbecue and said, "Ten more minutes."

"So what was it like upstairs?" Madge said.

"It's big," Lisa said. "It's big everywhere. The kitchen is huge and there's a separate breakfast room with French doors to the garden. Then there's a posh dining room, a study and an enormous sitting room with another set of French doors. Five bedrooms with high ceilings, large bay windows."

"But old-fashioned?"

"Very dated but not unpleasantly so."

Madge said, "So you were impressed."

"Anybody would be."

"But you haven't spoken to him since?"

"No."

Wally dished up and the three of them loaded their plates with salad and chutneys. They sat around Madge's patio table and the sound of next door's lawnmower pierced the temporary lull in their conversation.

"So, why do you think he wanted you to see the house, Lisa?" Madge said eventually. "I mean, he must have had a reason."

Lisa put down her knife and fork and did a little cough. She said, "I think I know what you're getting at, Madge. He wants my input on the refurbishment of some of the rooms."

"Is that it?" Madge said and put down her own cutlery. "Is that really all it was?"

"Yes."

"Wally, what do you think? Do you think that's all he wanted?"

Wally swallowed his mouthful of hot dog and said, "What are you asking me for? I don't know the man. How would I know what he's got on his mind?" He reached out for another sausage and rolled his eyes.

"Lisa," Madge said, "I can't believe for one minute that's all he wanted. He's biding his time now, hanging on waiting to see what you would change in the property to make it how you would like it. He's going to ask you to move in with him."

Chapter Fourteen

December

Two weeks before Christmas, Amy Miller finished her shift at Westgate Care Home and set off home with too much to think about. Usually the daily walk from work to her flat on Northgate Street took just long enough to clear her mind from workday issues. As a rule she'd be able to think out any leftovers from the day's problems and prepare for a relaxing evening in the comfort of home. Striding out in fresh air gave vent to any lingering frustrations. She'd stamp them out with each stride so that by the time she arrived she'd feel more human, more ready to share the day's news with her flatmate, Jessie. But today had been a bad day.

Normally her work gave her a sense of satisfaction. Sometimes there was real pleasure when things went well. On good days it was easy to use humour to lighten the load of administering to the needs of very elderly residents. She and Jessie often quoted the old saying, *you've got to laugh or you'd cry* but today it had been impossible to see the funny side of anything. Today a resident had been taken away. It was heartbreaking whenever an aged resident became too aggressive and had to be moved to a secure unit for everybody's safety as well as their own. Days like today were always difficult. Staff and residents all felt it. Staff had to try maintain a sense of calm while dealing with their own mixed feelings: relief that a dangerous situation had been resolved; guilt that they'd felt relief in the first place and sorrow at the deterioration in a resident's condition and how that was going to affect the rest of the loved one's family.

It was impossible to say what most of the remaining residents felt after one of them had been removed. Many didn't want to talk about it. Some simply couldn't express in words how they were feeling. They might be more agitated than usual instead, or more demanding, or more needy. Others appeared not to notice anything was any different. There was always a shift in the atmosphere, though, like an unspoken dread of what the future might hold, a palpable threat that permeated the communal rooms and corridors. Then, on top of everything else, the incident with the Old Feller's behaviour had been the last straw. On good days she'd have laughed it off. Today, Amy was glad to go home.

As soon as she stepped out of the building and crossed the staff car park instead of the relief of fresh air against her cheeks she felt worries hammering at her brain. Turning right out of the gates she strode with purpose but still felt a gnawing sensation in her stomach that wouldn't leave her alone. Her pace slowed as she breathed out thoughts of the Old Feller and her mind shifted to the problems with her mother, Lisa. Every day at work Amy saw exactly what the future held for so many people once they'd reached a certain age and whenever her thoughts turned to her mother the same questions rolled around time and again.

Hadn't Mum had enough troubles in her life? Hadn't most of those problems been to do with the men in her life over the years? At her age shouldn't she know better than take at face value a man she'd known only five months? First impressions can be a bit off to say the least, she acknowledged, but Amy was convinced that Aubrey *whatsisname* simply wasn't right for her mum: Mum, the number one person in Amy's life who deserved some happiness after all that had happened; Mum who'd seen Amy and her brother Danny through the toughest times and still come out smiling; Mum, who surely was entitled to something better.

As if she'd been on auto-pilot she found herself by her own front door. She climbed the stairs to the upper floor flat to find her flatmate, Jessie McNulty still wrapped in a bath robe. Jessie had worked the night before and looked as if she'd just got up. Amy liked the fact they sometimes worked different hours at the care home. The arrangement worked well. The one who got home first and had time to rest and wind down could offer support to the other. They both felt night shifts were often easiest once the residents were asleep.

A teatime radio show was playing golden oldies and Jessie, curled up on the sofa, was dunking biscuits in a large mug of something. Amy's stomach gurgled.

"Jessie," Amy said, "put the kettle on again, will you? I'm gasping."

"Hard day, hun?"

Amy rolled her eyes and said, "Don't get me started."

By the time Amy had showered, washed her hair and put on her dressing gown, coffee was waiting. She picked up her mug and sat beside her flatmate. She knew Jessie was watching her, waiting for her to say what was on her mind.

Jessie didn't wait long. She said, "So, come on, Amy, you know as well as I do it's best to talk about it. You've got to let it out. Repressed emotions and all that stuff." Amy sighed and closed her eyes. "That bad, huh?"

Amy groaned. "We said goodbye to Rita today. It was awful. You know what it's like. I know it's for the best. I know we have to think about everybody else, but it's still shit. Poor Rita. She hadn't a clue why or where she was going."

"And the Old Feller. How was he today?"

"Oh, don't ask. He's getting worse, Jessie," she said. "You know we always have to go into his room in twos now, don't you? Yes, well, God help us, it was me and Mrs Turnbull. Pauline. You know, the one with the Mini Cooper. Drives it like it was a petrol tanker. Always parks it on an angle."

"Yes. Go on."

"So we knock on the door and go in. The randy old goat is on his bed with a huge grin on his face, lying there stark naked. He must have been playing with himself. He had an erection like, I was going to say Nelson's column but, you know, bendy. *Come in ladies*, he says. *Who's first? Jump on.*"

"He didn't."

"He did."

"What did you do?"

"Pauline grabbed a facecloth and ran it under the cold tap. Slapped it round his willy. *We're not putting up with that*, she says. *You mind your manners, Geoffrey Atkin. Or you'll find yourself under an ice cold shower.* Then he said something about not being past it. He could manage us both. Honestly, the things we have to put up with." She shook her head and added, "We'll have to report it."

Jessie laughed. "But nobody's going to do anything about it," she said. "Perks of the job, Amy."

"It didn't feel like a perk to me. It put me off my tea break."

"Well, never mind. Drink up now and forget about it." Amy drained her mug and sighed again. "Sounds as though you've more on your mind, Amy." Jessie said. "Is it your mum again?"

"How did you guess?"

"Because I know how much you care about her."

"You know what? Sometimes I wish I'd never encouraged her. I should have left well alone. I thought she could do with a nice little break. If I hadn't pushed her into going away last June none of this would have happened."

"None of what? Nothing's happened yet."

Amy tutted. "This Aubrey whatsisname guy."

"Tennant."

"Aubrey Tennant. Who is he, anyway? We've met him, what? Once?"

"Twice."

"Twice then. In five months. What did he have to say for himself, huh? Not much. He hardly said a word."

"I expect he felt a bit awkward meeting you and Danny. Amy, some people take a while to get to know."

"But that's just it. We haven't got to know him. We know nothing about him. Where did he say he worked?"

"Cambridge, I think. Something to do with planes. It sounded like an important job to me. Quite exciting, I thought."

"Exciting? Aubrey whatsisname *exciting*?"

"Amy, look, I think you're making a mountain out of a molehill. There's no reason why your mum can't have a boyfriend."

"Oh, please. Don't call him that."

"Well, he is, isn't he?"

Amy shuddered and pulled a face. "You didn't meet the last one," she said. She leaned back against the cushions and stared at the ceiling. "You know, that bastard had us all fooled. What a charmer we all thought he was. We couldn't have been more wrong. Once she realised what a liar he was Mum kept it to herself. I wish she'd told us sooner." She remained gazing at the ceiling as if the past was painted there and if she stared at it long enough she could make it all disappear.

Jessie shuffled forward on the sofa and reached for Amy's hand. "You can tell me about it if you want to," she said.

"You've heard it all before."

"I know. But it's obviously still bothering you." Jessie got up to turn off the radio, took the empty mug from Amy's hand and put it on the coffee table. "Come on, hun, say what you're thinking."

Amy puffed out a long, slow breath and said, "I'm worried this new fella will turn out the same as the last one."

"A heavy drinker? I should think your mum's had time to find that out by now. She wouldn't fall for that again."

"It isn't just that," Amy said. She brought up her knees and hugged them hard. "I don't want her to be hurt again. I don't want her to think he's the best thing since sliced bread and then it turns out he isn't."

She waited for Jessie to respond. When Amy studied her flatmate's face she could see an expression like her mother used to wear when she was little and she or Danny had got themselves into another scrape.

"You want my opinion?" Jessie said. Amy nodded. "I think you're trying to reverse the roles here. You're not your mum's parent but you're acting like it."

The thought came as a shock. "Am I?" Amy said, her mouth dropping open. "Is that what I'm doing? How sad is that? I must sound like a complete idiot."

Jessie patted her hand. "You're not an idiot. You're a caring daughter. Your mum has had a lot to cope with in her life. So have you and your brother. It's only natural to be a bit worried."

"More than a bit worried. Sometimes it's all I can think about. I've got to stop it."

"Yes. Put it out of your mind for now and we can come back to it later if you need to. Right now we both need to tidy ourselves up and get ready."

Amy checked the time and said, "Danny will be here soon."

"Ah, I forgot to tell you. He called. Said he's running late so won't have time to come here first. He'll meet us there. At the pub."

Amy grimaced and said, "What kept him this time?"

"Dunno. He didn't say. Better wrap up. It's a big coats' night. And a scarf. I think a walk in the cold air would do us both good. There'll be nowhere to park up there anyway this time on Friday night."

They walked to the end of Northgate Street where Christmas lights twinkled as they swung from lampposts and window displays were full of festive sparkle. They rounded the corner into Fuller's Hill and sudden, stiff December blasts pushed them on, past St Nicholas' church and Priory Plain, toward Market Road and the bus station. Swirling wind sent fish and chip papers spiralling through the underpass and the smell of fried food made Amy's stomach gurgle again.

Warm air and Christmas muzak greeted them at the pub entrance. Danny was already seated at a table near the door.

"Hi, Jessie," he said. "Hi, Sis. Turned out I wasn't as late as I thought so I got your drinks in already. Hope I remembered it right."

Amy hugged her brother and he returned the hug with a peck on the cheek for both of them.

"Where is everybody?" Jessie said, looking around the half empty lounge bar. "I thought this place would be packed tonight."

"Could be office Christmas parties this weekend keeping people away, maybe. Or they're keeping tight hold onto their cash for a final blowout Christmas Eve. Who knows?"

They thanked him for the drinks and shuffled along a bench seat with their backs to the window.

Amy said,"You were working late, Danny. On a Friday night? How come?"

"Wedding rehearsal. Had to be tonight. St Nicholas is booked up for Christmas recitals and craft fairs or something."

"You doing wedding photography now, Danny?" Jessie said.

"Got to. It pays the bills, you know?"

"So why did they need you there tonight?"

"They didn't need me. I wanted to be there. I like to plan ahead. Find unusual angles for shots. So I have to make sure there isn't going to be anything in the way."

"It isn't the kind of photography you prefer though, is it?"

"No, not really. I'd rather be outdoors with my wildlife stuff but even so, I always want to make a good job of whatever I'm booked to do. Wedding albums are important to the couple getting married and both their families. We don't all get married as many times as my mother."

"Danny!" Amy shouted. "That was uncalled for."

Danny laughed. "Come on, Sis," he said. "You know as well as I do she's going to do it again."

"Do you mind if I say something, Danny?" Jessie interrupted. "Amy's been really worried about your mum. It doesn't help if you go off making fun of it like that."

"Well, that's what this meeting's all about, isn't it? I'm sorry if I was a bit abrupt. Let's order some food and calm down."

Jessie pulled a face and said, "Just a minute, Danny. I think you've got the wrong idea. We thought this was just a social evening. A bit of a catch up. You know. If you want to discuss your mum's business I don't think you should do it here, in a pub. What do you think, Amy?"

Amy agreed. "Let's get takeouts and bring them back to the flat," she said.

"Okay. Fair enough. There's not much atmosphere in here anyway. I'm parked on Market Place. What do you fancy? Indian? Chinese?"

Amy said, "I could murder a kebab."

The temperature had dropped further as they stepped outside. Late night shoppers hurried along the streets their collars turned up against northerly gusts. Christmas lighting swayed precariously in trees around the the market square. Amy tucked in her scarf and wished she'd worn gloves. They walked in single file along the pavements, the girls semi-sheltering behind Danny as he led the way. *Donna's Kebab* house was only a few doors away from the girls' flat. Amy texted ahead so their order would be ready as soon as they arrived.

They carried their spicy-smelling suppers upstairs to the flat, hugging the parcels close to keep them warm. Jessie organised plates and cutlery while Amy cleared space on the sofa. Amy's phone buzzed. A few seconds later Danny's phone buzzed too.

Danny was the first to speak. "There you go! What did I tell you? She's going to do it again."

"I can't stand much more of this," Amy said. "It's doing my head in. We have to do something." She handed her phone over to Jessie for a second opinion.

Jessie read aloud the most important part of the text message from Lisa.

'*Can we arrange a meet-up soon? I need to see you both. There's something I want to tell you. Love, Mum xx.*'

"That could be anything," Jessie offered. "It might not be about what you think it's about."

The Second Year

Chapter Fifteen

New Year's Day

On the top step at the entrance door to Laburnum House Lisa waited in anticipation for the guests to arrive. Out of sight of the house the double gates at the roadside stood open in expectation of their arrival and oil lanterns lit the way right around the drive to the parking area at the side. Aubrey had told her the lanterns were the same ones Uncle Vanguard had brought back from one of his trips abroad and she'd noticed how carefully Aubrey had polished up the brassware and set the lamps in place. When they were lit at dusk the glamorous effect of golden light flickering through bare branches was worthy of an Oscar, she thought, and told him so. He'd hurriedly thanked her for the compliment and rushed off. He was somewhere inside now. He'd be checking everything was in order or maybe still showing his friend Timothy around the place.

Timothy Reynolds' appearance earlier had been an unexpected event. It was obvious to Lisa that Aubrey had forgotten he'd apparently invited his work colleague to the house-warming. He later admitted he couldn't recall details of the conversation they'd had at the office before they came away for the festive season, but it was possible Timothy may have misunderstood Aubrey's intentions when the subject of the house-warming had come up. Timothy had arrived florid of face, flustered about how many times he'd taken the wrong turning on the way from Cambridge and how if only he'd remembered the postcode to put in his sat-nav his journey might have been cut by at least three quarters of an hour. Lisa noticed he carried an overnight bag. She'd stepped in to cover Aubrey's embarrassment, greeted the unexpected guest like an old friend and shown Timothy to his room as if she'd known the arrangement all along and had prepared the room especially for him. He was the only guest staying over; all the others had only a short journey's drive home.

Christmas had gone reasonably well, Lisa thought as she stood waiting, and even though Laburnum House wasn't ready for them to move in permanently, the house-warming party should help set things straight even though Aubrey had been reluctant to meet with Danny and Amy again.

"So soon?" he'd said.

"You'll be fine," Lisa had replied.

Aubrey scratched at his neck. "I don't like to keep doing family get togethers," he said.

"Aubrey," Lisa said, "you must understand that my children want to get to know you. New Year's Day will be the perfect time. New beginnings. Fresh starts. You know."

"I don't care to keep meeting other people's families."

"But you'd expect me to meet yours wouldn't you? If you had family, that is."

"That's different."

"How is it different?"

"Because I would know them."

"Well, soon you'll know my family too and then there won't be a problem."

"I'm not going to live with them."

"You're making a silly fuss over nothing," she said and he'd turned his back on her. "And now you're sulking. Aubrey, for goodness sake. Everything will be fine. My children aren't monsters."

She heard him gulp. "I'm uncomfortable meeting new people," he said.

"Why, that's nonsense. Look at all the new people you met in Torquay."

"That's different."

"How is it different?" She'd given him time to search for a way to explain but he'd simply stared at her. "This is a significant time in our lives, Aubrey," she said. "I think it's so important to mark these occasions with a celebration of some sort otherwise the day just slips by like any other as if it didn't matter at all."

"Well, to me it *is* like any other day," Aubrey admitted.

"You'll be fine," Lisa said again.

She didn't remind him about all the other people she'd invited to the house: he was already agitated enough, but she knew how she was going to handle any little awkwardnesses. In any case, it made sense to include their nearest neighbours-to-be. It wasn't as if they were going to be living in one another's pockets: the neighbours were all detached and out of sight behind their own high hedges and boundary lines. It was a matter of politeness as well as an opening to future discreet pleasantries: a nodded greeting when passing in the street; a friendly '*how are you?*' when they got to know each other better.

Inviting local business folk was a calculated move, she admitted to herself. If Aubrey and she were to patronise the few local businesses it made absolute sense to set the relationship off on the best footing. The local butcher had supplied high quality cold cuts for the buffet tea table and Aubrey had been impressed enough to call it *charcuterie* when he'd helped himself to a small sample without garlic. Surely that would give Aubrey some common ground to converse with the man. Similarly, the baker and his wife had accepted Lisa's invitation as well as the elderly pair who ran the fresh seafood kiosk up on the coast road. There'd be plenty of conversations for Aubrey to take an interest. He wouldn't have to be so worried about saying the wrong things to her children.

And tonight they were all going to be together but under very different circumstances and in very different surroundings. Amy and Danny had the gist of the situation now. When they'd had their get together a week before Christmas Lisa had been able to put their minds at rest. Amy had tried to be diplomatic when, as tactfully as she could, she'd asked,

"Is he stimulating enough for you, Mum?"

"I don't need stimulating, Amy," Lisa replied. "I prefer a more measured man."

"But, I worry about you. And so does Danny. We both do."

"Aubrey has asked me to consider marriage," she told them as the three of them squeezed together on the sofa in her tiny apartment, "but I don't want you to worry. I don't have much luck with husbands as you know so I've said I'll think about it. At the moment I'm not interested in marriage."

"Oh." Amy said. "What *are* you going to do?"

"Well," Lisa said, "it's like this. I don't want to be a kept woman. Now, you might think this arrangement unconventional by today's standards but in the past it wasn't unusual at all. I'm going to be housekeeper of Laburnum House and companion to Aubrey."

"What?" Danny said. "You mean a bit like downstairs at Downton Abbey?"

"Mrs Danvers in Rebecca?" Amy added with horror written all over her face.

"Certainly not. I won't be dependent on Aubrey financially because I'm keeping my job at Marshall and Simpson. Besides, I'll have another source of income when I let this flat."

After an uncomfortable pause Amy said, "And do you think this . . . arrangement is going to work out?"

"Mum already has it all worked out by the sound of it, Sis."

"Yes, but . . ."

"Nobody knows how anything is ever going to work out," Lisa interrupted. "But at least this time I'm in full possession of the facts. Aubrey is financially very sound so there'll be no problems there. I'll be better off as well with the monthly rent on the flat. I'll even be able to save. I don't want you to worry. I'm looking forward to being the lady of the house. You'll understand when you see it."

"Mum," Amy said, "how can you be sure, I mean, at your age, sorry but you've got to be realistic and with everything I see at work, how can you be sure he's not just looking for a nurse with a purse?"

"That's a strange thing to say," Lisa said. "Aubrey doesn't need nursing."

"It happens, Mum. I've seen it happen. People develop all kinds of problems when they get older. Look, just be careful. That's all I'm saying."

Lisa smiled and said, "I'll bear it in mind." But it *was* something she hadn't considered.

She brushed away thoughts of things that might happen as she and Aubrey grew older and looked behind her at her imposing new home. This evening her children were going to see Laburnum House for the first time. She sighed. Thinking back to when she and Aubrey first met she could understand how others might think it had all gone ahead too quickly especially when she'd often voiced her determination to stay well away from the opposite sex. But this arrangement was different. Surely Aubrey and she would be able to create a harmonious relationship, a pleasant sharing of the autumn of their lives without the encumbrance of emotional attachment.

The sound of a vehicle crunching over the gravel drive roused her. Madge and Wally Sparrow's car crept into view. Lisa waved as they parked.

"Bloody Nora," Madge said gawping at the house as she approached.

"I told you what to expect, love," Wally said and came up beside his wife.

"You told me it was big. You didn't say it was like Sandringham estate."

Aubrey appeared from inside the house. Lisa was surprised when he confidently took Madge's arm and, gliding gracefully like a country squire, helped her up the steps.

At the dining table Aubrey looked up from his plate and glanced around at the guests. Some had chosen to sit at his table where they could more easily help themselves to a tempting display of finger food, meticulously arranged by Lisa who'd used several of Uncle Vanguard's largest platters to create a most enticing presentation. She'd used plates in colours contrasting with the food they displayed, an idea that would never have occurred to him. It had filled him with a gentle sense of ease that she could be trusted, not only with Uncle Vanguard's precious majolica, but with the proper perception of occasion he wished the housewarming should encapsulate.

There were meats and pastries, prawns and other seafoods, crackers and dips, cheeses, grapes and a selection of vegetarian choices. Various bottles of wine and a small cask of ale filled the top of one of the sideboards at the rear of the room. It pleased him that

Lisa had so carefully planned his table for their guests. Perhaps it had been a sensible idea after all to introduce themselves to the Peachtree neighbourhood. So far he'd managed to speak with most of them without too much difficulty. He leaned back in his seat and made a mental picture as he surveyed the whole assembly.

Other guests were scattered around the dining room in little groups, holding plates and glasses and chatting among themselves. Timothy Reynolds from PPE was over in the corner with a small circle of tradespeople and the nearest neighbours from either side of Laburnum House were gathered by the fireplace. Aubrey was settling into a surprisingly contented feeling when someone tapped him on the shoulder.

"I was wondering whether you'd mind if I took some photographs, Aubrey? I don't usually bother at social gatherings but I think Mum would like to have some."

Aubrey looked up at Danny, Lisa's son.

"I don't mind at all," he said and surprised himself still further by the agreeable tone in his own voice. He wondered why he hadn't felt jolted by the young man's sudden approach.

"It's a beautiful house. And this room? It's like a banqueting hall."

"Thank you," Aubrey said and rose to stand alongside. "That was very considerate of you to think of your mother. May I see your camera?"

Before he realised what was happening Aubrey found himself in an interesting discussion about the pros and cons of digital photography and computer software that could remove blemishes or unwanted background objects. He listened, fascinated, as Danny described the various enhancements that could be produced at the click of a mouse. Apparently, one could even make a photograph look like an oil painting or watercolour. Danny had brought only his pocket-sized camera to the house-warming. His professional equipment could work wonders, he said, and Aubrey was keen to learn more.

"Fancy coming out with me some time on one of my wildlife shoots?" Danny said.

Aubrey had no hesitation in saying, "I rather think I do, young man. It's very kind of you to invite me along. I think I would enjoy that very much. Thank you."

He watched as Lisa's son moved around the room taking informal photos, asking people not to pose especially.

"Just carry on as if you don't see me," he heard Danny say as he slipped behind and between each small group.

A novel sensation warmed him. Should he think of this friendly young man as a stepson-to-be? Would that happen automatically after he and Lisa moved in together permanently or would it take place after the wedding? The marriage was only a matter of time. He'd convinced himself that he understood why Lisa was being cautious: she had already had two husbands. Losing the first husband to an untimely death must have been a severe trauma in her life. He avoided asking questions about the failure of her second marriage. He thought it improper. If she wanted him to know details of it, she would tell him. He frowned, though, at the thought of her delaying but everything else was going exactly to his preferred plan. He'd found the ideal partner with children who were not an encumbrance of any sort. Indeed, young Danny epitomised healthy confidence: a young man with things to do and places to go.

Aubrey tried to imagine himself at that age. The comparison jarred but it was nevertheless clear to him what a marvellous job Lisa had done in raising such an affable young person. Lisa's son had manners. He'd requested permission to take his photographs. He'd been gracious and open and honest. Lisa was to be congratulated. He had a sudden urge to speak to her.

He found her in the kitchen with her daughter and a friend.

"Lisa," he said. "There you are . . ."

"Aubrey. I was just explaining to Amy and Jessie here what plans we have for the kitchen."

"Ah. Yes," he muttered. Only the two words stumbled from his mouth but he felt as if he might choke. Inwardly, he cursed at the immediate discomfort of the sight of three pairs of female eyes looking straight at him, waiting for his response, expecting something appropriate to the occasion, triggering the familiar fear and accompanying shame.

"But we haven't firmly decided on colours yet. Have we, Aubrey?"

Gratefully he accepted Lisa's lead.

"There are so many themes these days. I find I'm quite out of touch with what is current in interior design."

"I wouldn't care about fashion," Amy said. "I think you should just choose whatever you like best."

"It's a fantastic property, Mr Tennant," Jessie added. "I think bang up-to-date units just wouldn't look right in here. Why don't you stick up some pictures on the walls? You know, cut some out of house magazines. It'd give you an idea what it might look like."

"That's an excellent idea. Thank you," Aubrey said and did a mini Captain von Trapp.

"I hope you and Mum will be very happy," Amy said next, completely out of the blue, elevating Aubrey's level of anxiety.

"Ah, that's nice," Lisa said and gave her daughter a hug.

Aubrey stood transfixed. His hands edged to the sides of his trousers. He resisted the urge to run his fingers along the seams and pick at them before he managed to say a quiet thank you. When the women drifted off he helped himself to a glass of water and stood with his eyes closed.

Some people were ready to leave. Lisa called Aubrey through to the hall and together they stood at the door to thank their guests for coming to welcome them to their future home. The guests made their apologies for the early departure due to working commitments next day. Others took their exit shortly afterwards. Madge and Wally Sparrow followed about half an hour after that. Aubrey saw Madge wink at Lisa and nod her head as she made her way out. He assumed they'd had a private talk earlier.

"I'll come into the shop tomorrow, Lisa," Madge called out as she walked towards their car. "There's something I want to exchange." Aubrey thought he saw another wink.

Danny, Amy and her friend Jessie were the last to go.

"Don't forget about the photography day, Aubrey," Danny said as he shook Aubrey's hand.

"I certainly won't. No indeed. I shall hold you to it," Aubrey replied and made a mental note to research the winter fauna of the area as he waved them off.

When they stepped back into the hall Timothy Reynolds was waiting for them.

"Would you have a moment, Aubrey?" he said. "I didn't want to mention anything earlier so I've waited until now. I have some rather disturbing news."

"Oh, dear," Lisa said. "Shall I make coffee?"

"Thank you. Very kind."

"Let's go into the sitting room, erm, Timothy," Aubrey said. "It's more comfortable in there."

They sat separately, the three of them; Aubrey in his favourite winged armchair, Timothy on one sofa and Lisa on the facing sofa nearest the coffee table. Aubrey waited for Timothy to explain. Lisa poured and handed out the drinks. Still Aubrey waited.

"It's been a lovely evening," Timothy said eventually. "It was so kind of you to invite me along. And put me up for the night."

"We're happy you've enjoyed yourself. Aren't we, Aubrey?" Lisa offered.

"Yes. Of course," Aubrey agreed.

"It seems so very wrong of me to put any kind of a dampener on your successful housewarming but I have a real problem and, to tell you the truth, there really isn't anybody else I can turn to."

Aubrey glanced at Lisa. His stomach was doing somersaults but Lisa looked perfectly calm.

"How can we help?" she said.

"It's Daphne," Timothy said.

"Your wife?" Lisa asked.

Timothy nodded. His voice dropped to a whisper as he added, "She's left me."

Chapter Sixteen

"Aubrey, I think now would be a good time to have something a little stronger. How about we have a glass of cognac with our coffee?" Lisa said and left the room to fetch it. Aubrey didn't see what was worth celebrating about Timothy's news but accepted Lisa's decision. She came back from the dining room carrying a tray with a bottle and three brandy glasses. She wasn't smiling. In fact, she looked very serious indeed. She wore an expression like he'd seen in hospital dramas when someone has been given a terminal diagnosis.

As the man of the house Aubrey knew it was his responsibility to serve the cognac. He'd successfully manoeuvred through a host of new experiences throughout the evening and here was yet another procedure where he must take control. He must be seen to do it properly. These things mattered. He scanned his movie memory bank for a suitable image. It needed to be something solemn to correlate with Lisa's demeanour. He decided on a scene from James Bond films when M always offered brandy when there were serious matters to discuss. That was before Judi Dench took over the role and offered bourbon instead. There would always be some difficulty going on in the background in those scenes in M's office with alcohol: an agent missing in action or a betrayal of trust. Perfect. He opted for the betrayal and poured accordingly.

"Thank you," Timothy said and took a sip.

"Is there anything we can do to help you?" Lisa asked again.

"Perhaps. I'm not sure. The thing is, you see, I don't really know what to do next. I thought perhaps talking it over might bring something to mind."

"Do you know where your wife has gone, Timothy?" Lisa said.

"Oh, yes. She's at her sister's in Dumfries. She says she doesn't want to come home."

"Did she say why?"

"Not really, no. She hasn't said much at all."

"I can give you some more recipes," Aubrey offered, "if that's what's bothering you. And Lisa has a much bigger repertoire than my own. I'm looking forward to sampling more of her dishes when we're together permanently."

Lisa coughed. "Aubrey," she said, "let's concentrate on how we can help your friend, shall we?" She got up and moved across to sit beside Timothy. Aubrey watched as she settled back on the sofa, folded her fingers as if in prayer and laid her hands in her lap. "Start from the beginning, dear," she said to Timothy Reynolds as if he were a long-standing friend. "I always think it's best to start at the beginning. You might remember something important."

Timothy took his time. He seemed to gulp at the air and his shoulders drooped.

"I suppose I knew it was coming," he said. "Daphne has not been herself for some time."

Lisa said, "In what way was she not herself?"

Again, it seemed Timothy needed to search for the right words.

"She lost interest."

"In you?"

"In everything. You just mentioned recipes, Aubrey, and I thank you for your concern. Yes, I know I have to eat well. That's what they say, isn't it? When you have emotional problems people always tell you to be sure and eat well."

"And are you?" Lisa said.

"I have tonight. Thank you both. I think being among company has helped me relax. But since Daphne left I haven't had much appetite at all."

Aubrey sat with his glass of cognac and observed the scene in his sitting room. He might have been at the cinema watching the drama unfold before his eyes. He could think of nothing to say that would be useful.

Lisa said, "You told us Daphne lost interest in everything."

"Yes. She wasn't interested in cooking. Couldn't care less about the house and garden. Didn't want to go anywhere, at least, not with me. She's visited her sister more this last year than in the last five years added together."

"I see. This is going to be a painful question, Timothy, but it's something you have to think about. Is there anyone else involved?"

Aubrey thought Timothy's response exceedingly curious. Timothy Reynolds threw back his head and laughed so loud and with such gusto he had to put down his glass for fear of spilling. Aubrey couldn't wait to hear what Timothy was going to say next.

"My dear Lisa," Timothy began, "it isn't a question I find at all painful. It is, however, a little delicate. Suffice it to say Daphne has never been interested in that side of a relationship. I gave up all hope of any intimacy many years ago. We never had children."

Aubrey felt the urge to join the conversation but decided against. He took another mouthful of his cognac and settled back to see the scene play out. He scrutinised Lisa's face but couldn't see any obvious change in her expression. She looked calm and composed as ever.

"I'll make fresh coffee," she said, gathered up their empty cups and left the room.

Aubrey took a chance with a question of his own.

"So, what do you think you might do? Take a holiday? I know a lovely hotel in Torquay."

"A holiday? I hadn't thought of that. I used to fancy travelling abroad. Daphne wasn't interested, though. I'm not sure I would enjoy it on my own."

"But you wouldn't have enjoyed it with her either if she wasn't interested."

"You're quite right. She would have found something to complain about."

Lisa came back with a cafetière and three fresh cups.

"Proper coffee," she said. "It'll go better with the brandy."

She chose to sit on the sofa facing Timothy rather than beside him, Aubrey noticed. Then she pressed down the plunger slowly and deliberately.

"I thought a holiday might do him good," Aubrey said.

"Practical matters must come first, I think. I've been in this situation myself, Timothy, and I know there are so many things you have to sort out," Lisa said with some conviction.

"Indeed," Timothy agreed, "and here we come to the crux of the matter. Daphne is demanding her half share of the house."

"To which she is entitled I suppose?"

"She is."

"And?"

"I haven't got that amount of money. We'll have to sell the house."

"I understand. May I suggest the quicker you get on with it the better."

"There's more to it. Where am I supposed to live? Half the value of our home isn't going to be enough to buy a place of my own. And what will Daphne do? She'll be in the same position."

"You must downsize, Timothy. For the time being. Or rent somewhere just long enough to see you through the transition period. As for Daphne, she isn't your problem. She's getting what she wants, whatever that is. You don't have to apply for divorce just yet. Let her do it if she's so keen to be away from you. Sit tight and concentrate on what's best for you. Make sure you take care of your future pension and revise any will you may have made."

Aubrey stared in amazement. Lisa was magnificent. She'd moved the conversation straight to the point and had all the answers. He'd made a good decision in choosing her. He allowed himself a congratulatory smile.

"I may take up PPE's offer," Timothy said. "Last year they offered me voluntary redundancy but I turned it down. Daphne thought their offer wasn't substantial enough. And, she seemed to think it was somehow derogatory, a blemish on her character, an embarrassment to have a husband who'd been made redundant. Well, I am redundant now, am I not? In every sense."

"Wouldn't a lump sum together with your half of the house be enough to buy a place of your own?" Lisa asked.

"I have a choice," Timothy said. "I can take the whole package in one lump sum or have a smaller amount and have the rest as a monthly pension."

Lisa said," Do you intend to retire?"

"Sometimes I think I do."

"I've handed in my intention to retire, Timothy," Aubrey said. "I'm looking forward to being at leisure and taking up some new interests."

"I haven't decided about my own retirement," Lisa said to both men. "It's too soon. I need the connection with my work and the people there. You must decide for yourself how much your work means to you."

"But in the meantime," Timothy said, "I have to decide what to do about the house sale and where I'm going to live once it's sold."

With some ceremony Aubrey raised himself in his seat and lifted his chin to speak. First, he did a little cough as Lisa had done earlier. He waited until he was sure they were looking at him.

"The house in Thetford will be available for rent, Timothy. It was my parents' house as you know and my intention is to let it as a family home. But I should be very happy for you to use it during your period of adjustment if you should choose."

He sat back and waited.

"Aubrey," Lisa said. "That's an excellent idea. What do you think, Timothy?"

"It could be an admirable temporary solution, Aubrey and I thank you most sincerely. I'll enquire into the redundancy package to see if it's still on offer and make an early decision."

"Good," Lisa said. "You sound as if you're a bit clearer in your mind."

"I am. It's going to be a huge change in my life. There's no point in putting it off, is there?"

"You'll get through it."

"Like you did, Lisa?" Timothy said.

"Twice."

"Twice? I wasn't aware."

"My first husband died very suddenly. We didn't even know he had a health problem. I managed as a single parent for many years. I made the mistake of marrying again about three years ago. He was an abusive drunkard."

"Oh, how dreadful for you. So you divorced him?"

Aubrey squirmed. Was Lisa finally about to reveal particulars of the end of her second marriage? He'd never found the best way to ask her outright as Timothy had. He gritted his teeth. He hoped her explanation supported the high esteem in which he held her.

"I didn't get the chance to divorce him," Lisa said lightly as if it were an afterthought, "although I was planning to leave him and get well away from him. Amy was going to help me. We had it all worked out. On the day it happened I'd been out with her. A day out shopping. It was the middle of winter and very cold. It was dark by the time I drove home. I reversed into the driveway as usual and thought I must have banged into the fence or hit a stone or something. The car bumped so I left it parked right there and went indoors to switch on the outside light so I could see better to get my shopping bags from the boot and see if I'd caused any damage.

Then I saw him. Under the car. He'd fallen down drunk in the drive and I'd just driven over him. He was dead, of course."

Aubrey heard Timothy gasp. He looked into Lisa's eyes for signs of . . . he didn't know what, some sign of something that would give away how she was feeling. Her eyes were bright and smiling. He couldn't make it all add up. Had she actually *murdered* her husband?

He felt he ought to say something next but had no idea where to begin. There was nothing in his store of practised phrases for this kind of situation. He turned his attention to Timothy who was still sitting with his mouth wide open. Aubrey leaned back in his seat and waited for one of the others to speak.

"So," Timothy began. "It was an accident. You didn't mean to, but you actually killed him?"

"Oh, no," Lisa said, her voice light as a feather. "It wasn't my fault at all. The post mortem proved he was already dead by the time I came home. Broke his neck when he fell. Naturally there was a commotion in the village where I lived then."

She paused and her expression lost its brightness. The light went from her eyes. Aubrey's stomach lurched at the thought of what she might say next.

"People stared when I walked down the street," she said. "They stopped talking when I went into any of the village shops. I felt unwanted, like I was a stain on the whole village. It soon died down but I always felt it was there hanging over me. I was always going to be somebody for people to talk about. I'd already decided to move away and, when I found out about all the debts he'd left me with, I had no choice. I had to sell. I bought the flat to be nearer to Amy and Danny."

"But still, it must have been a horrible shock for you," Timothy said.

She took quite a few minutes to reply.

"I've had to learn to live with it," she said. "Yes, it was a terrible shock the way it happened. I had nightmares about it. There were times I regretted not leaving sooner. But it was a bigger shock finding out exactly how much debt he'd left me in. He wasn't the man I thought he was, the man he pretended to be. Besides being a drunken lout he was also a liar. If I'd allowed myself to continue worrying about it all I might have driven myself berserk. I couldn't let that happen. I had to get on with my life. I can tell you now I've never missed that horrible man, not for a minute."

Aubrey felt an intense desire to hold her in his arms. He couldn't ascertain where the feeling had come from. All he knew was his admiration for Lisa was becoming overwhelming. Unfamiliar sensations filled him. He concentrated fiercely to make a rapid analysis of this new consciousness. She was a practical, well-organized woman; a woman who'd overcome so many hard knocks in her life. He couldn't imagine anything she wouldn't be able to cope with. And yet. And yet. A compelling yearning to protect her from further distress made him question how their relationship was likely to develop.

Chapter Seventeen

Lisa had little time to organise any breakfast the day after the house warming at Peachtree Rise. She'd been the first to go to bed once all the guests had left and after the conversation with Timothy Reynolds about his plans for the future. Both Timothy and Aubrey had seemed content to continue talking after she'd explained how the post mortem had cleared her of any fault. Her drunken second husband was already dead where he fell. She'd left the two men helping themselves to one last nightcap and discussing the miracles of modern forensic science.

When she came downstairs next morning there was no sign of either of them. The whole house was quiet and cold. It had been comfortably warm the night before. Perhaps that was because there were so many people filling the rooms. Shivering, she went to the living room. She drew back the curtains and removed the tray of brandy glasses from where Aubrey had left them. In the kitchen her fingers felt like ice. It was freezing outside and not much better indoors. A thin swirl of frost had patterned the north facing window above the sink. She went to fetch her coat and put it on before she cleared the dining room table and set about hand washing the precious antique majolica platters.

Standing at the kitchen sink, gazing through the frosted window, she imagined what life was going to be like once she'd moved into Laburnum House. The planned refurbishments included a dishwasher, thank goodness. Even so, she thought as she carefully dried Uncle Vanguard's ceramic pieces and set them on the kitchen table, there'd still be plenty of hand washing of antiques to be done. And then there was the heating system. They'd have to review plans about the ancient boiler and radiators too, whether or not efficient heating would be good for antique furniture.

She checked the time and remembered Aubrey and Timothy Reynolds had the rest of the week off before they had to return to work. She made a rapid decision. For breakfast they would have to fend for themselves. She rinsed the rest of the washing up under the tap and stacked everything by the drainer so it was obvious they needed doing. She scribbled a note to remind them what was available to eat and to ask them to finish tidying up the kitchen and empty the waste bin but couldn't find anything to attach the note on the fridge door. Carefully she wedged it between the majolica platters on the table. There was still neither sight nor sound of the two of them as she let herself out of Laburnum House and dashed for her car.

She checked the time again. Just enough to park at Addison's as usual, dash over the road to her apartment, change into her working outfit and walk back into the town centre for work. Briefly she pondered the question of where she would park her car once she'd left the apartment and had to drive into town from Peachtree Rise. Maybe she could come to an agreement with the supermarket manager as she had before.

She made it just in time. In the staffroom her Marshall and Simpson mailbox was full: price reductions; memos from management about upcoming changes to the staff rota; further amendments to the staff pension scheme; a planned deep clean of the canteen area which would see it out of commission for a day and a half with an apology for the consequent lack of a subsidised hot meal at lunchtime (drinks would still be available) and a reminder to put in requests for summer holiday weeks before the end of the month.

Lisa couldn't help feeling deflated. Even though the housewarming had been a success, Amy and Danny had got on well with Aubrey and there was much to look forward to, January second was always an unsatisfactory kind of day at Marshall and Simpson. The excitements of Christmas and New Year celebrations were over and there were only the long, dark winter days ahead before thoughts of Easter time off work. Staff came into work earlier on January second to make sure the end of season stock count was completed before the store opened. Then piles of stock had to be moved to make way for deliveries of new season's styles.

As soon as the doors opened a torrent of returns and exchanges spilled into the store and began its rush through the departments filling the aisles and customer service desks till closing time. Lisa often wondered why people waited until the new year to bring back unwanted gifts. Maybe they were hoping to find sale bargains with the cash from their returns. Perhaps they'd felt the need to hang onto the undesired items a little longer in order not to offend the giver. Whatever the reason, it happened every year.

The day had started as it meant to go on. Lisa had no time to take her morning tea break. She was called so often to supervise exchanges and cash refunds her allotted break time passed by. In between customer service enquiries there were all the hectic reductions to organise and sale rails to set up. She gave the job to Justine Belton and asked Mrs Waveney to keep an eye on her and make sure she referred to her display ratios chart. When Lisa next looked at the clock she realised it was nearly her lunch time. It was a relief to see Madge Sparrow on her way in.

"I won't keep you long," Madge said as she put her shopping bag on the customer service counter, "I know it's a busy day for you today."

"Madge, I'm rushed off my feet. I don't know whether I'm coming or going," Lisa said.

"Well then, what time's your lunch break? I'll meet you somewhere we can talk."

They decided on the burger bar near Market Place. Service was usually quick and reliable. Lisa could make it there, have a quick bite and be back at Marshall and Simpson in time to relieve the next person on the staff lunch rota.

There were only a few customers at Bar-B-Quick and plenty of empty tables. Service was super quick even though the young lad at the service counter looked as if he couldn't care less. Madge picked out a table and they offloaded their trays.

When they were settled Lisa said, "So what did you think of Laburnum House? Be honest. What did you really think?"

"Wonderful, Lisa. Just wonderful."

"So, it's definitely the place Wally remembers from years ago?"

"Absolutely. Yes. He says it's hardly changed at all. He went to have a good look at the kitchen. You know, that's the only room he ever got to see when he was gardening up there. He said he could swear it was the same tablecloth on that pine table. Red and white check. Like in an Italian street café."

Lisa laughed. "He remembers the tablecloth?" she said.

"That's right, Lisa love. He remembers that cloth on the table in the kitchen because that's where he used to stand waiting for a piece of cake to go with his cup of tea."

"From the lady of the house?"

"Yes."

"Whoever that was." Lisa took a bite of her chicken wrap and had an afterthought. She swallowed quickly and said, "You know, it very well might be the exact same cloth. I found it in one of the dresser drawers."

"I've never in my life seen such a massive pine dresser," Madge said. "You couldn't have something that big in today's new builds. It looks like it belongs in a stately home. Will you keep it?"

"We haven't decided yet. Early days."

Madge nodded. "It is," she agreed.

"So you like the house then?"

"It's out of this world, Lisa," Madge said in between chewing. "I can see why you'd be attracted to it."

"Yes. I'm looking forward to making it my home."

Madge hummed and looked uncomfortable. She took a moment before she spoke again.

"But will it feel like your home, though?" she said. "Living in a house doesn't make it your home. There's some fabulous pieces of furniture in there but what about your own things? Won't Aubrey want to keep all his own stuff? There won't be room for yours."

"There'll be plenty of space for the things I want with me," Lisa said. "I'm to have two rooms upstairs. Like my own apartment. Anyway, my things would hardly look right alongside all those antiques. Besides, I'm leaving most of my stuff to let the apartment as furnished."

Madge grunted and said, "It sounds odd, Lisa. I have to tell you because it bothers me. Aubrey seems like a solid sort of chap. He was the perfect gentleman last night but it sounds like you'll be living separate lives under the same roof. I don't think I could cope with that if it was me."

"Are you in another of your funny moods, Madge?" Lisa said. "I'm getting the feeling you don't approve."

Madge Sparrow put down her burger roll and stopped chewing.

"I'm worried about you," she said. "Look, all I'm going to say is please be careful. You have to know that as far as that lovely house goes you'll have no rights. No rights whatsoever. If he pulls a fast one on you he can have you out on your ear in a flash."

"I do realise that," Lisa said. "That's why I'm keeping the flat. I'll always have that to go back to if things don't work out."

"I suppose so. It just seems such a risky thing to do at this time in your life."

"Life is full of risks, whatever age you're at," Lisa said. "Sometimes it's good to get out of your comfort zone and try something new and different."

"Well, I suppose you have a point there. I can't remember the last time me and Wally tried anything new and different."

"So that's how I'm looking at it, Madge. I'm treating it like a bit of an adventure. It's an opportunity I want to take. It wouldn't have happened at all if Amy hadn't persuaded me to have that holiday last June."

Lisa took the empty cartons to the waste disposal and came back to finish her drink. Madge looked as if she were in a daydream, her head on one side and a faraway look in her eyes.

"Penny for 'em," Lisa said.

"I was just thinking . . ."

"I know you were. I could tell."

"I was just thinking about what you said about trying new things. Me and Wally haven't had a decent holiday for a long time. I think we've got a bit stuck in our ways."

"So, there you are then. Maybe it's time for a change of scenery. Where would you like to go?"

"Oh, I haven't got that far into thinking about it. I've been too busy thinking about you and your adventure up Peachtree Rise. What's going to happen next? What are you planning?"

"I'm staying in my flat until Aubrey's decided what he wants to bring from his mother's house. You remember Timothy, from Cambridge? He's going to rent it for a short time. Long story. Probably divorce. I'll spend weekends at Laburnum House while the alterations are going on and then when the kitchen and bathrooms are ready I'll move in permanently."

"I really hope all goes well, Lisa. Truly I do. Me and Wally. Both of us. We know you've been dealt a rough hand before. More than once."

"Thank you. I hope so too."

Madge Sparrow grabbed Lisa's wrists and stared into her eyes. "Listen to me," she said and increased her grip. "I'll be your friend forever. Whatever happens. I want you to know that. But don't you go letting out your flat on a rental contract for more than a year. We'll all know by then, won't we?"

Chapter Eighteen

March

One month into his retirement Aubrey Tennant was enjoying his new lifestyle. Seated in his favourite armchair in the rear sitting room, comfortably stretching his legs, he was letting his thoughts wander in an amiable fashion as he gazed through the French windows watching sunlight fading on this early spring Sunday afternoon. Deliciously sweet aromas were wafting from the direction of the kitchen and he could hear the chinking sounds of china cups and plates. He wondered what treat Lisa would bring to have with their afternoon tea. The thought made his mouth water. Yes, indeed. Life had certainly become very pleasing.

He hadn't much cared for the retirement send-off from Piper Precision Engineering but had gone along with it, not least because the whole event had been put together by Timothy Reynolds.

"It's by way of a little thank you," Timothy had said. "You will take it in good heart, won't you? If it hadn't been for you and your good wife, sorry, lady." He'd looked embarrassed and coughed before he began again. "If it hadn't been for the two of you I don't know where I would have ended up."

"I'm glad it's working out well," Aubrey replied and agreed to go along with Timothy's plans.

There'd been a small gathering in the CEO's office suite, a presentation of a painting by a local artist chosen by Timothy, one which wouldn't look out of place in

Laburnum House when Aubrey decided the best place for it, followed by a few snacks and soft drinks. Aubrey smiled to himself as he recollected how well he'd coped with all the unwanted attention. He let out a congratulatory sigh. Life was becoming exceedingly comfortable. He reached for the book on his side table and opened it at the bookmark.

The door opened and Lisa came in carrying a loaded tray. She took it to the small tea table near the window. Aubrey's eyes lit on the scones and he quickly put his book back.

"Ah, scones," he said as he seated himself at the table. "Just the ticket," and he readied himself to make his choice.

"I was wondering," Lisa said as she handed Aubrey a tea plate before she sat, "what you were planning to do with the chest?"

"Which chest?"

"Your mother's. The one you brought from her house. You know, the one you said Uncle Vanguard had gifted her. The one that's still in the hall."

"I hadn't decided yet," Aubrey said. "I'm not sure where would be the optimum place to put it. It is rather large."

"I'm so glad you agree," Lisa said. Aubrey wasn't sure what he'd agreed to. He waited. "It's far too big to stay where it is, Aubrey. I nearly tripped, banging into it just now coming through with the tray. And it's so heavy I can't move it when I'm cleaning."

"Ah," Aubrey said. Now he understood. "You would like it moved from its present position."

"I would. Now, don't get me wrong. It's a beautiful piece what with all that lovely carving on it. I do understand it has much sentimental value for you, Aubrey, but I think it would be better somewhere else."

"Hmm," he said, savouring strawberry jam and whipped cream, "I must give it some thought."

"I've already thought it through," Lisa said. "There's an ideal spot for it on the upstairs landing. I could make use of it there, Aubrey. It would make the perfect place to keep spare linens for the guest bedrooms. What do you think?"

It was an admirable idea.

"Top marks, Lisa," he said. "I think that's the perfect location. Mother used to keep it in her bedroom, you know, and I do believe she also used it for linens. Well done. First class. Couldn't have come up with a better idea myself."

Lisa cleared the table when they were finished and Aubrey re-settled himself in his favourite armchair. His appetite sated, he picked up his book and opened the section on Norfolk wetland fowl in preparation for his upcoming outing with Lisa's son. By the time she came back from the kitchen daylight had faded further. He could hardly see to read. He switched on the table lamp at his side. He glanced at Lisa to say something about turning on more lamps in the room but she had her head down looking at a magazine. He leaned back to get comfortable but something wasn't as it should be.

He sensed Lisa was watching him as he rose from his armchair and nudged it to its right. Satisfied, he sat down again. A second passed and then he got up once more and nudged the lamp on the side table next to the chair. He sat down again, opened his book and continued reading.

"Is anything the matter?" Lisa said.

He didn't look up from his reading but said, "No. Not now."

"What was the matter before?" she asked.

"Before what?"

"Before you got up and moved the chair and the lamp."

"I think I might move the chair and the lamp if that's what I choose to do."

"I'm interested in the reason, Aubrey," she said. "One minute you were reading and suddenly you needed to move them."

"That's right. That's exactly what I did."

"And the reason is?"

"Because I wanted to."

"But why did you want to?"

Aubrey sighed but it wasn't out of comforting ease like a few minutes before when he was contemplating an appetising cream tea. He wasn't accustomed to having to account for every movement he made. He was aware of a prickling sensation at the back of his neck and, quite suddenly, all the pleasurable sensations he'd felt earlier had been quashed and replaced with a distinct feeling of discomfort.

He closed his book and took a deep breath. He didn't want to say the wrong thing but he really had no desire to enter into a conversation about why he'd moved the chair and the lamp. He didn't want to have any conversation at all. He'd had a lovely afternoon complete with tea and scones and now all he wanted to do was read his book. Unfortunately the angle of light cast by the lamp had been less than the optimum fifty five degrees. Moving the chair had helped a little but moving the lamp as well had been necessary. He cleared his throat to speak.

"If the chair and the lamp had been put back in their original, correct positions neither action would have been needed," he said.

"I've been cleaning today," Lisa said. "You can't do it properly if you don't move things."

"Yes, I can see that. But I don't know why you have to clean on Sunday, Lisa. Mother never cleaned on Sunday. She was too busy in the kitchen. I have an idea," he said. "I shall draw up some spreadsheets and on them will be the layout of each room with the positions of all items of furniture clearly marked. I should think that would avoid such discrepancies happening again."

"Aubrey," Lisa said, "perhaps you've forgotten I'm at work tomorrow. I'm at work all week including Saturday. I've swapped my day off with Mrs Waveney. So I did some cleaning today. Is it so important to you," she went on, "to have everything in exactly the same place as it always was?"

"If it's the best place to be, why not?"

It took her quite a while to respond to his question. When eventually she spoke again her voice sounded different. He could imagine it was how one's voice might sound if someone was squeezing one's neck.

"I like to have a change about sometimes, Aubrey," she said. "I suppose you could call it a woman thing. We like to put our own stamp on a place. You know what I mean? Otherwise it doesn't feel as if it's your own home."

Aubrey puzzled at the change in the tone of Lisa's voice. It was higher-pitched and a bit staccato as if there was something catching at the back of her throat. It reminded him of a female teacher he'd taken a particular dislike to when he was at his first preparatory school. When he concentrated on the expression Lisa was wearing he couldn't make out whether she was feeling angry or sad. Either way, it became obvious to him that she was upset about something. He decided to change the subject slightly.

"I've been reading about the Norfolk Broads' fauna," he said, brandishing his book, "and in particular the kinds of birds we're likely to come across when I go with Danny at the weekend."

"Oh," Lisa said and her voice sounded more normal. "I see. That's next Sunday, isn't it?"

"That's right," Aubrey said. "I want to be a little more informed about what we shall witness."

"But, Danny will be able to tell you everything. He knows a great deal about our Norfolk birds and the ones that come visiting on their way from somewhere else."

"Migratory," Aubrey added.

"That's what I said," Lisa replied.

"It says here in this book," Aubrey said, carefully avoiding the opportunity to further correct her, "that March is a good time to spot our foreign feathered visitors. March is traditionally the month, it says here, in which chiffchaffs, sand martins, wheatears and Sandwich terns begin to return."

"And if you do see them Danny will remember which is which," Lisa said. "So you don't have to force yourself to learn all about them before you even begin."

"Force myself? I'm not forcing myself, Lisa. I enjoy learning new subjects. It's one of the things I was looking forward to about my retirement. I'm grateful to Danny for inviting me and I'm looking forward to a new experience."

He watched as Lisa got up from the sofa, smiled an odd sort of smile and left the room. She didn't say where she was going and what she was going to do and he didn't ask. He had the clear impression that something was troubling her. No matter. She would say if she wanted to. He shouldn't press her. He could draw up the furniture layout plans in due time and have them ready for Lisa's referral the next time she needed to move his chair and lamp table. Problem solved. He turned his attention to his reading and gave the matter no more thought.

The door opened and Lisa was there again.

"I've just had a quick word with Danny," she said. "When he comes to pick you up next weekend he'll give you a hand moving that chest."

Aubrey heard himself gasp. "What? Straight away?" he said.

"It's a whole week away, Aubrey," Lisa said with that same, strange smile on her face. "It gives you plenty of time to make sure you're happy with where I'm going to put it. Draw up your furniture layouts if you must."

"But I don't like being rushed into things."

"You had deadlines in your work at Piper Engineering, didn't you? Of course you did."

"That's different. It was work. Here, at home, I prefer to feel more relaxed."

"Well, the sooner the chest is moved out of the way, the sooner we shall both feel relaxed."

"But mother's chest . . .," he began.

"We've agreed, Aubrey, that mother's chest is in the way where it is now. And speaking of your mother, as you often do, don't try to tell me that when she wanted something doing in the house you didn't jump up and do it just as soon as you could."

She had a point. He was forced to admit it. "You're quite right," he said.

"Well then. Don't expect me to put up with anything less."

All he could do was nod his agreement.

⚖️⚖️⚖️

The following week on Sunday morning as soon as Lisa dressed and came downstairs she could see Aubrey was getting himself in a quandary. He'd been up since first light. She'd heard him padding about from room to room, muttering and opening and closing doors. She gave up trying to go back to sleep and found him still in his dressing gown fussing about footwear and rainproofs.

"Just keep warm today, Aubrey. It's often cooler up at the coast," she said. "I doubt you'll need a raincoat. Wear layers."

"Layers?"

"Layers of clothes, Aubrey. How about a tee shirt underneath a nice warm sweater?"

"I haven't got a tee shirt. I haven't worn tee shirts since I was in my twenties."

"A shirt then."

"I still need a waterproof."

"The weather forecast has given dry today."

"Can't be trusted," came his rapid response as he rummaged in the cloaks cupboard. "I'm sure I put a lightweight waterproof in here. You haven't moved it, have you?"

"I haven't touched anything in there, Aubrey. If you put it in there, that's where it'll be."

She left him to it and went to the kitchen, partly to make her first morning cup of tea and partly just to get out of his way and give herself time to adjust. A few minutes later she heard the cloaks cupboard door close. He came to find her and stood in the kitchen doorway, his eyes wide and imploring like a lost dog.

"What do you think?" he said, holding up a dark green jacket. "Will this do? It's quite old but it seems to be still in good condition."

Lisa was careful to show her deliberation of the matter so Aubrey could see she'd given appropriate consideration.

"That's a Barbour," she said, looking impressed and running her hand over the waxed fabric. "They never go out of style. It's perfect for where you're going."

"Is it, though? I don't want to look out of place. I want to look as if I . . . as if I . . ."

"You'll look exactly like anybody else you come across, Aubrey. In fact, Danny has something like that himself. I don't think it's an expensive one like yours but it's very similar in style."

Surely she'd given enough reassurance. She turned away from him to remove the tea bag from her morning mug.

Aubrey threw the jacket over the back of a chair and sat, looking as if he expected serving. Lisa put her tea in front of him and started making another.

"It isn't mine," Aubrey said. "I should try it on." He stood up and put it on, tugging at the sleeves. "They're a little short. Uncle Van wasn't as tall as I am. It's a little heavy too. I couldn't find my own lightweight. That would have been perfect. You can roll it up, you see. Carry it with you anywhere. Bring it out when you need it."

"It'll be fine, Aubrey. You probably won't even need a raincoat. Take it with you and keep it in the car. If the weather looks doubtful when you get there you can decide what to do then."

He finished his tea and dashed upstairs to finish preparing for his day out. Lisa sat with her own tea and took a deep breath. The doorbell rang and she went to answer it.

"Danny!" she said. "Come in, come in. Cup of tea, love? Kettle's just boiled."

"I might as well, Mum, thank you. Is he ready?"

"Not yet. He won't be long."

She switched on the kettle again then went to call upstairs to let Aubrey know Danny had arrived for their day out. When the tea was ready she sat with her son at the kitchen table.

"Tea up!" she said.

"Thanks, Mum. I didn't have time for a drink before I came out and I didn't want to be late." He gestured upstairs and said, "How is he?"

"I think he's really looking forward to today, Danny. He's had his nose in a bird book all this week. He bought it specially, I think. I've hardly had a word out of him."

"Excellent. I bet he's memorised everything he read."

"Well, it's funny you should say that. I think he has, actually. How did you know he'd do that?"

"Just a wild guess, Mum."

Lisa scrutinised her son's face for clues to any hidden meanings but Danny was cheerful as ever, leaning back in his seat, comfortable as you like.

"You won't forget to move that chest for me, will you, before you go?" she said.

"Let's have a look," he said and went out into the hall just as Aubrey was coming downstairs.

"Good morning to you," Danny said and shook Aubrey's hand.

"And a very good morning to you too. Have you come for breakfast?"

"I've come early to help with the chest you want moving."

"Ah, yes, of course," Aubrey said.

Lisa stepped forward. "Why don't you two make a start and I'll put some bacon on. I'll have breakfast ready for you before you go. I know you want to get away early."

"I prefer my bacon . . ." Aubrey began.

"Grilled. Yes, I know, dear," Lisa said and left them considering the best way to lift the bulky chest, manoeuvre it up the stairs and around the bend half way up. From the kitchen she could hear their exertions. Aubrey was red in the face when they came back. "Everything all right?" she said.

"Spot on. What did you think, Danny?" Aubrey said.

"I think it looks just right up there," Danny said. "It's a fantastic piece of furniture, Aubrey. Foreign, is it?"

"Chinese, I believe. My uncle, whose house this used to be, travelled very widely. He brought it back from one of his trips and gave it to my mother. It's been sitting in the house in Thetford all these years."

"Well, I think it's nice you have it now as a memory of your mother. What will you leave for me, Mum?"

"Thomas the tank engine and a light sabre," she said, "and a lot of the other toys you couldn't bear to part with. And old photographs of yours. Maybe you'd like them back now? I've still got them, you know. You can take them off my hands as soon as you like."

Danny laughed and said, "Not just now, Mum. I like that you're looking after them for me. And you can't complain any more about not having enough space for them."

They sat to eat while Lisa got on with making up packed lunches to take with them.

"Thanks for doing that, Mum. They'll be just what we need at lunchtime. It's surprising how hungry you can get when you're out in the fresh air for hours at a time. I usually call in at a pub when I've finished for the day," Danny said. "Is that okay with you, Aubrey?"

"I don't know," Aubrey said. "Won't that make us very late back? What time are we having supper, Lisa?"

"Oh, I won't be cooking tonight, Aubrey. I'm eating out today with Amy. At a carvery, I think. Or some Sunday lunch place. I won't want to eat another big meal today."

"You mean there won't be any supper?"

"We'll grab something in the pub," Danny said, finishing off his last rasher.

Chapter Nineteen

Amy Miller steered through the double gates, around the curved drive and pulled up outside Laburnum House. She noticed some of the rhododendrons either side of the entrance were in fat bud: a promise of things to come; spring well on its way; a joyful heralding of happy times. She frowned. She'd have to keep her true feelings in check today.

She sounded the horn. Within seconds her mother was hurrying down the steps and across the parking area to meet her.

"Morning, Mum. All set?" Amy said as Lisa wriggled into the passenger seat.

"You bet I am. Where are we going?"

"I thought I'd leave that up to you, Mum. Your choice."

"Somewhere by the water, please. Where the windows look out over a nice view."

"I know just the place," Amy said and reversed the car around. She turned out of the drive and drove along Peachtree Rise, down into the village, taking the main road away from the coast and inland toward the city.

"You very hungry?" Amy said.

"Famished," Lisa said. "I cooked breakfast for the menfolk this morning but didn't have any myself."

"Did they get away okay?"

"Oh, yes. I think Aubrey was a bit nervous about it to begin with, though."

"Why?"

"It's just the way he is, Amy. You've got to remember he hasn't much experience about family life."

"I want to talk to you about that, Mum," Amy said as they gathered speed. The words had tumbled free from Amy's thinking. She'd meant to bide her time, wait for the right moment. She'd have to be more careful and think it through before she spoke her mind.

Lisa said, "How do you mean?"

"Let's wait till we get somewhere comfortable, shall we?"

Deep in thought, wondering whether she'd already revealed her intentions, Amy took the Wroxham route which ran across country between acres of farmland bursting with spring green. Breezes buffeted trees and hawthorn hedgerows either side of the carriageway until the approach to the centre where the road dropped into the shelter of houses at the edge of town. Slowing, Amy drove along the main thoroughfare and turned into a narrow side street. The road curved behind a small shopping centre and into a car park at the rear of a hotel next to Wroxham bridge.

"Wait here a minute, will you, Mum? I have to go inside and give the car registration at reception. I don't want to be clamped."

It wasn't going to be the easiest thing broaching the subject of Aubrey Tennant's seemingly lacklustre experience of family life with her mother, Amy acknowledged as she made her way back to the car park. She wondered what was going to be the best way to begin. She could wait until Lisa brought it up herself to ask what Amy had meant earlier. That way Amy could be certain her mother was ready to talk about it. Or, she could wait until the end of their meal when they'd both feel more relaxed.

"Everything all right?" Lisa said as Amy opened the driver's door.

"Yes. It's all organised. I have to display this ticket in the windscreen," Amy said as she reached inside to secure the parking permit.

They linked arms with one another and Amy said it felt like old times going out to Sunday lunch with her mother. Lisa held her more tightly and squeezed her arm. They were met at reception by a charming young waiter who showed them to a table right next to the window overlooking the river and with a good view of the hump-backed bridge famous among the boating fraternity for its shortage of headroom. Swans gathered by the bank and a small family group were throwing scraps of bread.

"I thought you weren't supposed to give them bread," Lisa said, settling into her seat.

"That's all changed now, Mum," Lisa said. "I read it in the press just the other day. There's so little natural food for them now they'd starve to death without something to eat even if it is only bread."

"Did the article say why that's happening?"

"Not clearly. A number of reasons. Climate change. Too many boating visitors churning up the water. Pollution. Otters. Any number of reasons, I suppose."

The same waiter came to hand them menus and asked if they'd like a drink first. They chose one of many flavoured gins and were surprised by the size of the glasses when they arrived.

"You might have to help me out with this, Mum," Amy said, laughing. "I don't want to be over the limit."

"Don't worry, love. It's mostly tonic. It tastes very nice, though."

They made their choices from the menu and told the waiter they'd hold back on desserts.

"Where did Danny say they were going today?"Amy asked.

"Up on the north coast somewhere. He knows a lot of places up there where they have hides so they can get out of the weather and set up their cameras."

Their traditional English roasts arrived and conversation ceased for a while. Then Lisa spoke.

"What did you mean about wanting to talk to me about Aubrey?"

Plan one had presented itself. Amy thought carefully about how she was going to say it.

"Well,"she said, "I've been wondering about you both. It was really great on New Year's Eve. I thought it went so well for you. But we haven't heard much since. Everything is okay, isn't it?"

"Yes. I think it's working out just fine."

"Just fine?"

Lisa put down her knife and fork and said, "Amy, what do you want me to tell you about? We've had the central heating sorted out. We've put en-suites upstairs. The kitchen layout works better now. I'm still going to work. The tenants in my flat are lovely people, both teachers at the sixth form college. Aubrey and I have plans for the garden and the old boathouse. Is that what you mean?"

"Not really. Okay, then. I'd like you to tell me about why you think Aubrey doesn't have much experience of family life."

Amy waited as her mother took her turn to gather her thoughts. Then,

"There's nothing for you to worry about Amy." She looked around the room as if she was making sure nobody was listening. "Aubrey is different. He has some funny ways, that's all. Nothing I can't handle."

"What sort of funny ways?"

"Habits. I mean habits."

"What sort of habits?"

"Well, let me see. He is very particular. *Very* particular."

"Go on. Give me an example."

"Right. Okay then. He's how you might say, stuck in his ways. For example, he likes to have his chair and his table lamp in exactly the same position."

"Exactly?"

"Oh, yes."

"And?"

"Oh, lots of things, Amy. It's understandable. He's lived on his own for years since his mother died. Some people do get stuck in old habits. But, listen I really don't want you to worry. It's nothing I can't cope with. I've worked at Marshall and Simpson too many years to worry about precise measurements."

"He *measures* the position of his chair and lamp table?"

"Sort of, yes."

"Oh, Mum. How can you live with that? It's not normal."

"It's normal for Aubrey. You have to keep in mind what kind of work he used to do. It's always been important to him to be precise. You remember how Danny used to be when he was little? Always had to have his toys laid out just so."

"Mum, he was just a kid when he was doing it."

"Well, it seems similar to me, Amy. Aubrey gets out of his comfort zone when things don't go to plan."

"Does he get aggressive?"

"Good heavens, no. Is that what you've been worrying about? Let me tell you, Aubrey wouldn't deliberately hurt anybody. He'd be mortified if he knew that's what you've been thinking."

Amy lowered her voice and said, "Mum, you can't blame me for thinking about what could happen. He's never been married. He doesn't know anything about committed relationships. He's never shared his life."

"Well, he shared his life with his mother for a long time."

"And that, too! It's just not right. Mum, you must see that."

Lisa smiled and said, "Yes of course I see what you're getting at. I take it you don't expect this arrangement of ours to last long. Is that it?"

Amy sighed. She reached across the table and touched her mother's hand.

"What about love, Mum?"

"What about it?"

"Don't you want somebody to love?"

"I have you and Danny. Sweetheart, I haven't much interest in romantic love. If it happens in time, all well and good. What's more important to me at this time in my life is security. I already have all the love I need. One day there'll be grandchildren to love too."

"I need a decent boyfriend first, Mum. Look, I just want to let you know that if worst comes to the worst all you have to do is let me know and I'll be round there like a shot to help you."

"Thank you, Amy. Please try to stop worrying about me. Aubrey is doing his best to make it work for us. So am I. Time will tell. I know we'd known one another for a short time but when you get to my age what's the point of waiting? Life is for living, isn't it? As I said: time will tell. So can we get on with our meal now?"

"I hope I haven't upset you. I just wanted you to know I'll always be here for you."

"Oh, Amy, I know you will. I'm a lucky woman to have such a caring daughter."

"Aww, shucks," Amy said in an affected accent and batted her eyelashes. Lisa laughed but to Amy her mother's laughter sounded forced.

Amy sensed an uncomfortable silence hanging in the space between them. She wondered if her mother felt it too. She wanted to go further with her questions about how Aubrey and her mother were getting on together but instinct told her to leave it be. Maybe Jessie had been right when she said Amy was the one behaving like a parent. She picked up the menu and asked if Lisa wanted to change her mind about dessert. They ate in continued silence until Lisa broke it.

"I wonder how Danny's getting on?" she said. "I know he was hoping to take some special photographs today. There are some rare birds recently arrived apparently."

"Oh, yes?" Amy asked.

Amy couldn't listen to the details. She was aware her mother was changing the subject, avoiding the difficult topics of conversation, insisting there was nothing to worry about. But there were too many buts. How could her mother settle into such a strange relationship with a man she'd known for such a short time? Why had they heard so little from either Aubrey or her mother since New Year's Eve? Surely there was trouble ahead.

She couldn't wait to speak to her brother that night. She called him on his mobile the minute she arrived home. Danny's reaction surprised her. After she'd explained her thoughts and described what their mother had said about Aubrey measuring where the furniture should be, she expected some kind of validation of her doubts. Instead, all she heard was loud laughter. It sounded as though Danny was at a party. He was having to shout into the phone. There were other loud voices all around him and music in the background.

"You'll have to speak up, Amy," Danny said. "Can't really hear what you're saying. We're in The Dun Cow. Had a fabulous day out. Did you have a good day too? Aubrey's treating me to a posh dinner. I can hardly hear you, Amy. Better go. Tell Ma Aubrey might be a bit late home tonight. Great guy. Love ya."

Chapter Twenty

April

Lisa lost count of the ways Aubrey's behaviour surprised her during the following weeks. She'd become used to his moments of awkwardness in company and always somehow managed to smooth the way for him and help him with unfamiliar conversations with anyone he didn't know well. She understood his apparent need for everything to be so precise. It was perfectly understandable, bearing in mind the job he'd done and the way he'd lived his life before they met. Everybody develops habits of their own, she reminded herself. She had her own preferred way of doing things so why shouldn't Aubrey be the same? She expected it to take some time before he could relax into a different way of living with a new partner in a new home. Hadn't Mrs Waveney at work gone through a difficult phase with her husband straight after he retired? Lisa remembered how often Mrs Waveney had come into work in the morning and, even before she'd taken off her coat in the staff cloakroom, she made it clear she was still angry about something her husband had said or done that morning. Lisa understood all this and, she believed, was coping with this new life of hers reasonably well but she couldn't put her finger on exactly what was happening to make Aubrey behave so differently from his usual ways.

She stood at her bedroom window, gazing out at the garden below, puzzling at the changes in his behaviour. There were days when he seemed to act completely out of character. She took to looking at him more often, more intently, noticing changes in his expression, hearing warmer tones in his voice. Sometimes with amusement and at other times with curiosity, she watched him as if she were looking at him for the first time.

His days out with Danny continued throughout the spring months, not always at weekends. Occasionally, when she came home from work there'd be a note on the kitchen table to say he'd be back late and not to worry about supper as he'd be eating out with Danny. Afterwards, he'd talk non-stop about what they'd seen and who they'd met. He hadn't gone so far as to buy similar professional photography equipment as her son used but he'd treated himself to a better camera and enjoyed comparing the shots he took with the illustrations in the several bird books he now possessed.

He hardly ever mentioned his furniture layout plans. In fact, he'd never finished them. He didn't comment either on the furniture positions or Lisa's cleaning arrangements at all. He'd even begun taking on some household chores himself when she was at work. She noticed when he'd had the vacuum cleaner out because he always wound up the flex in the opposite direction to the way she did it. He unloaded the dishwasher and put things away. He took care of the laundry when his basket was full. She was aware he would have done all these things and more himself when he lived alone but the fact that he was doing them now made her feel that perhaps he did see their partnership as a relationship of equals.

He seemed to be a changed man. When she thought more deeply about it she realised the change was welcome. As she turned away from the window she caught sight of her reflection in the wall mirror and saw that she was smiling. This much more relaxed Aubrey was how he'd first appeared to her at the hotel in Torquay. She reminded herself how impressed she'd been by his voice and old-fashioned gentlemanly ways. His obvious lack of experience with women had seemed quite attractive at first.

She heard a blackbird's joyful call and turned to the window again. Outside, spring flowers were bursting into bloom everywhere. Spring had brought early warmth. The garden was brimming with a multitude of vibrant colours, almost like a symphony, each bright colour singing its own heady melody. In the rose garden behind Laburnum House buds were forming and through the wisteria tunnel, all along the supports, long racemes already hung low, ready to explode into spring blue. Summer was approaching fast.

Aubrey had kept on the gardener he'd employed the previous year but there was still work to be done to make the area around the boathouse safe. Then the house would be finished. She gazed at the time-and-weather-worn boathouse wondering what Aubrey would find to keep him occupied after everything was repaired. Would he spend even more time bird-watching? Her thoughts turned to holidays and how nice it might be if they were to spend some time away together. She hurried downstairs and found Aubrey in the kitchen. He was filling the kettle.

"I thought I would make us a cup of tea, Lisa," he said.

Another change in his behaviour.

"Lovely," she said. "Thank you. That's thoughtful of you. Aubrey, I've been wondering about something. If we decide to plan on an extra holiday this year, I need to know soon. I have to book my weeks off work well in advance. I might already be too late."

"I thought you'd already secured a week in June," he said.

"I mean the rest of the year. We might decide to take a later break as well."

"As well as what? I don't follow."

"As well as our week in June," Lisa said. "I assumed you'd want to revisit Torquay again."

His eyes opened wide as he said, "Why would I want to do that?"

"I thought you liked it there."

"I do. That is to say, I did. I don't see the point now."

"The point is having a break away from home, Aubrey. Don't you want to?"

He looked completely puzzled as he said, "I really don't feel the need. I have enough to occupy me here."

Her stomach sank. He hadn't given any thought at all to what she might like to do with her time off work. Worse, he hadn't even realised his lack of consideration. He was completely unaware that she'd have preferences of her own. When he took his tea into the living room she stayed at the breakfast table staring at the wall, thinking seriously and asking herself why she had so suddenly felt bereft when only moments before she had imagined they were becoming closer. She came to the conclusion it was because Aubrey was happy and relaxed only when he was doing what he wanted to do. Consideration of other people's feelings didn't seem to register with him. He talked about his preferred subjects or he didn't talk at all.

As April turned into May Aubrey seemed distant as if he had his mind on something else, on something she knew nothing about. He was spending a long time upstairs in his room and didn't want to be questioned about what he was doing. When, one Sunday afternoon she found the Highway Code on his side table she asked outright.

"Are you having driving lessons, Aubrey?" she said.

He grinned and looked embarrassed. "Yes," he said. "Danny is helping me understand the basics."

"When did all this happen?"

"Ever since I started going with him on his wildlife photography days. He let me take the wheel occasionally and I discovered I quite enjoyed being in control of a vehicle. It's exhilarating, isn't it? It gives you a sense of freedom I never knew existed. I've applied for my driving test. I've been swotting the rules upstairs."

His face was glowing with pleasure. She saw the brightness in his eyes and an expression so boyish it reminded her of when Danny was a boy delighted about something.

"Why didn't you tell me before now?"

"It was going to be a surprise, Lisa, and I'm sorry you've discovered my secret. I was going to take us out and drive us to a good restaurant to celebrate when I have my full licence. How did you guess?"

She brought out the Highway Code booklet from behind the cushion where she'd hidden it.

"You left this on the table," she said.

"Ah," he said. "How forgetful of me. I've ruined the surprise."

He looked truly remorseful. A surge of warmth rose up within her toward this awkward man whose old-fashioned habits and speech were capable of testing her patience to the limit.

"Never mind, Aubrey," she said. "You'd like to drive us out to a restaurant? That's something I'll really look forward to. Thank you."

He seemed pleased and gave her that military-style nod he sometimes did which she took as his way of showing a satisfactory end to the conversation. Later, she reprimanded herself for thinking the worse of him. He was only trying to keep a secret and didn't know how.

When she met with Madge Sparrow on her next day off she brought up the subject of holidays. "I don't know what you're complaining at," Madge said as they rode the Park and Ride bus into the city.

"I'm not really complaining, as such," Lisa said. "It's more like just being curious. I mean, he's going out with my son more than he does with me. They're off out again today."

"Well, that's what you wanted isn't it? He's getting on well with your children." The bus took a sharp corner and Madge's empty shopping bag toppled from her knee into the aisle. When she retrieved it and leaned back in her seat she was grimacing.

"What?" Lisa said.

Madge tutted. "That couple up the back of the bus?" she said. "They're listening to every word we're saying." She brought her finger to her mouth and faced forward, tight-lipped. They sat in silence till they reached the Castle Mall stop where they left the bus but not before Madge had stared hard at the eavesdroppers. "Nosey buggers," she said, "all bloody ears, they were. Craning their necks for a bit of gossip."

Arm in arm they crossed the road into Gentleman's Walk in the direction of the city centre. They stopped at a French style patisserie to buy cakes before heading off toward the market and after filling her shopping bag with eggs and vegetables Madge suggested a trip into the department store on the corner where they could have coffee and a sit down.

"So, go on then," Madge said as they sat at a table in the downstairs café with cake and coffee. "You were saying about him going out with your Danny more than he goes out with you."

"He does."

"And what do you want him to do instead?"

"I don't know."

"You see, Lisa. There you go. I don't think you know what you do want."

"Well, it would be nice if he wanted to go away on holiday somewhere. It's not as if we can't afford it."

"There you go again. There is no *we,* is there? Housekeeper and companion, Lisa. That's what you said. That's what you wanted. I thought you'd decided to give it a year to see how it goes. What happened to *I'm treating it like an adventure*? Lost your taste for getting out of your comfort zone?"

Lisa couldn't answer. She stared at the posters on the wall instead.

They returned their empty trays to the counter and wandered up the stairs from the basement café through the department store, Lisa lost in thought. Madge's words had brought her up sharp. Madge was right: she *was* confused about the nature of her and Aubrey's relationship. What had started as a clear cut arrangement between them had somehow shifted in her thinking, her expectations. She was hurt by Aubrey's lack of consideration yet knew she had no right to feel that way. She was going to have to sort herself out. She took a deep breath and let it go slowly, like a silent sigh, but it brought her no relief.

The way to the store exit led them through the cosmetics department where intoxicating perfumery reminded Lisa there was something she needed to buy.

"Hold on a minute, Madge," she said. "I want to buy a new lipstick. I've been using the same one ever since my makeover day at the hotel in Torquay last year. There's hardly any of it left."

"Well, I hope you can find another one like it, love. They keep changing the names of them, don't they? And just when you find a colour you really like they go and discontinue it. Tell you what, I'll just have a quick look round while you're deciding."

Madge disappeared in the direction of shoes and handbags. She came back after barely a few minutes holding out a coloured tourist pamphlet just as Lisa was paying for her new lipstick.

"Look what I found," Madge said, waving the brochure under Lisa's nose. "I'm going to book this for me and Wally as soon as I get home."

"What is it?" Lisa said.

"Trips to Cornwall. You know, that place with all the different climates underneath huge domes."

"The Eden Project?"

"That's the one. Look," Madge said, tapping at the brochure. "The girl at the kiosk over there says this company is promoting a special offer. They had late cancellations or something from a whole group of people. So they've a lot of places to fill at the last minute. Look at this holiday here. It includes a day at the Eden whatsit and another day to the Lost Gardens of Heligan. I saw some of that on the telly. And see, the coach picks up from here like when you went to Torquay last year."

"It's the same company," Lisa said, recognising the logo. "They're very well organised."

"So, what do you think?"

"I think it's a good idea, Madge. I can see how Wally would enjoy that too. He's always loved his gardening."

"And how about you?"

"I don't get chance to do much gardening. Aubrey has somebody come in to do it."

Madge laughed. "I don't mean that!" she said. "I'm talking about you coming with us."

"Oh. Well, I don't know . . ."

"Don't think about it too long. Places will be snapped up."

They picked up Lisa's car at the Park and Ride car park and started the journey home before the usual teatime rush. Madge talked with excitement all the way. She read aloud all the information in the holiday brochure she'd picked up and Lisa had to admit the idea was tempting. She wondered if perhaps Aubrey might change his mind about going away and decide to come with them. She planned to ask him straight away.

At Laburnum House she ran up the steps to the front door. She let herself in and went to find him. Aubrey was in the breakfast room and, from under the table, a black and white dog growled at her.

Chapter Twenty One

Lisa bent down to say hello to the dog under the table. She tentatively held out her hand but it backed away and grumbled at her again.

"He'll get used to you eventually," Aubrey said. "It took him a while to know me well enough to stop growling." He reached down with his hand outstretched and the dog came to him. Lisa watched in amazement as Aubrey stroked its head and the dog settled at his feet with its head on Aubrey's knee.

"You didn't tell me you liked dogs," she said.

"You didn't ask," he said.

"Whose is it?"

"Mine now. Temporarily."

She dropped onto a chair and stared as Aubrey took the Springer spaniel to the rear entrance to show it the garden where it promptly ran out past the roses and peed up against a tree trunk. He followed after it with a dog lead in his hand. Lisa could hardly believe what she was seeing as he bent and gently clicked the lead into the dog's collar. She saw a tenderness in him she'd never noticed before.

"I think you'd better explain, Aubrey. This has come as a complete surprise to me," she said when Aubrey came back with the dog following obediently at his heels.

"I always wanted a dog," Aubrey said. "But mother wouldn't have animals in the house. After she died, I did think about taking in a rescue but it wouldn't have been fair to leave him at home alone all day while I was at work."

"So, why is he here? Is he a rescue dog?"

"No, no. Danny told me about him."

"Danny did?"

"Yes. Toby, that's the dog's name, belongs to one of Danny's friends. An old chap from the birding group. Sam Overland. I'm sure I've mentioned him to you but I don't suppose you ever met him. I met him several times on our days out. Old boy, he is. Has long hair. Smokes a pipe. Proper Norfolk fella as they say in these parts."

Aubrey sounded excited. Lisa had never seen him so animated. He'd even taken on some of the local way of speaking.

"So why has this Sam given his dog away?"

"He hasn't given him away for good, Lisa. Poor old Sam himself needs looking after for a while. He's had a hip operation and the hospital wouldn't let him go home to be on his own. He's gone into a residential home for what they're calling respite care, although it's really convalescence. The trouble is they don't allow pets. Danny's been looking after Toby for a while but he has a big job coming up and needs to go away for a few days. He wondered if we'd like to have him."

Toby was still resting his head on Aubrey's knee, looking at him with adoring eyes.

"He seems to like you," Lisa said.

"I know. I think it's because he's used to me. Sam took him out with him everywhere. We'd often find ourselves walking along together with the dog when Danny was holed up somewhere with his photography."

"How long is Toby going to be here? You don't recover from hip operations in just a few days, Aubrey."

"That's right. I understand all that. It's only until Danny gets back from his assignment. Just a few days. We've plenty of space for him, haven't we? And, of course, I'm at home every day to look after him and take him out for exercise. I shall enjoy that."

Lisa could see for herself how much Aubrey was going to enjoy having a dog to look after.

"I see," she said. Was now the right time to mention the holiday in Cornwall? She didn't want to miss the opportunity to go. "Madge has asked if we'd like to go with her and Wally for a week's holiday to Cornwall next month." There, it was said.

"What for?" Aubrey said, paying more attention to the dog than what Lisa was saying.

"To see the Eden Project and other gardens."

"No, thank you. That doesn't really appeal to me."

"I thought you might enjoy it. You know, picking up ideas for the garden here, perhaps."

"I already have plans made out. In any case it would be better for me to be here. You know, there may be problems with the quay head and the boathouse roof. Far better for me to be around. Don't you think?"

"I don't know what to think, Aubrey. They haven't given you a firm date yet to start the work. You seem to be enjoying being vaguely mysterious. I take it you're not really interested in having a holiday with me but don't know how to say it."

Aubrey stopped petting the dog and looked at her. He was smiling. "Thank you, Lisa," he said. "You are quite correct as usual. The last thing I want to do is cause offence but I have to be honest with you. Madge and Wallace are *your* friends. I shouldn't be at all comfortable spending a whole week with them. I prefer my days outdoors with Danny and the birding fraternity. There's nothing to stop you going with them, though. Is there?"

Although his response was what she'd expected from him, his words still cut. It was true. There was *nothing* stopping her. Housekeeper and sometime companion: that's all she was.

"I suppose not, Aubrey," she said, shrugging off her disappointment. "I'll call Madge and let her know I'd like to go."

"Good," Aubrey said. He sounded genuinely pleased. "We've both found something to enjoy. I think that's a very reasonable conclusion."

She was just in time making the call. Madge was on the point of booking online.

"Oh, I'm so glad you've decided to come," Madge told her. "It'll do you good. I think it will do us all good. We have to pay in full as it's only a few weeks away. You can settle up with me later. I'll ring you back and let you know how much your share is."

"I can do an online bank transfer, Madge," Lisa suggested. "The money goes through straight away."

It was settled. She was going away without him. They spent a quiet evening watching a film on television but Lisa couldn't concentrate. She wandered into the kitchen and Toby followed her. She filled his drinking bowl and gave him his evening chewy treat. She went early to her room and wondered if she'd done the right thing about the holiday. Would Aubrey feel she was abandoning him in some way? Why would that matter, anyway, if all they had between them was the house where they lived under the same roof and she was nothing more than housekeeper and companion. Convincing herself he would really enjoy having Toby for company eventually helped her to fall asleep.

Toby didn't growl at her the following morning. He hopped out of his basket and went to stand by the rear door in the kitchen.

"Do you want to go out, boy? she said. She opened up and Toby ran to the tree he'd used before. When he came back he sat by his bowl looking hopeful. She wasn't sure of the dog's feeding routine so she gave him a handful of beefy dog biscuits. He ate them quickly and looked for more.

"That's enough for now," Lisa said. "Aubrey will see to you in a little while."

She shouted upstairs to let Aubrey know she was ready to leave for work and let herself out. Her working day kept her busy. There was no time to worry about whether she'd made a mistake booking to go on holiday without Aubrey. At her lunch break time she'd consigned it far enough to the back of her mind to concentrate on other things and even enjoyed the prospect of deciding what she should pack for the trip.

When Toby ran to meet her when she came home from work she crouched beside him and he licked her face.

"There. You see?" Aubrey said. "I told you he'd be used to you in time. It didn't take long, did it?"

"I think it's probably because I was the one to feed him last night and again this morning. But it is nice to be greeted like that whether or not it's just cupboard love."

The dog followed her to the hall and sat, waiting while she hung up her jacket. Then he followed her again when she took her cup of tea to the sitting room, curling at her feet and making snuffling noises.

"There you are! You have a new friend," Aubrey said. "You'll soon get used to his doggy attentions and, if you carry on like this, Lisa, you'll be sad when it's time for him to go back with Danny. I know I will." He finished speaking on a sigh.

"You'll still be able to see him though, won't you, when you go bird-watching?"

Aubrey nodded but looked as melancholy as a little boy who dropped his ice cream. His sad expression made her want to lift his spirits.

"Actually, Aubrey," she said, "I'd like it very much if I came out and walked with you and Toby. It's a lovely evening. How about I drive us to the nearest beach and we show Toby the sea? Supper's in the slow cooker and won't spoil."

"Would you?"

"Yes, if you like."

"I'd like that very much, Lisa. Very much indeed."

"And when you get your driving licence you'll be able to drive us yourself. If for any reason we look after Toby again."

"Or even find a dog of our own."

The word *our* made her smile. She said, "I think that could be arranged."

"Yes. That would be marvellous. You know, I'd no idea there was such a long wait to take one's driving test."

She couldn't stop smiling as he hurried for Toby's collar and lead.

Chapter Twenty Two

June

On the third Friday evening in June, exactly one year since meeting Aubrey, Lisa was reorganising her suitcase for the Cornwall trip next morning when she heard him coming up the stairs. He came to the doorway to her room and stood there, leaning against the door frame looking awkward.

"I'm just rearranging my packing," she said with a helpless shrug and gesturing at piles of clothes on her bed. "I think I've put too much in. But I won't be long. Then we'll have something to eat." She continued bending over her bed, lifting out clothes from her bag.

"There's no hurry. I know you have a lot to do. Lisa, I've just had a call from Danny," Aubrey said from the doorway. "He can't keep Toby. He's asked me to have him again."

Lisa straightened up and said, "Good grief. He's only just taken Toby back. Has something happened?"

"Another contract. They were so pleased with his work on the last assignment they want him again."

"Well, that's good news, isn't it?" Lisa said, refolding summer tops and placing them in a new pile on the bed. "Danny must be doing very well and you enjoy having the dog, so what's the problem?"

Aubrey groaned. "It's Sam," he said. "They're taking him back into hospital. He isn't doing very well. They're doing tests."

Lisa stopped her packing and turned toward him. "I'm sorry to hear that," she said. "I thought he was on the mend and would be able to go home soon."

"Danny is worried about him, too. So, I said he could bring Toby here tomorrow morning."

His face was the picture of misery. She hadn't realised how much Aubrey had taken old Sam's situation to heart.

"Come on," she said. "Let's go downstairs and eat. I can finish this later. I've plenty of time."

Lisa watched as he picked at his food. She tempted him with the chocolate dessert she'd made specially for him before she went on holiday but he said he'd save it for another time. She cleared the table and they went to sit outside on the bench above the rear rose garden. Down by the boathouse, water glistened in warm evening light and, beyond the Broad, rushes gave way to shrubs and taller trees backlit from the setting sun. They sat quietly gazing at the picture postcard view with its colours and reflections, sunlight and shadows. Aubrey broke the silence.

"The roses are looking particularly fine this year," he said.

"Yes. I love roses. They fill a room with such lovely perfume."

Aubrey shifted in his seat and said, "I hope Sam is going to be all right."

"He's in good hands, Aubrey. Did Danny tell you exactly what the problem is?"

"No, only that they expected Sam to be making more effort at walking."

Lisa lightly rubbed Aubrey's shoulder. "Perhaps he just needs the right kind of encouragement," she said. "You could visit him to see for yourself. Find out which ward he's on. Book a taxi and go see him."

She saw his expression change.

"That's exactly what I'm going to do. Thank you, Lisa." He slapped his knees and nodded his head. He grabbed her hand and kissed it.

Within minutes his appetite returned and he went to fetch two portions of chocolate dessert. He brought them outside and ate his quickly. He muttered something she couldn't quite catch then went inside to begin searching along the bookshelves. Lisa followed him indoors.

"Have you lost something?" she said.

"It should be here. I'm sure it's here," he said, fingering the spines of books as he searched. He found what he was looking for, pulled out a paperback and settled into his favourite chair. Lisa read the title. It was a book on country walks.

"I've often thought it would be nice to do all the walks in that book," she said. "You know, work your way through them. Once a month, maybe."

"I agree," he said. "If I'm to have Toby for longer this time I thought there might be something nearby as I'll have to begin from here."

"Hmm. That might be a problem. I seem to remember they all begin with how to get to the parking area before you begin the walk."

"Yes, I can see that now," he said. He closed the book and shook his head. "I need that driving licence, Lisa.

I've let my silly prejudices spoil far too much of my life."

He got up and put the book back on the shelf.

"Have you thought about what kind of car you'd like when it's time to choose?" she said. "You could do some research. You could book some driving lessons as well while Danny is away."

Her suggestion fired him. He was on his laptop, absorbed in his reading when she slipped away upstairs to finish her packing.

Madge and Wally Sparrow arrived at five a.m. next morning. Lisa was ready and waiting, feeling a mixture of excitement and apprehension, suitcase neatly re-packed. Aubrey carried her bag out to the car and helped her climb in the back of the taxi beside Madge. He held on to her hands and squeezed them before he walked back to the house and stood at the entrance door to wave her off.

She was gone. Aubrey went indoors and began to plan his day. He noticed the time and realised it wouldn't be long before Danny arrived with the dog. He went upstairs to shower. After dressing he couldn't resist looking into Lisa's room.

Her bed was freshly made and her bath robe hung by the en suite door. He stepped into the room. Without thinking, he moved closer to where her robe hung and reached out to touch it. The fabric of it was soft and fluffy, like a child's toy. He took hold of a sleeve and brought it to his nose. He closed his eyes and thought of her face. He stroked his own face with Lisa's sleeve and felt the comfort of its soft warmth.

The door bell rang and he hurried back downstairs. Danny had arrived early. He was out in the drive walking back to his car. Aubrey ran out to meet him.

"Morning, Aubrey," Danny said breezily, reaching into the back seat. "Is the kettle on? I'd love a coffee please. I'll just get Toby's things." He let the dog out and Toby jumped up at Aubrey to say hello.

"Come on, Toby," Aubrey said. "Don't get in the way. Let's go and see what we've got for you."

He moved toward the house and Toby ran on ahead to stand by the kitchen sink waiting for his bowl. Aubrey made a fuss of the dog, gave him a drink then set about making coffee. Danny came in with Toby's bed and a bag full of dog food. He put them on the floor.

"You're having an early start, Danny," Aubrey said. "Got far to go?"

"I'm off to Wales. Puffin island. It's up on the north coast."

"I've heard of it. I should think you'll get some fantastic shots. I envy you. I've never seen a puffin."

"Neither have I. Yes, I'm really looking forward to this assignment. It's for the tourist board. There'll be a few of us so it's likely to be a bit competitive but they're paying for my time anyway."

Aubrey put two mugs of coffee on the table and sat.

"I'm going to see Sam," he said. "Which ward is he on?"

"Ah, you'd better ring the hospital first, Aubrey. I spoke to the ward sister last night. They might be sending him back to the care home this afternoon. They said it wasn't too serious after all. An infection but it's responding to treatment. They've got him on antibiotics."

"I'm glad to hear it," Aubrey said. "I'll take your advice and telephone to see what's happening. I'd better have the number for the care home, too. Perhaps it would be possible to visit Sam there."

Aubrey took Toby out into the garden so Danny could get away without too much fuss from the old dog but Toby seemed happy enough sniffing around the trees. When they went back inside Aubrey checked the supply of dog food. He decided there were not enough chewy treats so he took Toby with him down to the village store. He fastened the dog lead around a post, the way he'd seen others do. Toby sat on the pavement and waited patiently. Then they walked the long way back home, through to the far side of the village and upwards, along the narrow track next to the primary school. Another narrow track led to a field at the top of the hill where he could let Toby off the lead. He laughed at the old dog's antics: running like a puppy, ears flapping behind, until he could run no more. When Aubrey caught up with him both of them were panting.

Lisa called later in the evening to say they'd all arrived safely after a tediously long day's coach journey. They'd had a meal at the hotel and were all aching to lie down and sleep. Aubrey told her about Danny and the dog and how Sam's situation wasn't as bad as he'd feared. He wished her a good night's sleep and they said goodnight.

The next day, Sunday without Lisa began enjoyably in a quiet way. The weather was too hot to walk poor Toby over baking pavements to reach the fields above the village where it seemed the whole village walked their dogs so Aubrey played ball with him at home on the grass. Even that had proved too much of an effort for the ageing spaniel. Toby stopped playing fetch and ran off toward the boathouse where he leapt from the decking into the water. He came back and shook himself all over Aubrey and, even though he was laughing, Aubrey missed not having Lisa on hand to tell her about it. It occurred to him how strange it was to be on his own again, to have someone in his life whose absence made a hole that only they could fill.

Toby seemed content to lie on his belly on the cold kitchen tiles for most of the afternoon so Aubrey spent the time at his desk in the study drawing up plans for a complete rebuild of the boathouse just to amuse himself. His thoughts drifted as he drew and he imagined himself and Lisa enjoying lazy afternoon excursions on a day boat they would choose together. Maybe it could be something a little larger than a day boat: a cruiser, perhaps, so they could stay overnight in a quiet backwater enjoying the wildlife and the wide Norfolk sky.

In their evening phone call they exchanged news of their different ways of spending their first day apart. Lisa sounded excited about her upcoming day out to the gardens but when she asked him what he was going to do the next day he didn't tell her about the plans he was drawing up and the one-bedroomed cruiser he'd been daydreaming about.

"I'll see what the weather's like," he said, "before I decide. It was too hot for poor old Toby today."

His thoughts returned to the one-bedroomed cruiser throughout the rest of the evening. Long since neglected, imaginations of amorous encounters disturbed his usual equilibrium. He had difficulty that night trying not to envisage himself in Lisa's bed in the room next door to his. Or, Lisa beside him in his own bed.

On Monday morning Aubrey was surprised to take an early phone call on the landline from Lisa's daughter.

"Hello Aubrey. It's Amy," she said. Her voice sounded bright and breezy. "I just thought I'd give you a ring. See how you're getting on."

"Me?" he said, surprised she should be concerned.

"Yes. You. Is there anything you need? Any shopping? Anything?"

"That is so kind of you, Amy," he said.

"Well," she said, "I know you don't drive and Mum's away for the week. I expect she's stocked up the fridge, but, you never know, there might be something she's forgotten."

"That is so, so kind of you," he said again.

"Is there anything? Would you like me to come over? Just for a chat?"

"You're very welcome to come at any time, Amy," he said. "Call first, though. I'm looking after a dog and I might be out with him."

"Mum told me about him. Toby, isn't it? What's he like?"

"He's a lovely old boy. No trouble at all. He might growl a little bit until he gets to know you, but that's all. He soon stops."

"I'll come with a doggy treat then."

"You've got it. That always seems to work."

"So, there's nothing you need?"

"Thank you, no. Your mother is very well organised. There are the village shops here, too. I can easily get fresh bread when I want some."

"What time does Mum get home on Saturday?"

"I'm not sure. It'll be late."

"How about I come over on Sunday? I'll cook for us. I'd like to do that. Would that be okay?"

Aubrey wasn't sure what to say. "To be honest with you, Amy, I'm not sure how that would go down with your mother. She likes to take charge in the kitchen."

"She'll be tired after the week away. All her washing to do and everything to get ready for work Monday morning. I think it would be lovely to have a family dinner. Don't you?"

Aubrey agreed. The idea appealed to him now that he knew Lisa's children better. He told Amy he'd mention the arrangement when next he spoke to Lisa. He was replaying the conversation with Amy in his mind to check if he'd faltered in any way when his mobile rang.

"Hi, Aubrey! I thought I'd let you know what's happening up here in Wales."

"Danny, hello," Aubrey said. "I've just been speaking to your sister. How peculiar you should both call within minutes of one another."

"Great minds think alike, eh? How's Toby?"

"He's settled in very well. No trouble at all. He knows how to get in and out of the water from the quay heading. He does love a swim, doesn't he?"

"Watch out for him rolling in smelly stuff. Have you heard from Mum?"

"Yes. We speak every evening. Have you seen the puffins, Danny?"

"Hundreds of 'em. I can't wait to show you the shots I got."

"I'd love to see them."

"Good. I'll be back late on Saturday but I'll come round next Sunday to welcome Mum home and have a family day. How does that sound?"

Aubrey paused to let his thoughts gel. "It sounds familiar, Danny," he said. "Have you and Amy been making plans together?"

"Of course we have. She's my sister. I'm her brother. It's what siblings do."

The conversation with Danny lasted nearly half an hour. By the time the call was finished Aubrey felt thirsty. He went to the cooler for some iced water. Toby looked up at him with beseeching eyes. Aubrey went for the dog lead and they set out toward the village.

By Monday evening he was feeling lost without Lisa. The morning walk with Toby had taken in the grand tour of the village and dog-walking fields and he'd spent the afternoon in his study. His plans for the new boathouse complete, he was longing to show them to her.

Chapter Twenty Three

On the fourth day, Tuesday, after Lisa left for her week away to Cornwall Aubrey had only just returned from his walk with Toby when the landline rang. Quickly, he kicked off his walking boots and padded into the hall. He recognised the voice immediately. Timothy sounded breathless. His voice came in little gasps.

"Aubrey, I'm so glad I've managed to get hold of you at last. I've been trying your mobile all morning."

"Ah," Aubrey said. "I didn't take it out with me. I've been out walking. Is anything wrong, Timothy? You seem a little anxious."

"It could be nothing at all so forgive me if I'm sticking my nose into your personal business," Timothy said, "but I think you ought to know."

"Know about what?"

"About the woman."

"What woman?"

"The woman who's just been here this morning. The woman who's looking for you."

"Looking for me? Who is? Timothy you're making a mystery out of it. I'm finding it difficult to follow what you're telling me. Why is a woman looking for me?"

"She didn't say. Oh, dear, I should have asked. Only, you see, it all happened in such a rush. She was here at nine this morning. I was still in my pyjamas. Had a bad night. Not slept well at all. I wasn't thinking clearly. My mind wandered and I was imagining all kinds of things. She could have been up to no good. You hear of these things. They send in a woman to scout out the place. You know, some female you'd never suspect but really she's there to see if there's anything worth stealing. Then they come back at night and . . .I'm sorry, Aubrey, I should have asked her to state her business."

Aubrey could hear the tension in Timothy's voice. He could almost feel the man's discomfort in his own gut. Fluttering sensations in his stomach made him want to tap out his apprehension.

"It seems to me, Timothy," he said, taking control of his own nervousness and sounding as calm as he could, "that something has put you into quite a state of agitation."

Aubrey surprised himself at his rapid summation of Timothy's situation. An idea formed itself and a strange thrill bristled at the back of his neck at the freedom of the unusual suggestion he was about to make.

"It's no good talking serious matters on the phone, Timothy," he said. "Throw some things in a bag and come on up here for a few days. Lisa's away on her holiday with her friends and, to tell you the truth, I could do with some company. You don't mind dogs, do you? I'm looking after one while someone convalesces. I'll tell you about it when you get here."

As soon as the details of Timothy's visit were agreed Aubrey took a moment to think. Here was something very new. Yet again, he was facing something he'd never done before and it was giving him nervous excitement. He could feel it from head to toe. How much planning would he need to do? He couldn't remember where he'd put his Torquay notebook with his daily planner and he took the stairs two at a time to search for it. As he reached his bedroom a sudden thought snapped in his mind. He stopped mid-stride and rested against the door frame.

I don't need to fall back into old habits. I don't need a notebook. I can do this.

He stepped into the room and sat on his bed to be still and clear his mind. He stared at the wall, hoping a solution would come to him. He concentrated on slowing his breathing until the twitching in his fingers had stopped.

What would Lisa do next if somebody was coming to stay? She would get the guest room ready. He didn't know where she kept linens for the guest rooms and looked in all the storage cupboards. The stack of sheets and towels in the main bathroom airing cupboard were the ones she used for their own beds. He recognised the colours and patterns on the duvet covers and recalled how she'd insisted on having all new bed covers for their new home together. *To clear away remnants of our past lives,* he remembered she'd said.

He crept into Lisa's adjoining rooms to continue his search and felt like an intruder amongst her personal things. He stood transfixed, looking at her belongings. She was using the smaller room for storage. Cartons and baskets filled the alcove one side of the chimney breast and the other was filled with shelves of books and smaller shoe boxes. Over the door she'd hung a canvas storage bag holding scarves all rolled neatly into little sausages. In her bedroom she'd put photographs of her two children at different ages all along her dressing table and, in the window sill, behind the upholstered seat in the bay window were odd ornaments of some kind. He moved closer to get a better look at them.

A peculiar, tortoise-shaped lump of wood had eyes and a smiling mouth burnt into it. He picked it up carefully to inspect: a child's handiwork without doubt. Next to the wooden tortoise was an underwater creature made of shells. Strange little paintings, put into photograph frames stood on their supports, proudly facing the room. Gently, he put everything back in its own place. He had a lump in his throat that made him cough.

He left Lisa's space in a hurry, not wanting to analyse the feeling that had come over him. It was alien to him, this deep longing for something he couldn't put a name to. On his way across the landing he noticed his mother's carved Chinese storage chest.

"That's where they'll be," he said aloud and opened the lid.

The chest was full to the brim. A pleasant smell of fresh air wafted from it. He found spare pillows and all the bed linens he'd need. He took them to the room Lisa had given Timothy at New Year, dropped them on the mattress and went back to the landing.

Would Mother have approved of the way Lisa was using Uncle Vanguard's gift? He stared down at the remaining contents of the chest and noticed the way Lisa had neatly folded and packed away the things inside. Something cold like a shiver made his fingers tingle as if they wanted to tap away the knot in his stomach but he bent and closed the lid quickly.

He made the bed for his friend and adjusted the window blinds. He wondered if he ought to find a dusting cloth and perhaps even use the vacuum cleaner but he could see there was no need. It was already done. Lisa had taken care of everything before she went away. Lisa. Practical Lisa. Caring Lisa. Pangs of guilt made him grimace at the discomfort they brought him. He hoped she was having an enjoyable time.

He wanted to think on it. There was a feeling gnawing at him and he needed to analyse it thoroughly to settle his mind. But there was no time. Timothy Reynolds was on his way and Aubrey needed to prepare a meal for them both.

Timothy arrived shortly after six in the evening. Aubrey heard the sounds of a vehicle on the gravel drive and went to stand at the door. Timothy was pulling an overnight case behind him and carried a small canvas bag in his other hand. Aubrey ushered him into the kitchen and offered to make tea as Lisa would have. Toby was busy at his feeding bowl and forgot to bark at the newcomer.

"I've brought something a bit stronger, Aubrey," Timothy said, settling at the table. He reached into the canvas bag and brought bottles of wine from two of the six compartments.

"Good choice," Aubrey said, eyeing the label, "but shall we have some with dinner shortly? It will be chilled enough by then. I've put you in the same room as you were in before, when you're ready to take up your things."

"Ah, yes. of course," Timothy said. "First things first. Nice dog, by the way."

He disappeared upstairs. When he came back Aubrey was waiting for him in the sitting room. He'd placed two cups of tea on the small table by the window. Toby looked up but didn't bother to growl.

"I've put the wine in the utility room," Aubrey said. "We have a cooler in there."

"Thank you. Good idea," Timothy said as he went to stand at the bay window. "It's a marvellous view you have here, Aubrey," Timothy said. "All the way down to the water. I didn't pay much attention to it when I was here before. Of course, it was winter then. But now? Look at that. It's remarkable. Is that a boathouse down there?"

"Yes, but it needs attention. It's on the list of things to do."

"I can see you're enjoying your early retirement."

"I am, thank you. You might say my life has changed considerably. Take a seat, Timothy," Aubrey said. "Anywhere you like."

Timothy chose to sit in the same place he had at New Year. Aubrey handed him his tea and silently searched his stock of appropriate phrases for a topic of conversation. He couldn't recall anything and found himself, once again, asking himself what Lisa would do.

She would encourage Timothy to say something about himself.

"How's your house-hunting going, Timothy?" he said.

"Not good. I'm used to having a bit more outside space than my budget allows. These modern new builds are so cramped, you know? They build them so close together. There isn't even space out front to park your car. You get an allotted space or two in a parking area that everybody uses."

Aubrey considered for a moment. "You may have to broaden your search area. In fact, when you think about it, it doesn't really matter where you live now does it?"

"I hadn't thought of it that way. Yes, I must look into it. And, Aubrey, I realise you must need me to get on with it quickly. I appreciate all you've done for me but I can't carry on living at such a nominal rent. The house in Thetford is worth much more than I'm paying."

"That is correct, Timothy but I look at it this way: you're like a caretaker. You pay the bills and you look after the house and garden. When it's time to find new tenants the house will be in good shape."

"I don't know how to thank you enough."

"There's no need. In any case, there could be legal issues in the offing. I have to visit with the family solicitor again now that I no longer live there. It's all rather complicated, I'm afraid."

"Nothing is ever straight forward, is it?" Timothy said. "Not when it comes to property. The only saving grace for me at the moment is I don't miss working at Piper at all. Not once have I missed the place."

"Neither do I," Aubrey agreed. "I miss Lisa."

He grabbed his cup of tea from the table beside him and buried his face in it. Had he just blurted such a personal feeling? His fingers tapped against the tea cup.

Timothy was saying something but Aubrey couldn't concentrate.

". . . and I'm happy for the two of you," he heard Timothy say.

Aubrey regained his composure with a small cough into his hand. "So, this woman," he said. "Tell me what happened."

"Well, I thought I heard somebody at the door this morning so I went to see who it was."

"The mystery woman."

"Yes. She was standing in the drive at the side of the house where I'd parked my car, looking at it like she'd never seen a car there before."

"So what did you say?"

"I said, *'hello, can I help you?'* She stared at me for a moment and then she said, *'who are you?'* Actually, she didn't say it like that at all. She swore, Aubrey. She said, *'who the fuck are you?'* "

"Not very polite, was she?"

"No, indeed. So, you see, because I was a bit taken aback by her rudeness I'm afraid I wasn't very polite in return."

"What next?"

"I said, *'none of your bloody business, Madam.'* I turned away and was going to go back in the house when she followed me up to the door."

"Yes?"

"She says, *'Where the fuck is he?'* I say, *'Where's who?'* She says, *'Aubrey.'* Well, I was immediately suspicious. If she had been an attractive *lady* I may have acted differently."

"What do you mean?"

"I mean, I may have assumed she was an ex-partner of yours, a lady friend from your past come to look you up. But this loud-mouthed, over-made-up creature, effing and blinding all over the place? No. I couldn't see any respectable man being in the least attracted to her sort."

"So, what did you tell her?"

"I told her nothing, Aubrey. She wanted to know how long I'd been living in the house and if I knew where you'd gone. She bombarded me with questions, one after the other like rapid fire in between muttering obscenities. I admit I was getting out of my depth. It was all such a shock. I didn't know how I should handle it. I've never come across anything like it before. I really can't remember much more. You don't owe anybody money, do you? She had such a look on her face. Can't describe it. Very nasty. Murderous even."

"Surely not."

"Maybe I've exaggerated a little. Aubrey, I cannot impress upon you enough how uncomfortable she made me feel. In the end, I'm afraid I sank to her level and told her to bugger off."

"I have absolutely no idea who that could have been. There was a lady from Cambridge on my last trip to Torquay but I didn't give her my address. It must remain a mystery."

Tantalising smells drifted in from the kitchen. Aubrey made a decision. "Let's eat in the breakfast room," he said. "There's no point setting up in the dining room, is there? Will you open the wine, Timothy? I'll show you where everything is."

Chapter Twenty Four

The drive to Sam's care home the next day meandered through Norfolk countryside beneath avenues of shady trees and over several hump-backed bridges crossing from one side of the river and back again.

"Bet you can't wait to pass your test, Aubrey," Timothy said as he negotiated another sharp bend on a single track road, "then you can have a go at these switch backs yourself. Have they given you a date yet?"

"No. It's perhaps a good thing they haven't. I'm unable to get much practice while Danny is away."

"Book some lessons with a driving school, Aubrey. Surprise him when he gets back."

"That's what Lisa said. I suppose I should. Yes, I will."

"Nearly there," Timothy said. He turned into a sweeping, gravelled drive and swung around into the parking area.

Broadwater Care Home nestled into a quiet backwater, a wooded area at the bottom of a narrow country lane overlooking one of the smaller northern Broads disconnected from the main waterways. Dappled sunlight flashed through branches overhead. Leaves rustled in a gentle southerly breeze. Only reeds swayed in the still waters devoid of afternoon tourist cruisers and day trippers.

"This must be a haven for wildlife," Aubrey said as he closed the passenger door of Timothy's car. "I wonder if Danny knows about it."

"From what you told me about him last night I should think he knows all the best spots for his photography," Timothy said. "We'd better let the dog out, Aubrey. He's jumping up and down in the back here."

Aubrey opened the rear door and Toby jumped free.

"Here, boy," Aubrey said and the dog obeyed. "No long walk today, Toby old boy. We've somebody to see." He fastened the lead and Toby shook his ears.

"It doesn't look anything like how I imagine a care home," Timothy said. "It's more like a very grand private house."

"I agree. Danny told me what to expect but I have to say it's quite imposing. Apparently Sam was extremely lucky to be offered a place here. It's part residential with a care wing. Danny said we must ring the bell and wait a moment. There's a key code they give to family. For security, you understand."

"Quite right."

"Thank you so much for offering to drive here, Timothy. I think it'll do old Sam the world of good to see Toby. Might even give him the inspiration to get his leg moving properly again."

A young woman came to let them in after they said who they'd come to see and identified themselves.

"Oh, he'll be so pleased to see you, Mr Tennant," she said. "After your telephone call last night I told him you were coming today. I kept your surprise about his dog, though, as you asked. We don't mind pets coming to visit but please keep him on his lead. If you walk around the building to your left there you'll come to the garden area at the back. Sam's already out there waiting."

They found him seated on a wooden bench near a colourful border of summer perennials. Alongside the bench a walking aid waited. Toby pulled on his lead as he recognised his old friend.

"Blust, that's my boy," Sam cried out as he caught sight of them approaching. "Come you here, my boy. Let me see you up close." Toby pulled harder but Aubrey held on tight.

"I won't let him off the lead, Sam," he said. "Doctor's orders. We don't want you damaging that bad leg of yours."

Sam wasn't listening. He leaned forward and took hold of Toby's head, brushing his face against the dog's coat and kissing its face. When he looked up again there were tears in his eyes. He brushed them away and sat up.

"They didn't tell me you were bringing my old Toby to see me," Sam said between sniffles.

"I thought it would be a nice surprise," Aubrey said. "I hope you don't mind."

"Mind? What're you saying? Mind? That's the best surprise I've had in a long time, longer'n what I can remember. Ah, Toby my best boy," he said and threw his arms around his four-legged companion again.

"Sam," Aubrey said, patting Timothy on the shoulder, "this is my good friend Timothy Reynolds. He's driven me here today especially so Toby could see that you haven't left him for good."

"If it weren't so bloody painful I'd stand up sharpish and I'd shake your hand good and proper," Sam said. "But I thank you deep and true for doing this good turn for a stranger today. My Toby means all the world to me, bless yer heart."

"I can see that, Sam," Timothy said, bending to shake Sam's hand. "It was no trouble at all. I'm very pleased to meet you. And, by the way, I'm not so young any more."

"Younger than I am. What are you? In yer fifties? Yer still a baby, young fella. There's a long way to go for you yet."

"How are things?" Aubrey asked. "What happened at the hospital?"

"Bloody infection in the old waterworks. That's all it was. The old plumbing system don't work as well as it used to. Sent me funny in the head, it did."

"But it's under control now, I take it?"

"Got to take tablets," Sam said with a grunt. "Antibiotics. Don't like taking 'em. Never liked taking tablets. I seen what happened to plenty of other folk. They get you on them things, you never get off 'em."

"It isn't forever, Sam," Aubrey said. "I should think you can cope with a course of antibiotics."

Sam grunted again and pulled a face.

"The sooner you finish the course, the sooner you'll be able to go home," Timothy offered.

"Well I wish they *would* let me go home. That's all I want. I don't want to be stuck in here twiddling me thumbs. I've got a vegetable patch needs watering."

"I can do that for you, Sam," Aubrey said.

"Not with old Toby, thank you. Bless yer heart, that's a kind offer but that might be a bit confusing for him going to his own home and not being able to stay on account o' me not being there. Do you see what I'm meaning?"

"I'm sorry, Sam. I hadn't thought of that."

Timothy said, "When *will* they let you home?"

Sam slapped his thighs. "When I can get off me backside and walk proper," he said.

"There's more to it than that and you know it," Aubrey interrupted. "You're not allowed to bend. Six weeks, Danny told me. You have to let that new hip settle in. No bending down at all. How would you feed the dog?"

"I'd find a way."

"Lets see what you can do, Sam. A stubborn old chap like you can't resist a challenge, I'll bet," Aubrey said.

Aubrey knew he'd said the right thing when Sam Overland stared hard at him, nodded his head and set his jaw. Between them Aubrey and Timothy hoisted Sam up from the bench and put his A-walker in front of him.

"Can't wait to see me on a Zimmer, eh?" Sam said. "Here we go then."

He set off along the path through the care home gardens, placing the walking aid in front of him and walking into its space, the two men walking close beside ready to lend a steadying arm. Aubrey kept Toby on a short lead and well out of the way. Progress was gradual but as they continued Sam grew in confidence and made better headway. Aubrey and Timothy maintained the conversation as they walked and by the time they reached the end of the walkway they were surprised to see nearly half an hour had passed. They turned back around and moved toward the bench where a member of the care home staff was waiting. She came to meet them.

"Well done, Sam," she said. "That was great. I'm so pleased you're doing so well. We'll have to keep an eye on you now in case you try to escape. I just popped out to let you know it's nearly teatime. You might want to come inside soon." She went back the way she'd come.

"Shame," Aubrey said. "I wasn't aware we'd come at a bad time. I promise I'll stay longer next time."

They walked with him to the entrance where Aubrey lifted Toby up so that Sam could say goodbye.

"I hate goodbyes," Sam said and trundled through the doorway pushing the walker in front of him.

Timothy was unusually quiet on the drive back to Laburnum House and Aubrey took to staring out of the passenger window, watching fields flash by as they reached the main road. They decided on eating out that night and booked a table at one of the village pubs. Afterwards they sat with a nightcap on the Laburnum terrace overlooking the rear garden and view to the boathouse, the silent reeds and still water beyond. Evening mist was forming over the water as the air cooled. Night-scented jasmine wafted its exotic perfume from one of the pergolas. Toby was indoors asleep in his basket.

"I've been thinking," Timothy said. "About Sam's situation. I have an idea, Aubrey."

"Yes? What is it?"

"Do you think he'd take kindly to having me as a sort of carer, more like an assistant really. Just until he's fit and well?"

"What do you mean exactly?"

"I mean I'd stay at his house and be a live-in carer. Just for a short time. I can take a break from house-hunting. I need to rethink my future plans on that front anyway. I'd be on hand to make sure Sam wasn't trying to do anything he shouldn't be doing and he'd be in his own home with his beloved dog. Wouldn't that benefit his recovery?"

Aubrey pondered the question. "I couldn't say whether he'd agree to that. I know he can be quite an obstinate old chap. We'd have to ask him. But I should think he ought to jump at the chance to be back in his own home, especially with Toby. Are you cut out to be a carer, Timothy? I don't think I'd be able to do it."

"You took care of your mother when she was ill."

"That's different. That's somebody close to you. Caring for a stranger isn't quite the same."

"It's not as if Sam needs medical care. He doesn't need nursing," Timothy pointed out. "I'd simply be keeping an eye on him and encouraging him to keep up with his exercises. What's more, I'll be there to look after his precious gardening plot."

Aubrey was about to say something else when the noise of a vehicle crunching over gravel disturbed their conversation. The sound grew closer to the house. A car door slammed. Heavy battering at the front door followed.

"Are you expecting anyone, Aubrey?" Timothy said. "I think that's someone at your door."

"Dammit," Aubrey said, holding his stomach in and grimacing. "I was just about to go to the bathroom. Actually, I can't wait to answer the door. Would you get it, Timothy, please?" He dashed away.

Timothy went into the hall and stepped toward the entrance door. The letterbox was making a clattering noise, opening and closing. It stopped for a moment then began again. Somebody was out there rattling the letterbox, possibly even peeping through. He slipped into the side study that overlooked the drive and craned his neck to peer out of the window. A tall woman was bent over at the door pushing at the letterbox attempting to see through into the house. She uncurled herself and stood with her hands on her hips, tapping her feet.

"Oh, my God," Timothy shouted. He ran back into the hall just as Aubrey reappeared from the cloakroom. "It's her, Aubrey. It's that woman who was looking for you. She's here at the door."

"Leave this to me," Aubrey said, searching his memory bank for an appropriate phrase and switching into Hollywood hero mode. "Stand back."

Summoning all his determination he opened the door to deal with the intrusion but he wasn't prepared for the shock. His eyes widened and his jaw dropped when he realised who was standing there. He took a step backwards. The woman was yelling at him.

"About fucking time."

"Sigourney?" he said.

Chapter Twenty Five

High heels clattering along the hall, Sigourney Tennant marched into Laburnum House and headed straight for the kitchen door. Toby jumped up from his basket and ran at her barking and snapping until Aubrey picked him up and held him in his arms.

"A bloody dog, Aubrey? Gone soft, have we?" She pushed her brother aside and thundered her way into the kitchen. "Ooh, nice kitchen, brother. What the fuck is he doing here?" she said pointing a manicured finger at Timothy Reynolds. The finger flicked a disdainful gesture. "Aren't you the idiot I saw at the house in Thetford? I thought I recognised the car outside. Your boyfriend is it?"

"Timothy, this is my sister, Sigourney," Aubrey said, still reeling at the surprise of his sister's sudden appearance. "The mystery woman. I haven't seen her for nearly thirty years."

"I thought I'd find you here eventually, Aubrey. I've driven up and down this bloody backwater all bloody day. Aren't you going to offer me at least a fucking drink?"

"I think I'd better leave you two to sort this out between yourselves," Timothy said and made his exit.

"Yes. Bugger off. You're not wanted whoever you are."

"Must you swear all the time Sigourney?" Aubrey said. "I don't remember you being so . . . coarse. You've changed. I hardly recognised you."

"Too bad, brother. I'll have vodka."

"I don't have vodka."

"What's this?" she said picking up the bottle of brandy Aubrey and Timothy had been enjoying moments before.

Aubrey found another brandy balloon and gave it to her. She poured herself a large measure.

"Excuse me one moment, Sigourney," Aubrey said. "I'll be back shortly."

He raced upstairs to find his friend. Timothy was sitting on the edge of his bed. He looked anxious.

"I'm so sorry, Timothy," Aubrey said. "I had no idea this was going to happen."

"No, of course. I'm sure you didn't. Quite a shock, isn't she?"

"I can see how you were thrown off balance when she confronted you yesterday morning. I hardly recognise her. Especially her foul mouth."

"Is there anything I can do to help?" Timothy said. "I'm feeling out of place here right now, Aubrey. I think perhaps I should leave straight away."

"No. Please don't do that. Please stay, at least tonight. I would appreciate some support. It's getting late. She's bound to expect me to invite her to stay for the night."

"You have another spare bedroom?"

"Yes, but it isn't made ready."

They took more bed linens from the chest on the landing and when they'd finished making the bed Timothy said he'd stay upstairs and have an early night.

"You do understand, don't you?" he whispered. "I think it would be better if I stay out of your way just now. I'll go and see the people at the care home in the morning, and Sam, of course, and put my idea to them. I'll ring you to let you know what we decide."

"Yes, yes. Thank you."

"If it's agreed that Sam can go home with me in attendance it might be a good idea if I shoot off to Thetford and collect a few more of my things first."

"Yes. You're right."

"How long do you think your sister will stay?"

Aubrey sighed. "I have a hunch she'll stay until she gets what she wants," he said. "Whatever that is."

"And you haven't heard from her in all that time?"

"Mother and I had postcards for a time and then they stopped. I really couldn't say where she's been or what she's been doing."

"So she won't know that you inherited this house?"

"Probably not."

"Well, there you are then, Aubrey. My guess is she's looking for her share. Like Daphne did. Be careful, my friend. You'd better fasten your seat belt."

Timothy smiled and gave him a nod of understanding. He put a comforting hand on Aubrey's shoulder and said goodnight. Aubrey stood at the top of the stairs dreading more confrontation with Sigourney. The back of his neck was burning hot and his fingers prickled. Slowly, concentrating on his breathing, he went to find her.

She was in the sitting room, lounging on one of the sofas. She held out her empty glass when she saw him enter the room.

"I'll have another one of those, Aubrey," she said.

He refused to take the glass from her but went to the kitchen to fetch his own glass and the bottle of cognac. He handed it to her.

"Here," he said. "Help yourself."

"Not very gentlemanly, are we?" she said and laughed at him.

"Enough of a gentleman to refrain from commenting on your right to call yourself a lady."

He searched his film memory bank. There was nothing to match what he'd just said. To cover his embarrassment he poured himself a measure and sat facing her.

"There now," she said. "That's better. We have a lot to catch up on, brother. It's been a long time."

Aubrey scrutinised her face, looking for any sign that matched his long-held memory of her. She was wearing what he could only describe as a rigid expression. Her mouth was stretched into a thin smile but there wasn't any friendliness in it. It reminded him of Toby baring his teeth. The attempted smile didn't reach her eyes. They were penetrating, dark and cold. He recalled what Timothy had said about the malevolent look she had. He'd thought Timothy was over-exaggerating, but it was true. Everything about Sigourney was disconcerting.

"Where have you been all this time?" he said.

She waved a nonchalant arm and said, "Oh, here and there. You know."

"No, I don't know, Sigourney. I'm asking you. I'd like to know what my sister has been doing with her life."

"You know I've been travelling. I like to see different places."

"You can't possibly have been travelling all the time. Where have you been living? What have you been doing? Haven't you been working? How have you paid for it all?"

She laughed. "I knew you'd soon get around to talking about money," she said and flicked a dismissive wrist.

Aubrey had the distinct feeling he was being manipulated. She seemed determined to avoid his questions when it was only natural he should be curious about his own sister. Wouldn't anybody feel the same seeing a family member after such a long absence? His stomach felt heavy with trouble. She was steering the conversation, deliberately putting her own interpretation on what he'd said, giving his words her own distorted meaning.

An old, forgotten memory of her when they were children flashed an image at him. His stomach sank further as he relived the scene: she was grinning while keeping secrets from him, hiding behind her back a bag of sweets meant for both of them to share. He recalled the feeling of shame he'd felt at his boyhood tears and then the glow of gratitude when she'd deigned to allow him to take one. More, similar scenarios jabbed at his mind. He could see her, tossing her head and grinning at him as he took the blame for something she'd done. He'd wanted to protect her but she'd seen his loyalty to her as weakness. She called him names and teased him about it.

He felt as though he was falling into a dark hole where vague images of hushed, long-forgotten memories lined the walls, grew thunderous and roared at him to be remembered. He rubbed at his temples to silence them. Without thinking he spoke what next came into his mind.

"What do you want?" he said.

"What makes you think I want something?" she said. She raised her shoulders in a callous shrug but her eyes flared annoyance.

Aubrey counted his breathing. He made it slow down. His stomach was churning. He was on his own: no notebook of handy phrases; no memorised, carefully timed responses apposite to the circumstances. He'd never faced a situation like the one before him. He had no choice but to speak freely and hope for the best.

"You've been gone out of my life for so long, Sigourney, I can think of no other reason why you would suddenly turn up. Mother and I had no way of contacting you. We could only hope that all was well with you and you'd come to no harm."

She laughed again. "Mother?" she said. "Don't talk to me about mother. You still sound like Mama's little soldier, Aubrey. Did you know that's what she called you? I couldn't wait to get away."

"You didn't even come to her funeral."

"How could I? I didn't know she was dead."

"You should have kept in touch."

"Well, I didn't come here to talk about mother, Aubrey. Not yet anyway. There'll be plenty of time for that." She leaned back against the cushions with the glass in her hand and scanned the room. "This place hasn't changed at all. Still the same old stuff," she said with a sneer. "Except for the kitchen. I approve of what you've done in there. Must have cost quite a lot. I'll see the receipts another day. I expect you've changed things upstairs as well? I remember the bedrooms were very out of date."

Aubrey struggled with the sensation growing inside him. What had happened to the memory he'd always kept clear in his mind of his beautiful sister with the sparkling eyes and burnished hair? He'd thought her exquisite, a sister to be proud of.

"I always admired you, Sigourney."

"I know," she said.

"You were everything I was not. Popular. Beautiful. Confident."

He watched her as she yawned and stretched out her limbs. She kicked off her shoes and said,

"Fetch my bags from the car, will you? I'm tired. Which room would you like me to take?"

"The corner single room. It hasn't been redecorated yet. You'll be disappointed with it but I can't help that. The other rooms are all taken."

"Running a guest house are we? I don't see any more guests."

"My friend Timothy is staying the night," he said.

Aubrey stopped himself from explaining further. As soon as he thought about who was using the other two spare rooms his words caught in his throat. He clapped his hand over his mouth. He was supposed to call Lisa before bedtime and tell her about taking Toby to see

Sam. Sigourney's unexpected arrival had made him forget all about his promise. He was relieved Sigourney hadn't noticed his abrupt pause mid-speech. She was halfway upstairs.

He carried Sigourney's bags to her room where he found her grumbling about the small bed and the ancient drapes at the window. He didn't want to respond. He had no interest in further conversation with her.

"You know where the bathroom is," he said. "I'll leave you to settle in. I hope you sleep well."

He returned to the kitchen and poured another measure of cognac then sat at the table trying to assemble his thoughts. He looked at the time. It was too late to call Lisa now. She'd be asleep. He didn't want to disturb her.

On Thursday morning the weather was bright and sunny, belying the way Aubrey was feeling. He paid no attention to the endless blue skies nor joyful birdsong from his garden. He let Toby out of the French doors and drifted into the kitchen to switch on the grill for breakfast. Absent-mindedly he put out bacon for two then, realising there were actually three of them in the house, he wondered if he should cook the whole packet. He listened intently for signs of movement from above. He heard a door close and the sound of someone coming down the stairs. Timothy appeared in the doorway. By the expression on his face it seemed he was in a similarly concerned frame of mind.

"Any signs of life from the corner room?" Aubrey said.

"No," Timothy said. "Nothing at all. Maybe she sleeps late."

Aubrey suggested they take their bacon sandwiches into the sitting room. He smiled to himself as he recognised that, apart from tea and scones or biscuits, this would be the first time he would eat food from a plate on his knee. Lisa had suggested several times that they might have what she called a carpet picnic when there was something on television she didn't want to miss. He'd always declined and now, here he was, suggesting exactly the same thing.

They sat by the window looking out at the garden and ate in uneasy silence. Toby ran back indoors looking for treats. Aubrey got up and showed him to his bowl in the kitchen. When he returned, Timothy had a look in his eyes as if he wanted to speak, but he appeared to let go of it and cleared his throat instead. Aubrey sensed his friend's discomfort. He got up to close the door into the hall in case their voices carried upstairs and was the first to speak again.

"Did you sleep well?" he said.

"Yes, thank you," Timothy said. "It's a very comfortable room. I expect you had a lot on your mind. Too much to sleep well, I imagine. Were you up till late?"

"Not particularly, but you're right about having a lot to think about. But I think I have it straight now. I believe I know where my sister's visit is headed and it isn't going to be pleasant."

"You'll manage. I really believe that. May I say something?"

"Go ahead."

"I've seen such a change in you of late."

"What change?"

"No, no. Please don't be offended. I mean it in the best possible way. What I'm trying to say, and making a complete mess of it as usual, is you seem much more open these days."

"Open?"

"Willing to discuss matters. At Piper we spoke very little and when we did it was about work. There was no, how can I say this without sounding ridiculous? There was no conversation beyond what was happening at the office."

"I should think that happens in most workplaces, Timothy. Although, I wouldn't know about that. I never worked anywhere else."

"Maybe I'm not explaining myself well. What I mean is, you have been a true friend to me. I appreciate it and I rather admire this new you. I'm thinking it's come about since you and the lovely Lisa got together. What did she say about your sister turning up so unexpectedly?"

Aubrey put down his empty plate on a side table. "She doesn't know yet," he said. "In all that dreadful business last night I completely forgot to phone her. I must tell her today. She's back on Saturday and I expect Sigourney will still be here then."

"It could be a little awkward, couldn't it?"

"I should think so, yes. My sister is nothing like the way I've described her to Lisa."

"How will you tell her? What will you say?"

"I haven't a clue. What would you do, Timothy?"

"I think I'd warn her what to expect. Remember how shocked we were. She took us quite off guard. I know I didn't handle it well. You wouldn't want to expose Lisa to the same kind of confusion. Much better to be prepared, I believe."

There was still no sign of Sigourney by the time Timothy left. Aubrey cleared the breakfast plates and readied himself to make the phone call to Lisa. He took his mobile phone outside and walked past the rose garden and down the lawn. Lisa answered immediately. She and her friends were planning a lazy day in the sun, she told him. She sounded so happy.

"I'm so sorry I didn't call last night," Aubrey said.

"It isn't like you to forget, Aubrey," she said. "Has something happened?"

"I've had Timothy to stay over and we went to see Sam."

"Good. I'm glad you have company. Is Sam on the mend?"

"Yes, but Timothy has gone now."

"Oh?"

"Yes. Sigourney is here."

"Your sister?"

"Yes."

"Oh, that's wonderful news. I'm so happy for you. You must be thrilled to see her after all this time. How is she?"

Aubrey cast a glance back at the house. He took a few steps further away.

"She's absolutely awful, Lisa."

"What?"

"Completely atrocious."

"Is she ill? Has something happened to her? Aubrey, what do you mean exactly by awful and atrocious?"

"The way she is," Aubrey said. "She is vulgar, Lisa. Vulgar. Uncouth. Odious."

"That's a lot of awful, Aubrey. Go on."

"She swears like a trooper for one thing. She is demanding, querulous and bossy. She has turned into the most disagreeable female I've ever known."

"But I thought . . ."

"I know what you must be thinking after I've always held her in such reverence."

"Oh, my goodness. It sounds impossible. Did she tell you why she's there? I mean, it sounds to me as if she hasn't really come to see you because she's been missing you."

"Exactly. I believe she's come to make trouble. Lisa, I don't want to spoil the rest of your holiday but I thought you ought to know what you'll be coming home to."

"You mean she'll still be there?"

"Undoubtedly. My guess is she'll stay until she gets what she wants."

"And that is?"

"I don't know for absolute certainty yet." He paused at a sudden thought and added, "She seems to think she has a right to see receipts for what I've spent on

Laburnum House. Lisa, are you still there? Did you hear me?"

"Yes, I heard you. Give me a moment to think." Aubrey waited. He heard voices in the background. Her friends were calling her. "Aubrey," she said, "please tell your sister I'm looking forward to meeting her. Try not to worry. We'll sort it out."

She said Wally and Madge were waiting and she had to go. Aubrey wished her a lovely day and returned to the house, dreading the reappearance of the odious Sigourney. He ignored Toby's obvious begging for his morning walk and took him into the garden instead. He didn't want to leave Sigourney alone in the house. It was terrible to think even for a moment that his sister couldn't be trusted but he wanted to stay present just in case.

While he emptied the dishwasher and put things away he could hear Sigourney moving about upstairs. He steadied himself for what was to come. She surfaced close to noon, looking for refreshment. He offered to make tea while she helped herself to brunch. She took yoghurt and cereal and he sat, silently watching her, waiting for the trouble to begin. It didn't take long.

She pushed away her empty cereal bowl, leaned back and folded her arms. "I can see where your boyfriend stayed last night. Sorry, my mistake, he's just a friend, isn't he? Separate rooms. I noticed." She laughed and said, "So who's using the other rooms? I didn't think you were serious about taking in lodgers. I hope you're charging them enough rent."

"It's none of your business," Aubrey said, taking a leaf from Timothy's book, "who I invite to stay here."

"No matter," she said. "There's no need to get precious about it. It'll all come out in the end."

"I've no idea what you're getting at."

"You can't keep hiding the facts forever," she said. "I'll see those receipts now, Aubrey."

He pretended he didn't know what she was talking about.

"Which receipts?" he said.

"You know damned well what I mean," she said with a frosty glare. "I need to see what you've already spent here."

"No, you don't."

"I have every right to see proof, Aubrey. I won't have you exaggerating expenses."

"You have no rights at all here, Sigourney. I'm sorry to disappoint you. I will not argue with you any further. And that's all I have to say to you."

He made toward the sitting room but she barred his way.

"So you won't come with me tomorrow?"

"What do you mean?"

"I made an appointment for us at Christopher Chamberlain's office tomorrow morning at eleven," she said. Her eyes were glittering with triumph.

Aubrey knew for certain in that instant what her game was. He didn't tell her how days before she arrived he'd already made that same appointment at that exact time to iron out the family's legal and financial affairs. He'd already booked his taxi. Judging by the supercilious demeanour in which she'd delivered her imperious message, Christopher Chamberlain had not yet put her straight. He didn't feel at all dishonest in keeping that information from her. She would hear the truth from the family solicitor and that would save him the trouble of doing it himself.

Chapter Twenty Six

Timothy Reynolds phoned with good news. Sam Overland was being discharged from local authority care as soon as his GP approved the caring role Timothy was offering. He was waiting for confirmation before he could collect Sam and take him home. Depending on the timing he would come pick up the dog first.

"I'm speaking from Thetford, Aubrey," he said. "I came back here straight after my visit to Broadwater. There was no point in hanging around. I needed to be back here and pick up more things. My bag's ready to go as soon as I hear anything."

"Thanks for letting me know."

"How is the situation with *you-know-who*?"

"It got worse. As I expected."

"Can you speak freely at the moment?"

"Yes. She's gone out somewhere for the afternoon. She didn't say where."

"Did you get to the bottom of what she wants?"

"Not yet, Timothy. She hasn't come out with it. She believes she has the upper hand but I'm afraid she's in for a big shock."

"Well, good luck with it. It can't be easy for you. Don't forget, if there's anything I can do to help you out . . ."

"Kind of you to offer. If I think of anything I'll let you know. Better let you hang up now in case you miss the call from the care home."

"I don't think it will be happening today. They told me it'll most likely be tomorrow. Maybe even later."

"Right you are. Keep in touch. I'm at a meeting tomorrow morning so best leave it till later. Leave a message on the landline, Timothy, please. I'll have my mobile switched off during the meeting."

Sigourney returned late afternoon. She breezed into the house carrying evidence of where she'd been and what she'd been doing. Each arm was loaded with various bags of luxury shopping: large designer clothes' logos covered every one. Toby ran to investigate the rustling noise.

"Get that bloody dog out of my way," she yelled and kicked out with her foot.

Aubrey picked him up and stood aside. He chose not to retaliate. There was no point. He watched as his sister reached the stairs then dumped the bags on the floor.

"Well? Aren't you going to help me?" she said.

Aubrey ignored the curl of her lip and her vexed expression. He closed his eyes to her. He put Toby in the kitchen and closed the door. Without a word, he picked up most of Sigourney's shopping and took the bags to the corner bedroom where he laid them on the bed. She didn't follow him. When he went back downstairs the other bags were still where she'd dropped them and she was helping herself to wine from the cooler. Toby had gone to his bed.

"It's hectic in the city," she said.

"Is it?" He knew his voice sounded flat and uninterested.

"There are never enough parking spots in that bloody place. And what the fuck are they doing with the new bypass? It's a fucking nightmare. The signage is pathetic. Have you seen it? No, of course you haven't. You still don't drive. I wouldn't bother learning now. You'd never cope with all the lanes going everywhere but where you want to go. I'm so glad I don't live here."

"So am I," he said.

She grinned and said, "I'll be gone soon, brother dear."

Not soon enough, he thought. The evening alone in the house with her loomed ahead like a storm brewing. He felt the weight of it bearing down on him. He said he was going to his study and he didn't want to be disturbed.

"What's for dinner tonight?" she said.

"Help yourself from the freezer," he said. "I'm not hungry. I'll get a sandwich later."

"You expect me to cook? I don't think so. Let's have a takeaway. I noticed there's a Chinese in the village as I passed earlier. Order me a Kung Po chicken for seven o'clock will you? They deliver, don't they?"

She was intolerable.

"Order it yourself,' he said and went to his desk. He closed the study door behind him and sat with his head in his hands. He heard Toby in the hall and let him in. It seemed even the dog wanted to get out of the way, didn't want to be left in the same room as the insufferable Sigourney. He leaned over to stroke Toby and the dog responded by creeping closer.

"Poor old boy," Aubrey said aloud. "Never mind, Toby, you'll soon be back home with Sam and everything will be all right again."

He straightened up and stretched his back. His head felt too heavy for his shoulders and his eyelids were drooping. He tried sketching some garden ideas but soon gave up. He couldn't concentrate on anything. Toby followed him out of the study and into the hall. Aubrey strode over the shopping at the foot of the stairs. Toby clambered through the pile, his paws slipping on the glossy plastic bags. Aubrey left them behind him in a crumpled heap. He let the dog follow him upstairs and climb up on his bed beside him. He kicked off his shoes and let them lie where they fell. He spread his limbs and felt his back sink into the duvet. Toby curled alongside.

Through the open window a warm breeze swirled into the room, buffeting against his skin and he lay listening to the swish of the drapes as they puffed and billowed against the window frame. He turned his head to feel its waft on his face and noticed the bowl of flowers on the window sill. The sight of them brought a catch in his throat. Lisa had put them there before she left: a cut glass rose bowl full of blooms from the garden. She'd had them in her own room but they were too good to discard, she'd said. He breathed in to catch their sweet perfume and his eyes closed with the small pleasure of it.

An abrupt flare of insight shot through him like a stabbing pain. He sat bolt upright and disturbed the dog.

Toby yapped his alarm call but soon settled as Aubrey calmed him. Aubrey brought his hands to his face to feel his fingers against his skin. They weren't twitching. He looked at his hands, rubbing his fingers with his thumbs. He felt all around his hairline but there was no heat, no prickling sensation at the back of his neck.

In that moment he understood, the notion as clear as one of his own draftsman's drawings, that through the appreciation of these small enjoyments: the comfort of his bed, the companionship of the warm, four-legged life beside him and the flowers Lisa had left for him, something momentous had happened to him. He sensed the enormity of it, the thrill of it: he was at a turning point in his life. The heaviness he'd felt downstairs in his study had lifted. A floating sensation was coursing through his body and all the way along his limbs. Although the cause of his burdens was still down there making herself at home, he knew he had the measure of the situation. Now he realised he was able to master it.

He settled back onto his bed and pondered the last few weeks. Even though his schedule had been completely disrupted he had found his way through without resorting to lists and plans and calculations. He'd done it by himself. Notwithstanding the aggravation of his sister's unexpected arrival and the depth of his disappoint in her, something that would have had him plucking at the seams of his trousers not so long ago, he had not resorted once to picking at himself. He hadn't tapped. He hadn't scratched at his neck. Moreover, he hadn't even searched for words and phrases from his film memory bank. He'd spoken his mind freely and yet it was going to be all right. He hadn't had to act being normal. There'd been no need for pretence. He had simply been himself and it had happened naturally, without conscious effort.

It was nothing short of a revelation. Timothy had noticed it. Hadn't he mentioned how he'd noticed more openness about him and how much he liked the new Aubrey? He sat up again and looked at his shoes on the floor. He acknowledged he would straighten them when he stood up but not because of the rigid rituals he'd imposed on himself all these years. It would be a simple act of making something look tidier. There'd be no need to have them exactly lined up, perfectly placed as if they were warding off some unseen misfortune. He could step away from absolute control of everything in his world: a thought unthinkable for so many years of his life.

He heard someone moving. The sounds were coming from the direction of Lisa's room. There was only one person it could be. He went to confront his sister. He found her at Lisa's dressing table handling a bottle of perfume, inspecting his lady's personal things.

"How dare you?" he shouted from the doorway. "Put those things down. At once!"

"A lady lodger, is it?" Sigourney taunted. "Or is she something more than that?" She put down the perfume bottle and walked to the window. She picked up the little wooden tortoise and laughed.

"Good grief," she said. "She has poor taste in perfume and everything else judging by this monstrosity. What the fuck is it?"

He articulated his reply clearly, enunciating each word, each syllable, each consonant with deliberate precision.

"It is a child's gift to a cherished mother, Sigourney. Given with the purest of love. Something you would know nothing about. The only monstrosity in this room is you, my dear."

She spun on her heels to face him. "Grown a pair, have we?" she said through clenched teeth. She applauded slowly. Her laughter grated on him. He'd had enough of her. He'd been on the point of telling her about Lisa: how they'd met, how they'd found things in common that drew them together. He'd been on the point of sharing how he felt about Lisa: how he still hoped for marriage. But Sigourney would find a way to use it against him. She would select something to ridicule and she would enjoy causing him pain. She would cache the knowledge he'd just given her and hide it behind her back like a bag of sweets to torment him with later when it might inflict the most suffering.

"Get out," he said. "I don't even want to look at you. Drive yourself to the solicitor in the morning. I'll take a taxi."

⚖️⚖️⚖️

Aubrey contemplated what Sigourney would do after the meeting at Chamberlain's solicitors. There would be continuing trouble. Of that, he was certain but the notion was no more than an inclination of wonderment rather than a permeating sense of dread. All the same, it would be better to be prepared for further upsets. Sigourney had shown a propensity for delivering nasty surprises. He couldn't be sure how she would react to being on the receiving end of one.

Surely she'd pack her bags and leave straight away. There'd be nothing left for her to stay and fight about. She was a poor loser. In defeat wouldn't she hurry away to hide her embarrassment? It would be better for everybody if his sister took her leave. Lisa would be home the day afterwards and he still hadn't told Sigourney anything about her. He'd need to find a plan of action soon.

And yet, he wasn't anxious about the uncertainty of it. He ruminated on the reasons he wasn't worried about this unfinished business. He couldn't explain the light-heartedness he was feeling since the epiphany of his experience confronting his sister. He simply accepted that by releasing tight control of everybody and everything in his world, life would happen anyway and he would be perfectly fine with it.

The next day dawned bright, Norfolk blue and the temperature was climbing steadily. To avoid Sigourney at the breakfast table he took an early taxi into town and asked the driver to drop him in the centre. He would walk the rest of the way. The taxi dropped him by the Market Gates shopping centre and he thought about how Lisa would see this part of town every day on her way to work. Did she park on the pay and display now or in the supermarket car park as she had before? He hadn't asked. He turned the corner toward Regent Street questioning himself why he hadn't shown more interest in her daily routines. She was the woman who had become so vitally important to him and yet he knew so little about her.

There were so many things he hadn't taken the time to find out about Lisa. If it hadn't been for Timothy Reynolds he wouldn't know anything about her second husband and the unthinkable way he'd died. Lisa had dealt with such trauma throughout her life yet she seemed to have come through it with true grace.

He stopped at the pedestrian crossing and suddenly noticed the number of people waiting there for the light to turn green. They looked as if they were on their way to the beach, carrying children's toys and rolled up beach towels. Some had babes in push chairs. When the traffic stopped he followed on after them, listening to their excited chatter. These people lived in a different world from the one in which he had lived his childhood. Apart from the times Uncle Vanguard had taken him and his sister away, he couldn't remember family holidays like the men and women in front of him were enjoying. His father was so often ill and couldn't leave the house. In truth, Aubrey couldn't remember a time when father was in good health.

His thoughts shifted to Lisa again. She probably had cheery family holidays with her children when they were young. He could imagine Danny as a child running along beside his mother and getting excited like the children in the crowds around him on their way to the beach. He castigated himself for putting so little effort into learning about Lisa and her background. Why had his own needs always taken so much of his time? Why had he almost always felt it so necessary to concentrate on himself? He made a mental note to put that right but it sat uneasily in his mind.

He was in danger of losing the geniality he'd set out with. He mustn't let thoughts of his own past ruin the carefree disposition he'd only recently discovered. He looked for somewhere he could take his own breakfast in peace.

Peace and quiet, he discovered, was out of the question. On the last Friday morning in June, the seaside town was packed full of tourists. He let the crowds overtake him and he ambled along Regent Street, taking in the souvenir shops and fast food outlets. The place had changed considerably since his last visit to that part of town. He came out at the seafront promenade and walked as far as the Victorian water gardens, newly refurbished and looking splendid beneath a cornflower blue sky. He stopped at a beach side café where the smell of a full English tempted him inside.

"On your own, lovey?" a woman in a full-length white apron asked him.

"I am," he said.

"Would you mind taking the small table at the back there? I'll come and take your order in just a tick."

He followed her request and sat in the back corner next to the window where he had a view along the beachside walkway all the way to the Britannia pier. He picked up the plastic menu and made his choice. He knew the bacon would be fried, not grilled, but he didn't care. Here he was, in the back corner again just like the backroom boy at Piper Engineering, but feeling more alive than ever he could remember. He almost laughed out loud.

"Now then, lovey," the woman interrupted his thoughts. "What's it to be? The Full Monty? Have I guessed right? How do you like your bacon?"

"Actually," he said. "I prefer it grilled."

"Oh, I'm right there with you. All nice and crispy, lovey? Ent nuthin nicer than that. Two eggs? You've come to the right place."

He couldn't help smiling. His future was rosy after all. He would eat his meal, deal with the meeting and when it was finished his life would follow a smoother path. He would say what was on his mind without fear of offending. He would continue to be more *open*, as Timothy Reynolds had put it. Moreover, he would tell Lisa how he felt about her. It was time to put things right between them and not leave her feeling he was taking her for granted.

First, he had Sigourney to contend with. They met outside Christopher Chamberlain's office building five minutes before the due time. Sigourney arrived with a manila folder of paperwork. He spotted her coming along the pavement from the direction of the pay and display parking area with the folder under her arm. She swaggered as she walked and as she approached threw him a supercilious grin. He turned his head away.

"Always punctual, aren't we, brother dear? Thank you so much for making me feel so welcome this morning. It's a good thing you put that stupid animal out of my way. I helped myself to breakfast, by the way."

He ignored her. He didn't want to sink to her level. "Cat got your tongue?" she added.

They sat facing the family solicitor whose desk took up almost the whole width of the room that smelled of old books and leather. Chamberlain shuffled some papers and greeted them.

"Good. Glad to have you both together," he said, his voice the epitome of authority. "It will be better this way rather than seeing you separately as I have before."

Aubrey stared at Sigourney. He wanted to interrupt and ask her when she'd visited the office by herself. She'd been missing for an age. Had she returned to the UK to see the solicitor without letting him know?

"When I last saw each of you it was to discuss the first part of your late uncle Vanguard's last will and testament and to reveal to you the immediate monetary provisions he made for you. As executor, it is now my duty to bring his instructions to completion."

"There's more to come?" Sigourney said. "The old dog. I knew it." She twisted around to smile at Aubrey as if to say, *I told you so*, but he remained unmoved. He sat calmly, his hands in his lap.

Christopher Chamberlain turned to Aubrey.

"First let us make clear your deceased relative's reasons for us holding this meeting today. It was his express desire that you should both be present," he said before angling his head to look at Sigourney. "Ms Tennant, are you still at the same address abroad as your previous communications with this office?"

"Yes."

Aubrey couldn't stop himself from speaking out.

"You've been in touch here all this time?"

"Yes, of course." She rolled her eyes and wriggled in her seat.

"Then that is where we shall send your copy of this final bequest," the solicitor said. "And now, Mr Tennant, I understand you have taken up permanent residence at Laburnum House."

"As well as all his lodgers," Sigourney added.

"That is of no consequence, Ms Tennant. Your brother may do as he wishes with his own property."

"What?" Sigourney bellowed. She jumped up and pulled a document from her folder. "Show me where it says Laburnum House belongs to him." She spread the document on Chamberlain's desk and rapped at it with her fingers. "Show me where it says that on this copy of his will."

Chamberlain glanced at it and slid it back across the desk. "I don't know where you got that from," he said, "but it is not the will that went to probate, Ms Tennant."

"He gave it to me himself."

"Ah, but it's now invalid. He changed his will a few years ago."

"What? Why?" She was incandescent with rage.

"My dear lady," Chamberlain said, "I do not wish to be drawn into family dispute. I am here solely to fulfil my duty. What I am at liberty to say to you both is your late uncle envisaged just this kind of disagreement. It's why he wanted me to see you both together. You must know his intention to be fair. He wanted to treat you equally. At the time of this will the two properties bequeathed to your brother amounted . . ."

"*Two* properties?" Sigourney gasped. "Which two?"

Aubrey spoke up. "The house in Thetford. I was to inherit on Mother's death. I didn't expect it, Sigourney. I assumed our childhood home would be for us to share. I had no idea our parents never owned it in the first place. It was in trust. I didn't know I was also due to inherit Laburnum House as well on Vanguard's death."

"For which your brother paid a considerable amount in inheritance tax, Ms Tennant. Your late uncle had taken all this into account when he assigned the properties here in Norfolk to your brother and the three blocks of holiday apartments in Thailand to you. The values were and are still today, equitable."

Aubrey stared hard at Sigourney. She lowered her eyes and remained silent, like a sulking child. He had an urge to explain the depth of his disenchantment with her now that he could see the extent of her deceptions. She hadn't simply been looking for her fair share of inheritance: she wanted to cheat him out of his. If the existence of the other properties abroad hadn't been made known to him just now she would have used some kind of twisted game against him. He could imagine her performance playing wronged victim to make him feel sorry for her. And he would have given in. He would have signed over half of his own inheritance to his sister.

Chamberlain gave each of them a sealed envelope and said Vanguard had asked him to pass them on at the conclusion of the meeting. He stood and shook hands with Aubrey. Sigourney twisted away. She tore her letter open and scanned through it. Aubrey slid his own into his jacket pocket.

"What rubbish. Sentimental twaddle," she said and stormed from the office out into the street, crashing the doors behind her.

Aubrey shook his head in disbelief at his sister's behaviour in front of the family solicitor. "I am truly sorry for that outburst," he said.

"There is no need. I assure you," Chamberlain said kindly. "It was expected. Your uncle was a wise and clever man. Over the years I came to know him quite well."

Aubrey thanked him and followed Sigourney outside. He found her waiting for him. She was leaning against the wall and smiling at him as if nothing had happened.

"Let me give you a lift home," she said. "We may as well go together. There's nothing to hide now."

He agreed and walked with her to where she'd parked her hire car. He knew she wouldn't give in so easily. Her fake, sweet voice didn't fool him. She'd be hatching new plans with every step she took.

Chapter Twenty Seven

There was a call waiting on the answerphone when he let himself in but he could hear Toby scratching at the kitchen door. He quickly hung his jacket in the cloaks cupboard, greeted the dog and let him out into the garden. Sigourney followed Aubrey into the house and went to the sitting room. Aubrey noticed how quiet she was. He assumed that meant she was devising something.

The phone message was from Timothy to say he hadn't yet heard anything from Broadwater. He planned to call them himself if there was no news by teatime. Aubrey put the phone in its cradle and steadied himself for his sister's machinations.

"Anything I need to know about?" Sigourney called out.

"No," he answered. He joined her in the sitting room and sat in his favourite chair.

"Well, I'm so glad the boring legal stuff is all out of the way. We can get on with our lives now, can't we?" Sigourney said. She wore an innocent look on her face, eyebrows raised, her head tilted to one side. He waited for her to continue. "What will you do, Aubrey?"

"Carry on as before," he said, choosing to be vague and non-committal.

"I'm glad things have worked out well for you. Really, I am. I know we haven't been seeing eye to eye these last few days but it's all been such a strain, hasn't it?"

He looked straight at her. "I don't think you let anything bother you, Sigourney. I can't imagine you ever feeling strained."

"So, now we can spend some pleasant time together. I'm looking forward to meeting your friends. The lady who rooms upstairs, for instance. Where is she?"

He searched for a way to escape from telling her.

"None of your business," he said.

She laughed at him. "Oh, Aubrey," she said. "You are so predictable. So easy to read. She's special to you, isn't she? What's her name?"

He watched her expression change as she launched into her new subject with which to ridicule him. She threw back her head and her eyes narrowed. He would have to be careful.

"Her name is Lisa."

"Well, if she's so special to you, why isn't she here?"

"She's on holiday."

"Oh, brother. You poor thing. You mean she went away on holiday and left you at home all on your own? And you sleep in separate rooms? Sounds like a strange kind of special to me."

She shook her head and feigned sympathy with a pursed mouth and conciliatory eyes.

"It's so kind of you to be concerned for me," he said, copying her tone, "but I can assure you there's no need. In fact, Lisa asked me to tell you how much she's looking forward to meeting you."

"Wonderful!" she said and clapped her hands. "I can't wait. When does she get back?"

"Tomorrow."

"Then we must plan something to welcome her home, Aubrey."

"I don't think so."

"But I insist. A special meal perhaps or an outing. Could there possibly be a decent cocktail bar in this old town?"

"It will be too late in the day by the time she returns. And she'll be tired after a long journey."

"Nonsense," Sigourney continued arguing. "All women enjoy being made to feel special. I know I do. If some man was offering to do something memorable for me I'd jump at the chance no matter how tired I was. Especially if he was a millionaire bachelor like you."

She leaned forward waiting for his response. Her eyes were glittering and she couldn't disguise the twisted sneer at her mouth. Aubrey saw how her lip curled. He stood up and stretched. He looked down at his sister and concentrated on keeping his voice courteous.

"I'm just going to give the dog a little exercise in the garden," he said. "Would you like to join us?"

He knew she'd refuse. He collected a packet of cheesy treats and took them outside. He found Toby sniffing around the rose garden and the dog ran to him, gambolling beside him as they criss-crossed the garden. Aubrey threw the dog treats ahead of him for Toby to chase and find. He called the dog to him and they walked together down toward the boathouse. Aubrey picked a safe spot to sit on the decking, took off his shoes and socks, and dangled his legs over the side. He dropped his feet into the cool water and didn't care he was getting the bottoms of his trousers wet. He leaned back and turned his face to the sun. Toby sat beside him.

"She is truly a monster, Toby," he said. "I don't blame you at all for keeping out of her way."

He pulled the dog in close beside him and kissed his head. Toby seemed content to stay tucked under Aubrey's arm. "What are we going to do about this emotional mess, boy?"

He reached into his trouser pocket, took out his phone and called Lisa. He had no well-rehearsed words: they flowed from him in a continuous stream. He told her how much he had missed her and couldn't wait to have her back at home with him. It didn't make him feel the least uncomfortable to express himself so willingly. He described his breakfast at the beachside café and how he would enjoy it very much if they went there together for afternoon tea and cakes. It was homely and delightful, he said, and the woman there was completely charming. He outlined the visit to Chamberlain's office and his surprise at learning about Sigourney's inheritance abroad. He apologised for casting a shadow over Lisa's last day's holiday. He explained how determined Sigourney was to meet her, to make some sort of welcome home celebration and how she wouldn't take no for an answer. When finally he paused Lisa told him she'd missed him too and the sound of her voice comforted him.

"I don't want you to worry about anything, Aubrey," she said. "I've dealt with plenty of overbearing supervisors and awkward customers in my time at Marshall and Simpson. I suggest you concentrate on getting through this last night with her and tomorrow we'll sort it out together."

"I have a terrible feeling she'll want to stay much longer," he said.

"We'll see about that," Lisa said. "Just for tonight, go along with her. Play the game. Let her think you've forgotten every nasty thing she's said. When she's still off hand with you behave as though you haven't noticed anything. How about the two of you going out for a meal? You must have emptied the fridge between you by now. I hadn't counted on leaving enough for two."

"She likes Chinese apparently."

"There's a Thai restaurant in town. I've heard it's very good."

"Even better."

"There you are then. I'll see you tomorrow about six o' clock. I'll text you if there's any change."

They said their goodbyes and Aubrey put his phone away.

Go along with her; play the game, Lisa had said. But it felt wrong and gave him a sour taste in his mouth. It was as bad as telling lies. His new-found confidence faltered and his fingers fluttered. Was this what being normal meant? You had to pretend to like people? And yet, he thought, he'd been pretending for most of his life anyway so what was the difference? He stuffed his hands in his trouser pockets.

He paddled his feet in the water below him and watched as the circle of ripples he'd created radiated outward, winking in the sunlight as they spread.

"We need a bench to sit on down here," he said to the dog. Toby cocked his head as if he understood. "Lisa wouldn't always want to hunch down on the grass, would she, boy? Don't know why I didn't think of it before. I'll order one right away."

He stood and looked for something to throw. He found a small, flat flake of flint and skimmed it into the Broad. Toby stood on the bank and watched it fly.

"Not interested in getting wet today, Toby?" Aubrey said. "I'm not really interested in going out tonight with my sister, either, but needs must."

The dog turned his back and made for the house. Aubrey picked up his shoes and socks and followed. He threw the remaining cheesy treats ahead and Toby picked up speed to find them.

"Enjoy your little exercise?" Sigourney shouted from the sitting room as they came into the house. Barefooted, Aubrey padded across the hall and stood at the door, leaning against the frame in what he considered a nonchalant posture.

"I've been thinking," he said, folding his arms in front of him, "about something you said. You rather fancied a Chinese meal, didn't you? I'll book a table at the Thai restaurant for this evening. Seven thirty good for you?"

⚖ ⚖ ⚖

Sigourney Tennant's descent of the baronial staircase at Laburnum House was remarkable, Aubrey thought as he watched her. In the manner of the final scene in

Sunset Boulevard, she glided down each step, striking a *Norma Desmond* pose as she moved. He half-expected her to declare herself ready for her close-up, Mr de Mille but quickly dismissed the thought when he remembered what had happened to the writer, Joe Gillis.

She was wearing a tight-fitting ensemble in some sort of shiny fabric with a neckline that dipped rather too low and she carried another swatch of fabric, loosely draped over one arm. Her shoes seemed to be giving her some trouble as she negotiated the turn in the staircase.

"You look ravishing, my dear," he said, swallowing the lie with a little cough and hoping she hadn't noticed.

"Thank you," she said. "I thought I should dress nicely for the occasion so I decided on one of the new dresses I bought. After all, it's a red letter day, eating out with my brother again after such a long time apart. I'm so looking forward to it. My favourite food, too. I shall feel quite spoiled."

Aubrey noticed her smile still didn't reach her eyes no matter how wide she stretched her mouth. It was merely a device, a trick to deceive. She teetered toward him and said, "I really shouldn't drive in these shoes, Aubrey, dear. May we take a taxi?"

"It's already arranged," he said. "I wouldn't dream of expecting you to drive this evening. We shall enjoy a few drinks and there'll be no need for you to risk your licence."

"Thank you," she said again.

He didn't mention that when he'd telephoned the restaurant to book a table he'd first made sure there were choices without garlic. He didn't want to find himself in the embarrassing situation of choosing the wrong thing. They said they would make something especially for him and were happy to explain to him exactly what would be in it.

"Will you need a coat or a jacket, do you suppose?" Aubrey said.

"I have my wrap," she said. "They are so useful, you know. This silk and cashmere one was a gift. It goes so well with the dress, wouldn't you say?"

"Admirable," he replied and von-Trapped. As soon as he inclined his head he became conscious of what he was doing: playing the same game he'd been playing for years, only this time with a different reason.

He wasn't trying to make himself look acceptable in company, copying words and actions he'd seen in films in order to fit in with society. He was doing it to deceive, in the same way his sister was pretending everything was perfectly fine between them before she launched into her next volley of vitriol. The cold realisation of his artifice made him shudder. He pulled down on his cuffs and resisted the temptation to scratch at his neck. He wanted to discuss the whole scenario with Lisa. He needed her to tell him everything about her own experiences of playing this disingenuous performance. How could a whole year have passed and yet they still knew so little about one another?

Aubrey settled Toby in the kitchen and closed the door. The taxi arrived and he helped his sister into the rear, taking the front passenger seat for himself beside the driver.

"Lovely evening," the driver said and whisked them away. "Would you like to book me for the return journey?"

Aubrey agreed and they set the time. Two and a half hours ought to be more than enough. As they rode the short distance into town Aubrey made a mental list of conversation topics. He didn't want to leave any awkward silences in which his sister would have the opportunity to take control.

At the entrance to the restaurant Sigourney stood back as though she was waiting to be introduced. Aubrey gave his name to reception.

"Ah, Mr Tennant," the young man said, "we are happy to welcome you. Chef tells me we have a special menu for you tonight. We want you to be happy. Please follow me. We have prepared your table."

"They know you?" Sigourney said. "I am surprised." He let her believe it and they took their seats. The tables were separated by small palms in mosaic-covered pots. Leaf fronds, rippled by the air conditioning and uplit from below reflected their moving shapes in silver-framed mirrors around the walls. "It's a most attractive place, Aubrey. The decor seems quite authentic."

"Indeed," he said. "You would know of course, having spent so much time in the country. I suppose you must return there to your business interests."

"I haven't really decided yet. I have an agency to handle all the tenancies." She looked as if she was about to continue but stopped abruptly.

"And the apartment blocks," Aubrey said, pressing her to say more. "Are they all in the same location?"

"I don't want to talk about work tonight, Aubrey," she said and dismissed the subject with a flick of her wrist. "Let's relax a little. Shall we have drinks now?"

Aubrey signalled the waiter and placed their order while his sister perused the menu. With carefully focused consideration he watched her facial expressions as she gushed at the waiter and pulled another cosmetic smile that never went further than the corners of her mouth.

"Oh, my!" she said when the food arrived. "Doesn't that look wonderful?"

The meal was excellent, she said. It was the best Thai meal she'd ever had in England. The service was superb; the table setting delightful. Sigourney Tennant spent at least half an hour comparing and contrasting the quality of her restaurant experiences. She complimented the tiny side street establishment where they sat, on each and every single detail, right down to the bamboo design of the bronze cutlery handles. Aubrey barely noticed how delicious his own food was.

"We must have a plan for tomorrow," she said, unexpectedly changing the subject.

"Sorry? What plan?"

"To welcome your lady friend home. Eliza."

"Lisa."

"Have you decided where we shall go?"

"No, Sigourney. I told you . . ."

"Leave it to me. I'll think of something."

She wasn't going to cease forcing her agenda. That much was obvious even if he didn't yet know exactly what the agenda was. He carried on with his meal and let her ramblings wash over him.

⚖️⚖️⚖️

Lisa, Madge and Wally had an early evening meal in the small restaurant within their hotel. None of them wanted anything too heavy and the simple menu in the downstairs bistro offered enough choices for their last night's stay. Afterwards they took a table in the bar area but Wally passed on anything further to drink. Lisa took a sip of her blackberry gin and agreed with Madge.

"That is so good," she said. "And they make it here in Cornwall?"

"So the man said," Madge replied. "What do you think of it Wally?"

"Very nice," he said, tasting from his wife's glass. "Maybe a bit fancy for me, though."

"Well you'll be back on your usual tipple this time tomorrow, love," Madge said. "It's been a fantastic week, ent it? I've loved every minute of it. Still, it's always good to get back into your own bed."

"I don't know about you two ladies," Wally said, yawning, "but I'm done in. We're up at the crack of sparrow tomorrow, so if you don't mind I'll say goodnight now and take myself off up to bed."

"I won't be far behind you, love," Madge said as he bent to peck her on the cheek.

"Goodnight, Wally," Lisa said. "Sleep well."

"I meant what I said about being glad to be back in my own bed," Madge said. "What about you, Lisa?"

"I agree with you. We all like our home comforts, don't we?"

"Have you given much thought to what it'll be like meeting Aubrey's sister?"

Lisa nodded. "Oh, yes I've been thinking about it but I've no idea what I'll be walking into when I get back home."

"Has he called you tonight?"

"No. I didn't think he would. I suggested he take his sister out for a meal. I thought it would be easier for him than being alone with her in the house. You know, being in a public place you'd expect her to know how to behave."

Madge stroked Lisa's shoulder and said, "I think he must have had a queer sort of a childhood. Don't you think so? I'm sorry, but I think I might have misjudged him. From what you've told me it sounds as though the poor chap didn't have it easy with the women in his family. There's no wonder, really, why some of his behaviour might have seemed a bit odd. And he's never talked to you about it much?"

Lisa shook her head. "Only what you already know, Madge. He told me he was sent away to boarding school when he was seven and I can't see him enjoying that at all. From the little I know about boarding schools it's enough to upset most children. Especially if they're sensitive types. You know, I couldn't have parted with Danny at that age. Anyway, as I said, he doesn't talk about it."

Madge hummed and agreed. "I've never understood why parents would send their children away from home like that. Maybe that's what happened to his sister as well."

Lisa didn't know. She couldn't remember Aubrey telling her anything more about their childhod other than holidays with their uncle.

"You thought she must be absolutely gorgeous, considering what he'd already told you about her," Madge said.

"Yes, I did. It's very strange. Part of me can't wait to see for myself what she's like now and there's another part of me absolutely dreading it."

"I know what you mean. Have you decided how you're going to deal with it if she starts putting on her parts with you?"

"Not yet. It sounds awful discussing his private life like this, Madge. You won't say anything, will you?"

"God forbid, Lisa. What are friends for if you can't help each other out?"

Lisa smiled and continued. "I had a word with Amy on the phone last night. She knows more about these sort of things. She's done a lot of courses in psychology."

"I know," Madge said, nodding in agreement. "She's a clever girl, your Amy. What did she say?"

"To be honest, I can't remember the names of all the things she told me. You'd never believe how many different fancy names they've got for people's behaviour. Amy said there are some people who are born to be different. Well, you remember, don't you, how Danny used to be when he was little? Anyway, she said other people are made that way while they're growing up. Then, I suppose there are people who are a mixture of both. The one thing I can be certain of is I'm fully expecting trouble from Aubrey's sister, but I don't know yet how she's going to go about it. Aubrey's told me all the ways she's been difficult with him but I've just got this feeling she'll take a different tack with me."

"Well, you know where I am, love. If you need anything . . ."

"Thank you, Madge."

Madge nudged Lisa with her elbow. "Hey," she said, "I could come over to yours and sort her out, you know. I think I'd enjoy putting her in her place."

Lisa smiled and said, "I don't think it'll come to that. After what Amy's suggested I don't think Sigourney's the type you can sort out. It might be professional help she needs. I'll have to be careful what I say. I don't want to cause Aubrey any more trouble than he's already had."

Chapter Twenty Eight

Wally Sparrow was asleep with his head lolling on Madge's shoulder as the coach approached the services on the journey back to Norfolk from their week's holiday in Cornwall. Madge's head was nodding too and her eyes looked heavy. Lisa, in a seat across the central aisle, looked at her watch, leaned sideways and tapped Madge on the shoulder.

"We're coming up to the service station," she said. "Wakey, wakey, you two."

Madge shook her head and nudged her husband. He groaned but she nudged him again.

"Come on, Wally," she said. "We don't want to be at the back of the queue." He snorted loudly and made spluttering noises. Madge apologised to the people in front. "Wallace!" she said. "Wake up."

He roused and sat up.

"What time is it?" he said and looked at his own watch.

The coach slowed and swung into the parking area reserved for larger vehicles. The driver clicked on his microphone to make an announcement.

"Ladies and gents," he said. "As you're aware we're running a bit late after the hold up earlier but I'm sure you'll all be glad to hear there are no further roadworks ahead. Unfortunately there won't be time to take the full rest break this afternoon if we want to be back on schedule. Can I ask you to take a twenty minute break only? Please be back here at four thirty."

Wally looked at his watch again and repeated, "Four thirty. Right you are."

"There won't be time to queue for drinks," Madge said. "We could get a takeaway, though."

They followed the other passengers from the coach park along the path to the entrance. Madge and Lisa looked for the sign for the ladies. Wally followed the other sign. They met afterwards by the self service shop.

"Madge will you get me a carton of apple juice and a packet of cheese and onion crisps, please? I think I'll just sit here a minute and send Aubrey a text to let him know we could be a bit late."

Lisa found a space to sit and fished out her phone from her bag. By the time she'd pressed *send*, Madge was on her way back with the shopping.

"Here you are," Madge said. "Apple juice for you. Coke for Wally and orange for me. Crisps all round. Ten minutes to spare. Has he got your message?"

Lisa's phone pinged. She read Aubrey's reply.

"He's having a hard time with her. He says she's complaining about everything."

"You've got your work cut out there, my lovely. I don't envy you. You're going to have to get rid of her as soon as you can."

"I know."

"Lisa, if we are a bit late getting back I think we'll have to change our arrangement, if you don't mind. I know we'd planned to share a taxi with you from the coach station but . . ."

"That's all right, Madge. I was going to suggest the same thing myself. We need to go in different directions and if you drop me off first it'll make it very late for you getting home."

They walked through the busy foyer and out towards the coach park, Wally scurrying on ahead.

Madge said, "I'll call you in the morning. You know, if you feel you have to escape? You know where I am."

"Thank you. I'm sure we'll be okay."

Lisa's taxi pulled up in the drive of Laburnum House at seven p.m. Through the rear window she could see Aubrey waiting for her on the top step. He was pacing about with his hands clasped behind his back and seemed anxious.

"Perfect timing, Aubrey," she called out as she climbed from the passenger seat. "It's so lovely to see you there waiting for me."

Aubrey stopped pacing and ran down the steps to greet her.

He grasped both her arms and said, "Lisa, I must warn you. . ."

He had no time to finish what he was about to say as the driver opened the boot and handed over Lisa's bag. Aubrey took it and was on his way with it toward the house when, just as he reached the top of the steps, a figure appeared, elbowed him aside and scurried down to the drive.

"You must be Eliza," the woman said.

"Lisa."

"Oh, my darling girl. You must be exhausted. Come in. Do come in."

Aubrey's sister quickly took hold of Lisa's arm and led her up the steps, through the hall into the house. "My brother's told me all about you and I just know we're soon going to be the best of friends. Aubrey, please take Eliza's bag upstairs for her, will you? Sorry. It's Lisa, isn't it? We want to get better acquainted, don't we, dear?"

Lisa smiled and nodded to give herself time to think of a suitable response. Over Sigourney's shoulder she could see Aubrey's apologetic expression as he backed away and retreated upstairs.

"And you must be Sigourney," Lisa said eventually, wearing her Marshall and Simpson bright-eyed and interested face. "I've been looking forward to meeting you for so long."

"Welcome, welcome. You are so welcome here at my uncle's home. You must need a drink. What can I bring for you?"

"Oh, a cup of tea, no sugar would be perfect," Lisa said, making her way into the sitting room and settling into her usual place.

Okay, then, Lisa thought. *What have we got going on here? What is she up to?*

Rapidly, she tried to make sense of what had just happened. She already knew to expect some sort of manipulative game from Aubrey's sister but she needed to think about each fine detail. It had happened so fast. From the moment of Lisa's arrival Sigourney had manoeuvred herself forward. She'd pushed her brother out of the way and taken over. She'd claimed the kitchen too, as if she was inveigling herself in as number one female in the house. Also, Sigourney had called the house *my uncle's home*. Why would she say that? She knew it was Aubrey's home now.

Lisa considered some of the suggestions Amy had given her in the phone conversation while she was in Cornwall and an idea began to form itself. She hardened herself for what could happen next. Sigourney came back with one mug of tea and the cafetière with two china cups on a tray. Lisa watched Sigourney's every move intently.

"We'll wait for my brother, Lisa. He likes his coffee properly infused."

A command, Lisa reflected. There was something insulting about the tone of Sigourney's voice. Lisa couldn't think of the word to describe that kind of voice: like an emperor. *Imperious,* that was it.

*She's telling me what I have to do. We **will** wait. Not shall we wait? Definitely a command. Then she finds it necessary to tell me how Aubrey prefers his coffee. As if I didn't already know.*

Lisa felt herself growing angry at Sigourney's pretence at some kind of private intimacy with Aubrey. It felt like she was being marginalised. She could have said, *yes, I know how he likes his coffee. I've been living here long enough to know how he likes his coffee.* She could also have said, *I'm having tea. I don't need to wait for the coffee* but either of those responses was what Sigourney expected her to say.

"So, tell me about yourself, Sigourney," Lisa said. "I'm dying to know all about your adventures over the years."

"Oh, it's not so exciting," Sigourney said as she settled into Aubrey's favourite arm chair. She crossed her legs and gazed up at the ceiling. "When all's said and done, travel can become quite tedious, can't it?"

"I think that depends on your reasons for travelling," Lisa said and cocked her head to one side as if she was expecting a relevant response.

"Those are pretty little earrings you have on, Eliza. I couldn't wear them unfortunately. I can wear only high quality gold. I'm allergic to cheap metals."

Lisa took a quick sip of her tea, stood up and stepped away from the coffee table. "I need to pop upstairs now, Sigourney," she said. "Thank you for the tea. I'll be back shortly."

She didn't give Sigourney time to intervene. She strode from the sitting room and dashed upstairs. Aubrey was standing at the door to her room. She grabbed his wrist and pulled him inside, closing the door behind her. She put her fingers to his mouth to stop him from saying anything.

"Aubrey," she said, "there's no need to apologise. I know what she's up to. She's trying to make me feel insecure and put a wedge between you and me. We'll talk about it in more detail later. For now, please go down and tell her I needed to freshen up. I know she thinks we're going out. She's made coffee for the two of you. I won't be long."

He kissed her cheek and said, "Lisa, I'm glad you're home."

Lisa undressed quickly and took a shower. She threw washing into the laundry basket, put on her pyjamas and robe, fished her slippers out from under the bed and went downstairs. From the hall she could hear Sigourney giving Aubrey a comparison between dress jewellery and the real thing and how you could tell the difference. She walked into the sitting room and interrupted the conversation.

"Oh, that's better," she said, ignoring Sigourney's annoyed expression at the intrusion. She made a point of ruffling her wet hair and shuffling along the carpet in her slippers. "Now I can relax in my comfies. It's so good to be home. That's what they say, don't they? It's oh, so nice to go travelling but it's so much nicer to come home."

She flopped onto the sofa beside Aubrey, linked her arm through his and rested her head on his arm.

"Oh," Sigourney said. "I thought you were dressing for dinner. We're going out tonight. Didn't Aubrey mention it? We decided . . ."

"Tonight?" Lisa intervened. "Oh, no, Sigourney. I think you're mistaken. We settled on a home delivery, didn't we Aubrey? Good old fish and chips for me, sweetheart," she said, winking at Aubrey, "fish and chips for all of us. I'll make myself a fresh cup of tea now while you're having your coffee and then we can have supper. Have you placed the order yet?"

"Not yet," Aubrey said. "I'll do it now. I don't have the number in my mobile. I, erm, forgot to put it in. I'll call from the hall."

"Thank you, sweetheart."

"Fish and chips?" Sigourney said when Aubrey had left the room, "when you could have had fine dining?"

"Why not? It gets so boring having fancy meals all the time. We like fish and chips occasionally. They're very good from the local chippy and it's great they have a delivery service. Anyway," Lisa said, lowering her voice and winking, "Aubrey and I've been apart for a whole week. We have a lot of bedroom business to catch up on. You will excuse us, won't you if we have an early night. I'll try not to make too much noise."

Sigourney spluttered on her coffee. Lisa thought, *you can't beat me on that one,* and went to the kitchen to make her fresh cup of tea.

Early on Sunday morning Lisa dressed quickly. Quietly she opened her bedroom door and listened. All was still. She tapped gently on Aubrey's door and let herself into his room. She closed the door gently behind her. The room was hushed and dark.

"Aubrey," she whispered. "Are you awake? I can't see you."

"Yes. Stay there. I'll open the window shutters."

She heard him moving and then morning light poured into the room in slices of flickering amber. Aubrey put on his robe over his pyjamas and sat in the window seat.

"Are you okay?" he said.

"Yes, I'm fine. I just wanted to talk to you about your sister before she gets up so we can speak freely about our plan."

Do you think it's working?" he said.

She sat beside him in the window seat.

"I don't know yet," she said. "I know she was shocked last night when we came up together. Did you hear her come up later?"

"I did, yes. I think she stood listening at the door."

"I thought she would. Listen, I've made up my bed so it looks as if I never slept in it last night and I've left my bedroom door ajar so she can she it when she walks past." She curled up beside him and hugged her knees. "It's bit exciting this, isn't it?"

Aubrey laughed. "Lisa," he said, "if when we met you'd told me that one year later I would be hiding away from my sister, sitting here conspiring in the window seat, I wouldn't have believed you."

"Me neither. But it's been fun, though."

His face twisted and became serious. He reached for her hand.

"Lisa," he began, "there are so many things I want to talk to you about. To tell you. To ask you."

"I think I know, Aubrey," she said. "I feel the same."

"Do you?"

"Yes. We've spent a year together now. We both took the risk of it. And it was a big risk. It might have been a disaster but it isn't. I'm not saying everything's been perfect, but . . ."

"But there's still so much more we need to talk about."

She stroked his face and said, "That's right. We do. But not just now. The thing is, I don't want to carry on this pretence. To tell you the truth I regret what I did and said to your sister last night. I think I went too far. I've been having a good think about it."

"And what have you decided?"

"Well," she said. "I can't take back what's already done. But I can stop it from going any further. I don't know the real reason why your sister has become so . . . difficult, but couldn't it be because she's been badly hurt?"

"Go on," Aubrey said.

"I think she was planning to spoil things for us, Aubrey. She didn't get her own way over your inheritance so she was determined to ruin something else. Now then, what kind of person wants to do things like that? Hurt people hurt people, so they say."

"So what are you suggesting?"

"I think we still have to be careful. I've heard about some people who are so stuck in their ways there isn't a lot you can do about it. They like to take advantage of peoples' kindness. They enjoy winkling out other people's weaknesses so they can make use of it. I think we should completely ignore her barbs and innuendos. We mustn't react to what she might say."

They waited until they heard Sigourney going downstairs before they came out of Aubrey's room together, Aubrey still in his dressing gown.

"Good morning, Sigourney," Lisa called over the bannister. "I hope you slept well."

"Oh, fuck you," she heard Sigourney mutter.

"We're coming down for breakfast. Just a light one this morning. We're having a big family lunch later."

Aubrey pulled her back to face him. "How did you know about that? I'd forgotten all about it. I was supposed to tell you but so many things have happened lately it went completely out of my thoughts."

"Ah, we women have our little ways," she said. "Danny never could keep secrets from me. He's looking forward to showing you his puffins."

She didn't mention the phone call she'd had with Amy, their discussion about Sigourney's behaviour and how to deal with it. That was something else to be discussed with him later. He said he was going to get dressed and asked her to wait for him so they could make a united front going downstairs together.

Sigourney hadn't dressed: she'd come down in a diaphanous housecoat with elaborately embroidered, floaty sleeves and was drifting about from room to room like a nineteen thirties Hollywood drama queen complaining about the dog following her.

"Can't you lock him up somewhere?" she said. "He keeps sniffing at me."

"It's what dogs do, Sigourney," Aubrey said. "He just wants to get to know you." He let Toby out into the garden and closed the door.

"Tea or coffee this morning, Sigourney?" Lisa called from the kitchen.

"Don't you have fresh orange juice?"

"Sorry. No."

"That's the first time she's asked for that," Aubrey whispered to Lisa.

"Take no notice, Aubrey. She's looking to make more trouble. Remember not to react."

Sigourney wandered into the kitchen and sat at the table. She kept shifting her weight and sighing every time she moved.

"I'll have peppermint tea," Sigourney said. "I know you have that. I saw some in the cupboard. I don't think I could stomach coffee yet."

Aubrey said, "Why? What's the matter?" and regretted it as soon as the words left his mouth.

"If you must know," Sigourney whimpered, "I'm feeling a little queasy this morning. It must be all that greasy food we had last night."

"I didn't think it was greasy," Aubrey said. "I thought it was delightfully crispy. And very tasty."

"You must understand, Aubrey, I'm simply unused to eating that kind of food. It doesn't agree with me."

Lisa produced the peppermint tea and made drinks for Aubrey and herself. She tuned in to the radio for Sunday morning light music to help lift the brooding atmosphere.

"Oh, please," Sigourney said. "Must we have that dreadful caterwauling on first thing in the morning?"

Lisa prevented Aubrey from responding by stepping in front of him.

"Oh, yes," she said. "We like to sing along sometimes. And jig about a bit."

"I'll go to the drawing room, then. I can't bear to listen to that cheap trash."

Lisa watched her slink away, rolling her hips as if she were on a fashion catwalk. She noticed Sigourney made a point of using Aubrey's favourite armchair. Lisa crossed the hall and pulled on the sitting room door.

"If we keep this door closed," she said to Sigourney as brightly as she could muster, "we can let Toby back into the house and he won't be any trouble to you."

She closed the door fully and went back to the kitchen where Aubrey was sitting with his head in his hands.

"It isn't easy," he said, "this not reacting business. Can't we simply ask her to leave?"

"I don't think we'll need to. She'll soon get bored with the way we live."

They heard a groan from the sitting room. Aubrey went to investigate. Lisa followed him. Sigourney was sitting doubled up in Aubrey's chair, rocking from side to side and holding her stomach.

"Are you ill?" Aubrey said.

"I don't feel at all well, Aubrey. Such pain in my stomach. I may need to be taken to emergencies."

"Why not try something to settle your stomach first?" Lisa suggested. "We've a full first aid kit and I know we've something for upset tummies."

"You want me to take unprescribed medication? What are you trying to do? Kill me? Aubrey, is this how you want to treat your only sister?"

Lisa went to fetch the medical box and brought it back to the living room. She put it on Aubrey's side table where Sigourney could reach it.

"Aubrey," she said, forcing a smile in front of his sister. "You were right. It isn't easy. I'll leave you two to sort it out. I've things to do upstairs."

"Have you?" Aubrey looked confused.

"Yes. I think it would be a good idea to make up a spare bed in case any of my tribe decide to stay over tonight."

It was a good enough excuse to absent herself. She left the room and almost ran upstairs. Everything Aubrey had recently said about his sister was true. She was completely insufferable. It was Amy who'd suggested the non-reaction response to Sigourney's attempts to cause unrest. Amy had lots of experience with difficult patients. She'd studied people's behaviours for years and had psychiatric qualifications for her job. But it wasn't working. When Lisa and Aubrey disregarded one thing, Sigourney manufactured another. The woman was impossible to deal with. Perhaps Aubrey was also right when he'd suggested they simply ask her to leave. But what if she refused? What would they do then?

There was nothing Lisa could do at that moment. Her family was coming shortly. They'd all have to muddle through. She focused on changing the bed Timothy Reynolds had been using and getting the room ready for any unexpected house guest.

She stripped off the bed for washing and went to the airing cupboard in the main bathroom. She was short of two pillowcases should she need extra pillows. She remembered there were some at the bottom of the carved chest. They were old but made from fine fabric, still in good condition.

The chest was half empty. She lifted out the remaining sheets to look for pillowcases beneath. There they were: plain white linen with a hand-embroidered motif. She lifted them out and gave them a shake to loosen the fold lines. She decided they'd be fine. She heard raised voices from downstairs.

"I'm not ready to leave yet, Aubrey," she heard Sigourney shout. "I will not be rushed out of my uncle's home."

Lisa sank to her knees. *Oh, Aubrey,* she thought. *You've jumped the gun and asked her to leave. She'll be more determined than ever now.*

Lisa stopped what she was doing to listen.

"This is not Van's home any more," Aubrey was saying. "This is *my* home. Why can't you understand that?"

"Because he promised it to me," Sigourney yelled back.

I'll bet he didn't. Oh, Aubrey, she's lying. Please don't let her get to you.

Lisa reached into the chest intending to put back the sheets and smooth them flat. Something was sticking out from inside a satin pillow sham. She lifted it out. In a heavy damask brocade design the pillow sham could have been straight out of the nineteen thirties. She couldn't imagine using them now. She pulled at the corner of the piece of paper jutting out from the opening. An unsealed envelope came out. She opened it. Inside was a handwritten sheet of writing paper.

She could still hear shouting downstairs but it was all Sigourney's voice. Aubrey had fallen into silence, it seemed. He needed support. She should hurry and go down to help him. But the letter was still in her hand. Gingerly she unfolded it. She didn't recognise the handwriting. It wasn't Aubrey's. She'd seen his handwriting often enough to know. Her eyes fell on the opening line:

My darling girl,
I'm going to miss you terribly . . .

Chapter Twenty Nine

Lisa was on her knees listening from her position on the landing, the hidden letter from the linen chest still in her hand.

"I will not be rushed into making a decision that could affect the rest of my life," Sigourney was screaming at her brother. She sounded like a banshee. The high-pitched shriek of that voice burned right through Lisa, as if it could pierce her skin and get into her bones.

"What kind of man treats his sister the way you're treating me?"

"I'm not listening to you, Sigourney. You're being irrational."

Aubrey had found his voice again.

"Irrational? Me? Look at yourself, brother. You were never so callous, Aubrey. You used to be so kind and thoughtful. What's happened to you? What kind of beast has *she* turned you into?"

"What? How dare you? Lisa is the best thing that has ever happened to . . ." Aubrey's response was thunderous.

"Oh, come on, Aubrey. Can't you see what's going on here?"

"Stop it, Sigourney. Stop it now."

"Somebody has to tell you if you can't see it for yourself. She's obviously playing you. Planning to get all she can out of you. Where was she before you found her? Living in some run-down apartment somewhere, scratching around to make ends meet. No wonder she jumped at the chance of getting together with you."

Lisa's mouth soured. She felt sick. The pounding in her head made her dizzy. She got up from her knees and stood still for a moment to steady herself. She went to her room and sat in the window seat. The letter fell from her hand to the floor.

She must call Amy and Danny to put them off. A lovely family meal and get together couldn't happen in these circumstances. Sigourney would be bound to kick off again. Lisa didn't want Amy and Danny to witness all this trouble. Hadn't they seen enough problems with the men in their mother's life? But what would she say to them? How could she explain the brutality of what was happening downstairs? You had to see it to believe it.

But maybe there was another way. Amy wasn't afraid of difficult situations. She dealt with them almost every day in her work. Danny would probably ignore it and do his own thing. He got on so well with Aubrey that, perhaps, Sigourney wouldn't be able to cause problems as they'd be heavily into talk about bird watching and Danny's time in Wales. Most likely they'd spend hours going over Danny's photographs. Sigourney wouldn't have an audience.

Lisa made up her mind to go downstairs and carry on as if nothing had happened. She stood up and noticed the letter on the floor by her feet. She picked it up and slid it back in its envelope. *My darling girl* would have to wait. She put the envelope on her dressing table and went downstairs.

Aubrey was by himself in the kitchen.

"How are you?" he said as she came in. "Did you hear any of that?"

"Yes. Are you okay?"

"I think so. What do you think we should do now?"

"Nothing, Aubrey. We don't change anything. That would be like giving in to her. We're going ahead with our plans for the day and your sister will just have to take a back seat. Where is she now?"

"Upstairs. Getting dressed, I suppose."

"I didn't hear her come up. I was in my room. I suggest one of us takes Toby for his morning walk. Give him a good run. Tire him out. Laburnum House is going to be hectic this afternoon."

"I'll take him, if you don't object to being left here with my sister."

"No problem," Lisa said. "Amy will be here soon anyway so I won't be on my own for long."

Aubrey called the dog and they went out. Lisa went back upstairs. She could hear Sigourney in the corner bedroom speaking to someone and surmised she was on her mobile phone. She went into her own room and closed the door. The envelope was soon in her hands. There was no address on it. No name. No date. It was a simple, blank envelope.

Her hands trembled and she stopped. She had no right to open it. It was wrong to read someone else's private thoughts. She should hand it over to Aubrey and tell him where she found it. That would be the right and proper thing to do.

She couldn't resist. Softly she pulled out the paper and unfolded it. The letter was brief.

My darling girl,

I'm going to miss you terribly. Try not to think too ill of me. It's time I went away and stayed away. Know that I have always loved you in my own way. My brother loves you to the end of the earth. But for all our sakes I must end our arrangement.

Here is my promise to you: I will take care of the children's futures. I won't forget them. You have all brought such pleasure to my life. My brother is a lucky, lucky man.

Van

Lisa folded the slip of paper and put it down. Her fingers were cold. Immediately she bristled. What she had just done was so wrong. These were private words. She had no right to read them. What good could come of it? Quickly, she put the letter back in the envelope then wondered what to do with it. Should she put it back in the linen chest? Should she tell Aubrey what she'd done?

But what had she actually discovered? She didn't know anything about the reasons behind such a letter. Images flashed through her mind of all the times she and Aubrey had sat watching films on television together; the hours they'd spent eating together; the discussions about the garden and his plans for the boathouse area and the endless *settling in* conversations they'd had deciding what to put where in the home they shared. Not once had they talked in any detail about their pasts, their childhoods and schooldays, their parents. They'd shared so little about themselves. A huge void occupied the space at the heart of their relationship. They'd lived in the moment, in a permanent present where the past hardly existed and only the future mattered.

The realisation of such an important emptiness in their knowledge of one another shocked her. And now Aubrey's past had pushed through the boundaries they'd unwittingly set. Here, in a secret letter to Aubrey's mother, the past had ripped through the veil they'd unconsciously fabricated.

Lisa's imaginings rioted in her mind. Had Uncle Vanguard been in love with his own brother's wife? That much was obvious from the wording in the note: *know that I have always loved you.* But what about the *in my own way?* What was that supposed to mean? She wondered if they'd had an affair: two brothers who loved the same woman. Did Aubrey already know about it and why would his mother keep such a letter for the rest of her life?

Now, look what you've done, she thought. *As if things in my life aren't complicated enough, you go and open up another can of worms.* She heard a voice calling from downstairs.

"Mum? Are you there? Can I come in?"

Lisa slipped the envelope into a drawer and hurried away. Amy was standing just inside the front door, two large shopping bags at her feet.

"Amy!" Lisa said, casting aside all thoughts of Uncle Van and Aubrey's mother and hugging her daughter. "You're in good time."

"Well, it's a big joint to cook. Can't leave it till the last minute. I know you had a great time in Cornwall. Did you have a good journey home?"

"Lovely, thank you. I'll tell you all about it later. Fancy a cuppa? Aubrey's out with the dog. He won't be long."

"I've brought some doggy treats in my bag," Amy said, kissing her mother hello and taking the shopping through to the kitchen. "Aubrey told me it's a good way to get in Toby's good books. Has Danny called you?"

"No. Was he supposed to?"

"I just wondered what time he'll turn up. You know what he's like." Amy emptied her shopping bags while Lisa made drinks. By the time the kettle had boiled the worktops were overflowing with food: a whole leg of lamb fresh from the farmer's market, vegetables for roasting and greens for the steamer, locally grown asparagus for starters, grapes and crackers and an enormous black forest gateau to defrost for dessert.

"Anything more to tell me about Aubrey's sister?" Amy said as she washed her hands at the kitchen sink.

"Not just now, Amy. She's upstairs on her phone." Lisa lowered her voice and continued. "She's been giving Aubrey a terrible time. I hope she doesn't try to spoil our day."

"Mum, don't worry. We'll just take it as it comes. You go sit down. I'm cooking."

"I'd like to do it together, Amy. I'd enjoy that. It would feel like old times," Lisa said. "You just delegate and I'll be sous-chef."

"Mum," Amy said, "I hope you don't mind but I've invited someone else to eat with us."

"Who? Jessie?"

"No. His name is Ryan. He wants to meet my family," Amy said and stretched an embarrassed smile.

Lisa nodded and said, "I don't mind at all. There's enough here to feed the whole village. But are you sure he'll be all right with the lot of us?"

"He'll be fine. I hope you like him. He means a lot to me."

"We'd better all be on our best behaviour then. Have you known him long?"

"Actually, yes I have. I guess I just started looking at him in a different way."

Lisa was about to mention the risk of further trouble from Aubrey's sister when she caught a waft of strong perfume. She turned in its direction. Sigourney was standing in the doorway. Lisa nudged Amy with her elbow.

"You didn't tell me we were having guests," Sigourney said, her nose in the air. "Aren't you going to introduce me?"

Amy stepped forward. "No need," she said. "I'm Amy. And you are?"

"Well, I didn't expect that. How quaint. I see you do things differently from what I'm used. Lisa?"

Lisa said, "Amy this is Sigourney. Aubrey's sister."

Sigourney stepped into the room and held out her hand. Amy took it and shook it vigorously.

"Lovely," Amy said. "Have you come to help us in the kitchen? We could do with an extra pair of hands. There's a lot of preparation to do."

"Preparation?" Sigourney said and screwed up her face.

"Yes. Peeling vegetables, making Yorkshire pudding batter, chopping herbs. You know. Preparation."

Sigourney took a step backwards and ran a hand through her hair, smoothing it as if she were preparing for a photo shoot. "I'm hardly dressed for kitchen work," she said and inspected her fingernails. "I'll just keep myself occupied. I wouldn't want to get in your way. Surely you have something of interest I could look at. A magazine perhaps? No, don't put yourself to any trouble. I'm sure I'll find something."

She drifted off and out of sight. Lisa puffed out a sharp breath, looked at her daughter and rolled her eyes.

"Hmm," Amy said. "I see what you mean."

Lisa put on some music and they set to work together.

"It could be awkward for your Ryan," Lisa said. "Are you sure about this?"

"Mum, he's a consultant at the hospital. There isn't much about family life he hasn't already seen."

"Quite a bit older than you then?"

"Not much. He's thirty six."

There were no further interruptions from Sigourney as they worked together in the kitchen. Amy told her mother how her flatmate Jessie was thinking of giving in her notice at work and moving to another area where there might be more chance of promotion. A bigger city ought to offer bigger opportunities. They were in the middle of discussing Amy's own prospects at work when the front door opened closely followed by loud voices and the sound of dog's paws clicking their way through the hall. Danny and Aubrey had arrived together.

"Look who I found outside," Aubrey said as he came into the kitchen wearing a broad smile and an outdoors flushed face.

Toby was jumping about with pleasure and was so busy running around to greet everybody he didn't notice there was a new presence in the room. He rushed at Amy to greet her too, ran back to Danny and nearly fell over himself in his efforts not to leave anybody out.

"Hello Aubrey," Amy said. "Hi, Danny. So this is Toby. I thought you said he was an old dog. He's running around like a puppy."

"I think he's happy to see me," Danny said. "Have you changed your car, Mum? There's a different one out front. Looks like a hire car. Not having problems with yours are you?"

"Ah, no, love. That one isn't mine. I put it in the garage before I went away. The hire car belongs to Aubrey's sister. She's around here somewhere."

"I have news," Aubrey said. "Let's give old Toby a drink first to calm him down." He filled the dog's bowl with water and put it down in the utility room. Toby followed and when he'd had his fill Aubrey let him into the garden.

"I forgot to ask," Danny said. "Have a good holiday, Mum? Come here. Give me a hug."

"Danny Miller, look at my hands. You'll get flour all over your shirt."

"So?"

He grabbed his mother and lifted her off her feet. Suddenly the house was full of clamour. Aubrey and Danny kept up the conversation they'd started before they came indoors. Lisa caught snatches of it: puffins and other birds, photographs, cameras and lenses, rain and wind and sun, ferry boats and lively seascapes, Toby pawing at their feet for attention. Amy was singing along to the radio channel, clattering pots and pans as she moved around.

"Good heavens," Lisa said. "It feels like Christmas in here today. I love it."

Aubrey interrupted. "I almost forgot my news, Lisa," he said. "Can you prepare for another two? Timothy is on his way with old Sam."

Chapter Thirty

There were going to be eight hungry bodies to feed. Lisa, mentally reorganizing her plans was busy finding extra matching tableware. Toby was watching from his basket, hoping for treats.

"Do you think we'll have enough food, Mum?" Amy said.

"We'll manage. A slice less meat each and more vegetables," Lisa suggested. "Maybe an extra Yorkshire pudding. Aubrey, will you and Danny set up the table in the dining room, please? We may as well do it all properly. Let's extend it to give everybody more space. We'll need a different tablecloth too. Make it feel more special."

"I think Mum really means she'd like us to get out of the way, Aubrey," Danny said. "Good chance to show you some of my shots."

"So everything worked out as you'd hoped?"

"A few too many tourists. But I just set my alarm and got up earlier."

Aubrey said he and Danny would take themselves and Toby off to his study but to give them a shout if help was needed for anything else. They stepped into the hall just as Sigourney came out from the sitting room. From where she was standing in the kitchen, through the open door Lisa could see them almost bump into each other. She heard Danny speak first in his usual upfront way.

"Hi. I'm Danny. Lisa's my mum. Do you want to come and see my photographs?"

Sigourney looked down her nose and said, "What photographs?"

"Wildlife, mostly birds."

"No thank you."

"Sigourney, this is Danny, Lisa's son. Danny, meet my sister. He's an excellent photographer, Sigourney," Aubrey added.

"If you say so," she said and looked away. She sauntered back into the living room muttering about young people and manners and closed the door behind her.

Amy stifled a laugh. "Well done, Danny," she said. "Don't forget to lay the table before you disappear. Mum, is that your mobile ringing?"

Lisa quickly wiped her hands and picked up her phone. It was Madge calling as promised.

"Thanks for calling," Lisa said. "Everything's fine. Amy and Danny are here and we're expecting another three people. It's a bit hectic. Can I call you back later?"

Danny popped his head into the kitchen to say he was sorry but he didn't know where anything was and Aubrey didn't know which tablecloth to use. Could Lisa spare a minute? She dashed away to delegate and hurried back to the kitchen where Amy was reading a message on her phone looking disconsolate.

"What's the matter?" Lisa asked. "Has something happened?"

"It's Ryan. He's had to go back into work. An emergency complication. He won't be able to make it until later."

"A complication?"

"An emergency Caesarean. He's an obstetrician, Mum."

"Oh, wow. I didn't realise. I can't wait to meet him. It's a shame he's been held up. Never mind, Amy, we can make up a plate for him. Give it a quick zap in the microwave when he gets here."

Sigourney was conspicuous by her absence as Lisa and her daughter worked together finalising the preparations for Sunday lunch. Lisa set the timer for the oven to switch itself on. Amy cleared away the last few things and loaded the dishwasher.

"That's it. Everything's done," Amy said. "What do we do now, Mum? Do you think we should go and be sociable?" She tilted her head in the direction of the sitting room and popped her eyebrows.

"I don't think so. Let's go outside." Lisa led the way through the rose garden and set off down the expanse of lawn toward the water. "I don't feel like being sociable with Aubrey's sister," she said as they walked. Briefly, it crossed her mind whether she should tell Amy about the secret letter she'd found in the linen chest but rapidly decided against. First, she had to make up her mind whether or not she was going to admit to Aubrey she'd been prying into his family concerns.

"What have you decided to do about the work down here?" Amy said as they reached the edge of the Broad.

"Aubrey keeps changing his mind," Lisa said. "At first it was going to be a simple refurbishment. Replace the boarding on the quay heading to make it safe. The roof on the boathouse needs looking at as well. I thought it might make a lovely summer house down here. You know, somewhere to come to sit near the water and read or just to watch the birds on the Broad. I'd like to see a kingfisher but I haven't been lucky yet. Anyway, now Aubrey's talking about digging out a larger lagoon area to take a bigger boat."

"He wants to buy a boat?"

"I think so. Nothing too fancy, just something to use for days out on the water. Probably second hand."

"Mum, that sounds amazing."

"Yes. I think I'd like that a lot. The trouble is, I'd always be worried about going too far from home and not getting back in time to get ready for work the next day."

Amy stopped walking. She took her mother's arm.

"Let's sit down a minute," Amy said and led the way around a weeping willow near the water's edge where the garden fanned out wider creating an attractive arbour with beds of hydrangeas.

"When did this bench get here?" Lisa said. "I haven't noticed it before."

"I don't suppose you can see it from the house," Amy said. "It's kind of tucked behind the tree here. It's brand new by the look of it."

"Aubrey must have done it while I was away," Lisa said. "It's lovely, isn't it? And what a good place to put it. Sometimes he can be very thoughtful like that."

They settled on the new bench where they had a clear view across the narrowest stretch of the waterway. A small group of coots paddled near the bank below them and near the far bank, in a small clearing in the rushes, a heron was scrutinising the shallows looking for his lunch.

"Does it feel good to be back home?" Amy said.

"Yes, it does. Who wouldn't feel good in a place like this?"

"And are you happy, Mum?"

"Yes. Thank you for asking. Aubrey and I are reaching a better understanding of one another. His sister isn't helping matters, though."

"Do you think she'll stay much longer?"

"Oh, I hope not. I don't know how much more I could take of her shenanigans."

"She glides about the place as if she was the lady of the house, doesn't she?"

Amy's words were like a gunshot. Immediately, they ricocheted through Lisa's thoughts. *The lady of the house.* In an instant, the peace in the garden was shattered; its boathouse, the water birds and Amy sitting beside her, all evaporated behind the flashing intrusion of an image so clear it brought a lump to Lisa's throat. *The lady of the house.* Wally Sparrow remembered being given tea and cakes from her.

Then another sharp, more recent memory stabbed its way forward. *Know that I have always loved you.* Was that secret letter written to the same woman? Could it be that Aubrey's mother had spent time here? Was that the reason the sitting room curtains at Laburnum House were exactly the same as at the house in Thetford? Had *the lady of the house* sewed both?

"Mum? Are you okay?"

"What? Oh, yes love."

"I thought you were going to faint. You've gone really pale."

"Have I? Probably a bit overtired, that's all."

"Mum, here's something for you to think about. Do you really need to work full time? Why don't you reduce your hours if they'll let you. Give yourself a long weekend. Just think, if you get that little boat you were talking about you could spend as long as you like on the water."

"Well, I don't know."

"Promise me you'll think about it."

It sounded ideal. Lisa could imagine spending lazy days out on the water, maybe mooring at a lunchtime pub or finding a good place to watch the sunset.

"Okay. I promise," she said.

Aubrey's sister was still lounging on a sofa when they went back indoors. Amy checked the oven and reported all was as it should be. A car horn sounded out front. Aubrey came out from his study and went to open up. He came hurrying back inside.

"Danny will you move your car over, please?" he said. "Timothy needs more space to park. Sam is struggling to get out."

"Sorry," Danny said. "My fault. I should have remembered." He ran outside and immediately ran back up the steps and indoors again, shouting, "Car keys. Where did I put my car keys?"

"Are these yours?" Amy shouted back. "On the worktop in here. Take mine as well in case you need them."

Danny grabbed them and hurtled back outside again. Toby ran into the hall to see what all the noise was about and was beside himself when he saw who was coming into the house. Danny rushed to pick him up. Timothy Reynolds stayed behind Sam to guide him over the threshold and Amy stood in the kitchen doorway. Her phone buzzed. She went outside to take the call.

"Toby's a trip hazard," Danny said, juggling the wriggling dog who was doing his best to escape the strong arms holding him. Sigourney appeared at the sitting room entrance, took one look at the gathering in the hall and made an affected gasp of surprise.

"I thought you weren't interested in having lodgers, Aubrey," she said in a tone of voice to match the expression on her face.

"Blust me," Sam said as he manoeuvred his walking frame ahead of him slowly along the hall. "You've got yerself a house full here, missus."

Aubrey said, "Lisa, I would like to introduce Sam, our friend from the birding group."

"Toby's dad," Danny added.

"Sam, I'm very pleased to meet you and it's wonderful you're up and about and on the mend," Lisa said. "Let's get you comfortable in the sitting room, shall we? Excuse us, Sigourney. Sam needs a comfortable seat."

Sigourney grimaced and shrank back.

"I thank you very glad, missus. Bless yer heart." Sam said.

"Is there anything I could get for you?" Lisa asked.

"I could murder a cuppa tea."

Sam said the winged armchair would be the best bet for his temporary disablement if they could put in an extra cushion to make it higher and, as soon as he was seated, Danny set the dog free. Wagging his tail furiously and yelping with excitement, Toby rushed to be near his old friend. Timothy cut across the room to supervise.

"We've a special high seat chair arriving tomorrow at Sam's place," Timothy said, "and there's somebody coming to assess the house for other mobility aids."

"I ent planning on being an invalid for long," Sam argued, "but I do thank you very glad, Tim, for getting all this sorted out so's I can go home, bless yer heart."

"That was Ryan on the phone just now, Mum," Amy called out above the clamour. "He's able to make it after all."

"Oh, good. Amy, would you put the kettle on please? Sam's longing for a cuppa," Lisa said.

"Okay. Anybody else fancy one?"

"Who is Ryan?" Aubrey said.

"Ryan is Amy's friend," Lisa said. "He's a doctor. He was called away so we didn't know if he was going to make it. Well, he can, and he's on his way."

"Danny," Aubrey said, "would you and Timothy make sure there's enough space for another car out front, please."

"Dear God," Sigourney said, "It's like a bloody circus in here." She swept past them all and went upstairs.

The last of the Sunday lunch visitors had left and Laburnum House relaxed into gentle serenity. Aubrey sat silently at his desk in the study; the letter from Chamberlain's office lay opened in front of him. He leaned back in his chair and listened to the quiet house.

Lisa was somewhere sorting laundry and getting her work outfit ready for next day. He knew she'd enjoyed the family day so much. He'd waited until she was busy elsewhere in the house before going to the cloaks cupboard and retrieving the letter from his uncle. He didn't want anything to sour memories of the joyful afternoon he'd savoured. He smiled and chuckled to himself at the atmosphere she and her family had created. It felt as though Laburnum House had been brought back to life, overflowing with good-natured humanity. He wanted more of it.

Amy had produced a wonderful meal. Her mother wouldn't take any credit for it.

"No," she'd said. "I was just the assistant. Amy is the chef."

He'd seen the way Amy and Ryan had looked at one another and wondered if Lisa had seen it too. Ryan was the kind of young man any mother of a daughter would be happy to welcome into the family. Danny's silly joke at the dining table had set them all laughing.

"I've got a nickname for you two," he'd said when Ryan explained his work and Danny compared it with Amy's. "Hatch 'em and dispatch 'em."

"Danny!" Lisa had warned.

"Well, it's life, Mum. No point in pretending otherwise, is there?"

Then Sam had added his viewpoint and everybody joined in. The good feeling permeating the room had been almost tangible. Uncle Van's dining room had been lifted out of its history and deposited right at the heart of a powerful expression of human connection such as Aubrey had never before experienced.

He picked up the letter his uncle had sent through the family solicitor and read it again. In Chamberlain's office Sigourney had opened hers and immediately dismissed its contents. He wondered whether it carried the same message as the one he had in his hands. He would never know. Sigourney had left before lunch. She'd made up some nonsense about checking something in her car and, while they were all moving into the dining room, concentrating on who was sitting where and making sure Sam could be comfortable with Toby's basket nearby, Sigourney had made her move.

"One last request, brother dear," she said to stop him from following the others. "You can tell them whatever you want afterwards but right now I would appreciate your help."

"They're waiting for us. Lunch is ready."

"I'm not staying. Would you please bring down my suitcase and put it in my car?"

He didn't ask her any questions. He did as she asked. Before she drove away he said,

"Where are you going? Will we see you again? Ever?"

"I booked my flight this morning. Got to go. Goodbye, Aubrey."

He followed her car toward the gate and was left standing, limply watching her disappear around the curve in the drive. Briefly, he felt dazed by her sudden departure. Then, the haze in his mind lifted and he saw more clearly what she'd plotted. She'd wanted a dramatic exit, he thought, as if she were playing a part, a role in a stage play. She'd had it all planned. She'd always known she wouldn't be staying. All that ridiculous playacting earlier about an upset stomach. All lies. She'd probably had her flight booked all along, from the moment she arrived.

Lisa came to find him. He knew she sensed straight away what had happened.

"She's gone, hasn't she?" she said. He took her arm as they walked back to the house.

"Yes," he said. "I think she wanted to make this afternoon be all about her, not you and me, our family and friends. She staged it, Lisa. She wanted to leave us with something we would have to explain, to make the conversation all about her even though she isn't here."

As they reached the steps Lisa stopped. "So, what will you tell everybody?" she said.

"The truth, Lisa. I will never take responsibility for my sister ever again."

"I'm so sorry, Aubrey. I know it's not what you would have liked."

"She always called for a lot of attention, even as a child. I convinced myself she was well-liked, popular with her friends. Now I realise she was just demanding."

"It's up to you, but you don't have to say anything at all if you don't feel at ease with it."

Lisa had been so understanding, so kind. She said nothing further about his sister even though she had every right to complain. Together, they joined the others in the dining room and took their places. It transpired that it was enough to tell everybody that his sister had had to leave. He offered nothing more. Nobody pressed him for further details. The only reaction came from Danny who loudly expressed his interest in having second helpings from any leftovers now that there was a spare serving.

And now everybody was gone. But it didn't feel like an ending. He held within him a growing sensation of belonging, of being part of a family of honest, caring people. One day he would bring out one of his old photograph albums. He knew where they were. He would fetch one and share it with Lisa. When the time was right he would show her the letter too and hope she would understand. Surely she would see for herself how much he resembled his uncle. He would tell Lisa all about the secret suspicions he'd harboured for most of his life.

But not today. He had new prorities now. Generations past had made their own decisions and they'd had to live with them. It was time to shape his own life without the encumbrances of other people's past mistakes. He put the letter back in its envelope, dropped it into a drawer and closed it firmly. He heard Lisa coming down the hall.

"Aubrey, do you fancy a cup of tea?" she said as he came out of the study to meet her. "Are you okay? You look a bit worried. Have my lot worn you out?"

He took hold of her hands and shook his head.

"I've had the most exhilerating afternoon, Lisa, and all thanks to you. Come and sit down with me."

He sat beside her on one of the sofas and they talked. They drank tea and they talked more. There was no mention of confessional letters and secret suspicions. He told her how much he cared for her, for Danny and Amy and how much happiness they'd brought into his life. Later, neither of them had the appetite for another full meal so they ate buttered toast and talked again.

He fell into listening to Lisa as if they'd known one another forever. He watched her eyes shine as she recounted her own childhood, the birth of her children, her years of joy and terrible loss. He watched her mouth move as she talked and felt his heart swell at her kindness, her common sense, her fortitude. She was nothing short of resilience personified.

Later still they took coffee and cognac to the rose garden and made plans for their future together. He let go of all notions of checklists and preferences and pre-rehearsed things to say. Lisa accepted him for all his foibles and now he knew it was perfectly fine to be imperfect.

He yearned for physical closeness. He kissed her and her mouth was soft and yielding. He knew she also felt the same longing.

He took her hand as they went upstairs together.

"Your room or mine?" she said.

"Lisa," he said. "It's been a long time since I . . . you know."

"Same here," she said.

THE END

ABOUT THE AUTHOR

Celia Micklefield has worked in an accountant's office, a high street retail store, a textile mill and a shoe factory as well as short stints in a fish and chip shop, behind the bar in a pub and running a slimming club. She studied for a degree in education and went into teaching at high school, became a partner in an import and wholesale business and ran a craft outlet at a country shopping experience. She returned to teaching where her last position was at a sixth form college.

Celia was born in West Yorkshire and has lived in Aberdeenshire and the south of France. She currently lives in Norfolk.

MORE BOOKS BY CELIA

PATTERNS OF OUR LIVES - a dual timeline, historical saga 1935 to 2010. From a pre-war northern industrial town to the post war peace of the Nofolk countryside this is a heartwarming, heartbreaking story where secrets from World War Two surface generations later. Keep tissues handy! (Some sexually explicit scenes)

TROBAIRITZ THE STORYTELLER - dual narrative, contemporary fiction. A present day female troubadour (trobairitz) leads a nomadic life driving long distance haulage in Europe. At an overnight truck stop she dodges questions about her personal life and instead tells a fascinating story. Her themes are those of the original trobairitz - tradition, current affairs, the role of women in society, but these are the very subjects causing problems in her own life.

She says, "I like men. I really do. Wasn't it Dorothy Parker who said 'there's nothing quite so much fun as a man'? And I've had my share of fun. I'm no angel."

THE SANDMAN AND MRS CARTER - a psychological mystery. When Wendy Carter was nine years old the Sandman came to help her sleep. Now in her forties with a failing marriage and difficult relationship with her ailing mother, Wendy feels she needs a lover. Five named characters tell Wendy's story from their own viewpoint. She never speaks for herself but who is the mystery narrator who seems to know everything about everybody?

ARSE(D) ENDS - a collection of shorter reads inspired by words ending in the letters a.r.s.e.

Why is Ted sick to death of Judy's hobby?

Why does Don spend so much time in the basement?

Why is John such a control freak?

What did Ahmed learn about the real world?

Whose world ended on 21st December 2012?

Why are they burying barry in his Elvis outfit?

Six stories with twists and stings - some outright funny - some darker.

QUEER AS FOLK - a second collection of shorter reads, full of people's quirks and foibles because life's like that.

PEOPLE WHO HURT - non fiction. Part memoir, part informational, outlining the patterns of behaviour of persons with personality disorders.

A MESSAGE FROM CELIA

All my books are available in paperback versions and for Kindle. You can Follow Celia on my Amazon author page, my Facebook author page and @CMicklefield on Twitter. My website is https://celiamicklefield.com

Please let people know how you've enjoyed my books. Even the briefest review can help so much.

Thank you.

Printed in Great Britain
by Amazon

37141138R00189